"GOOD LORD!"

Alex exclaimed. "John Moore, by all that's wonderful!"

They shook hands and Moore added, his smile fading, "Although I could wish that our reunion were taking place in happier circumstances. Have you not realized the perilous state we're in? You would have been better off in Lucknow, my dear Alex."

"My wife and infant son are here. The baby was born prematurely less than three weeks ago. For his sake I dared not risk the journey. Why are *you* still here?" Alex asked curiously.

"It's not from choice, I assure you. I'm in command of our invalids, and I'm responsible for the wives and families who were also left behind. Would that I were not! You'll find it alarming here. Why in God's name the General didn't choose to defend the Magazine I'll never know! We could have held out there for months with little danger to the women and children . . . but old Wheeler insists that reinforcements are on their way and will reach us in less than a week. His main reason for choosing this site, he says, is because it's close to the Allahabad road and he doesn't want the reinforcements to have to fight their way through the city in order to reach us. He has a point, of course—*if* they reach us soon and in sufficient number. But if they don't . . ." He made a rueful grimace.

"May God help the poor innocents we are pledged to protect!"

MASSACRE AT CAWNPORE

by
V. A. Stuart

For John B. Hayward, who shares my love of military and naval history . . . and in memory of those brave men and women who made history during the siege and massacre at Cawnpore.

Weep not: he died as heroes die,
The death permitted to the brave;
Mourn not, he lies where heroes lie—
And valour envies such a grave.

MASSACRE AT CAWNPORE

Copyright © 1973 by V. A. Stuart

All rights reserved, including the right to reproduce this book or portions thereof in any form.

A Pinnacle Book published by special arrangement with Robert Hale Limited, London.

First printing, November 1973

Printed in the United States of America

PINNACLE BOOKS, INC.
116 East 27 Street, New York, N.Y. 10016

CONTENTS

AUTHOR'S NOTE

Based on accounts published by survivors of the siege of Cawnpore, everything recounted in this novel actually happened.

The only fictitious characters are Alex Sheridan and his wife Emmy: all others mentioned are called by their correct names and their actions are on historical record, although, of course, conversations with the fictitious characters are imagined.

Accounts by survivors are by J. W. Shepherd, commissariat clerk; Lieutenant, later Captain, Mowbray Thomson, 56th Native Infantry; and Lieutenant Henry Delafosse, 53rd Native Infantry. Maps are from the published account by J. W. Shepherd, kindly lent by Mr. J. B. Hayward, to whom this novel is dedicated.

PROLOGUE

By mid-afternoon on Friday, 5th June, 1857, the last of the sepoy corps to join in the mutiny of the Cawnpore Brigade—the 56th Bengal Native Infantry—formed up in readiness to follow the rest of the brigade on the long march to Delhi.

The 56th had hesitated, mindful of their long tradition of service to the Company and reluctant to betray the trust reposed in them by their British officers. Some of their number had fought to defend the Magazine, when the sowars of the 2nd Native Cavalry—dogs of Muslims —had endeavored to plunder it of its weapons of war. They, with a section of the 53rd, had held off the men of the Nana Sahib's bodyguard, to whom responsibility for the safety of both Magazine and Treasury had been confided, refusing to believe the arrogant claim—made by Azimullah Khan, the Nana's Mohammedan *vakil*—that the sun had set on the British Raj and on the great John Company, which had ruled all Hind for a hundred years. Yet the General Sahib, to whom their native officers had gone to offer assurances that the regiment would remain loyal, had ordered a cannon to open fire on them, as they waited in their Lines, and this inexplicable act of hostility had broken the ties which bound them to their allegiance.

With the exception of a handful of older men—who, despite the shower of grapeshot which had rained down on them, had elected to join the British in their entrenchment—the 56th Regiment had now thrown in their lot with the mutineers and they were in good heart as they swung along the dusty road which led to Kalianpore, where it had been agreed that the brigade would bivouac for the night. The drums and fifes were playing a familiar British march, *Over the hills and far away,* and without any conscious sense of irony, the sepoys kept step to the lively air. In their scarlet tunics and white crossbelts, with muskets shouldered and shakoed heads held high, they looked the picture of a well-disciplined corps as they marched, four abreast, out of Cawnpore, the cheers of an excited crowd from the native city ringing in their ears.

Behind them, to mark their passing, pillaged buildings—once a symbol of British power—smoldered into extinction, and a few pathetic corpses, already bloated by the heat of the sun, lay unburied and, it seemed, unmourned. The heavy iron-bound door of the Treasury sagged drunkenly on shattered hinges; the jail and the courthouse were in flames and the Magazine had been systematically denuded of military stores. A part of its outer wall had been blown in and reduced to a heap of rubble in order to facilitate the passage of the fieldguns and ammunition tumbrils which the mutineers had seized and which, harnessed to bullock teams and elephants, were now heading towards Kalianpore, as the sepoys were, on the first stage of their 270-mile journey. Every man knew that there could be no turning back: the die was cast, the mutiny of the Sepoy Army of Bengal no longer a pipedream but stern reality. Victory would mean freedom, but defeat, they were well aware, would mean death for those who had betrayed their salt . . . the British would not forgive what had been done here this day, any more than they would forget what had been done, almost a month before, in Meerut and Delhi.

They had everything to gain and nothing to lose, their

8

native officers told them, and there was no reason to linger here when their comrades were awaiting them in Delhi, so they stepped out smartly, booted feet kicking up the dust, as the cheers grew fainter and finally faded into silence.

A mob from the bazaar, composed of unruly elements, had been hovering on the fringe of the crowd, cheering as lustily as the rest but, as if the sepoys' departure were a signal for which they had been waiting, they now separated from it and spread out, bent on turning the situation to their own advantage. This was an opportunity to pay off old scores and to take possession of the plunder the sepoys had left—too good an opportunity to be missed. The mutineers had burdened themselves with guns, they had not touched the cantonment bungalows or those in the Civil Lines. . . . Running swiftly, the rioters made for the walled enclosures at the river's edge and derisive shouts greeted the leaping flames as they set torches to thatched roofs and sun-dried timbers.

Uniformed police mingled with the newly released convicts and with the city riff-raff, making no attempt to deter them from their purpose and turning a blind eye to looters and fire-raisers alike. Even when the hapless family of a railway engineer was discovered, hiding in a godown, the police were deaf to their cries. Thus encouraged, the hate-crazed mob hacked the unfortunate mother to pieces and, flinging the children from one to another, disposed of them as mercilessly, finally letting the tiny bodies fall into the trampled mud at their feet, as if they were broken toys.

Sitting his horse a short distance away, the Nana Sahib —Dundoo Punth, self-styled Maharajah of Bithur— watched them, his round, plump face devoid of expression. His thoughts were of the meeting he had just had with a deputation of native officers from the four mutinous regiments and of the promises he had made to them when he had accepted an invitation to become their leader. His acceptance had, of course, been conditional on the mutineers' return to Cawnpore . . . he had no intention of leading them to Delhi to support the cause of the Mogul Emperor when, with their swords at his back, there was a kingdom here which could be had for the taking, once the British had been driven out. *His* kingdom, long promised to him by his adoptive father, Baji Rao, last of the great Mahratta Peishwas—his kingdom which, with Baji Rao's pension, the British had denied him, despite all his efforts to show himself as their friend and ally. . . . His dark, curving brows met in a scowl.

How he had worked to cultivate good relations with the British! He had entertained the Cawnpore garrison lavishly, had given dinners in their honor, organized picnics and hunting parties for them, making expensive gifts to their whey-faced womenfolk, enduring the boredom of their company and of their conversation—in a language he neither spoke nor understood—for hour after endless hour. And all to no avail, although time and again old General Wheeler had assured him that he would make representations on his behalf to the Court of Governors of the Company, and the General's wife, who was of his own caste and creed, had begged him to be patient. He *had* been patient, the Nana told himself. He had waited, whilst his coffers emptied and he had been compelled to call on the moneylenders to supply him, at exorbitant rates of interest, with the means to live in the manner to which his position entitled him, and to support the thousands of retainers who were dependent on him . . . fifteen thousand of them, the majority useless old men, responsibility for whom had been bequeathed to him by Baji Rao.

Yet nothing had been done. He had sent his young aide, Azimullah Khan, to London at great expense, to put his case to the Governors of the Company and they had rejected his claim, refusing to recognize the Hindu ceremony of adoption that, under ancient Indian law, gave him the same rights a natural-born son of the Peishwa would have enjoyed. He had been permitted to inherit

10

Baji Rao's private fortune and his palace at Bithur, with his debts and his retainers, but that was all. The Peishwa's generous pension was deemed to have died with him and his private fortune, never as large as the British chose to believe, had long since been dissipated.

He had had no choice, the Nana Sahib reflected bitterly, no choice at all in the circumstances but to embrace the mutineers' cause. He was in much the same position they were, with little to lose and everything to gain by severing his ties with the British. Crippled by debt, continually hounded by rapacious moneylenders, in what other way could he hope to recoup his fortune or regain his lost throne? He had for a time, it was true, toyed with the idea of ranging himself so staunchly on the side of the British when the sepoys rose that the Company would be in honor bound to reward his loyalty by recognizing the justice of his claim and paying him the pension they had for so long refused. But the success of this maneuver would depend on the British emerging victorious from the struggle, and events in Meerut and Delhi had convinced him that this was unlikely—a conviction to which General Wheeler's ludicrously inadequate preparations for the defense of Cawnpore had added weight. Wheeler, for all his glowing record, was proving as unfitted for command as Hewitt had proved in Meerut.

Had the old General decided to defend the Magazine, it might have been different, but as matters stood . . . The Nana Sahib smiled to himself. Most of the Company's generals were too old and Wheeler was in his dotage— he had refused to listen to advice, had rejected all attempts to persuade him to move his troops into the Magazine for fear of showing mistrust of the sepoys which, he had insisted, might offer them an excuse to mutiny. So, obstinate to the last, he had built what he was pleased to call an entrenchment out on the open plain which was, in fact, nothing more than a deathtrap for the nine hundred souls he had herded into its confines . . . and the sepoys,

11

neither waiting for nor requiring an excuse, had mutinied just the same.

Clearly Wheeler was mad or too senile to understand the gravity of the situation. Of those now sheltering in the entrenchment, close on four hundred were women and children. Burdened by these and by noncombatant civilians, railway engineers and a horde of frightened Eurasian Christians, with a scant two hundred trained British soldiers, a handful of British and native officers and a few loyal sepoys to defend them, what chance did the old man imagine he had, behind his crumbling mud walls? The British admittedly fought best when the odds were against them, but this time surely the odds were too long: with the sun beating down on them and some four thousand sepoys, with heavy guns, attacking them day and night, how could any of the motley garrison hope to survive?

The Nana's smile faded as he considered the odds. The hot weather had begun and, with each day, the temperature would soar. The recently built barracks and the new European hospital block, on which the defenders were depending for shelter, were of flimsy construction and would not long withstand the pounding of shot and shell . . . and the hospital was roofed only with thatch. The barracks were overlooked by other, as yet unfinished new blocks, from which the sepoys could fire down with impunity; the old General had not laid in adequate stocks of food or of ammunition for his eight light field-guns and there was only one well within the whole of the three-acre entrenchment. A few marksmen, carefully positioned, should be able to keep the well under continuous fire during the hours of daylight and, deprived of water at the height of the Indian summer, not even the British could hold out for more than a few days. A week, perhaps, at most, and if he offered a reward to any man who succeeded in setting the hospital roof ablaze, then . . . The Nana Sahib's smile returned.

Azimullah, he recalled, had named the entrenchment *The Fort of Despair* during the course of its construction, and thus it would prove, if the mutineers abandoned their foolish desire to go to Delhi and agreed, instead, to return to Cawnpore. Their leaders had assured him that they would; they had gone ahead of him in order to inform the sepoys of the proposed change of plan and he was only waiting for a summons to ride out to Kalianpore and place himself at their head. With their aid, he would build up a great power for himself here; he would march, as a conqueror, down the valley of the Ganges and, as more regiments threw off the Company's fetters and came flocking to his banner, he would fight a new Plassey. Above all, he told himself exultantly, he would teach these Christian dogs what it meant to flout a Mahratta. He . . .

"Highness!" Azimullah Khan's voice broke into the Nana's thoughts. His handsome young Mohammedan aide had been deep in conversation with his elder brother, Bala Bhat, and with the Moulvi of Fyzabad, Ahmad Ullah, for the past twenty or thirty minutes, and the Nana studied him with suspicious eyes as he approached. The Moulvi was a teacher of the Islamic faith. He had been useful in sowing the seeds of sedition in the minds of the Light Cavalry, who were of his faith, and he had done good work in Lucknow and elsewhere in Oudh, but he was ambitious, a smooth-tongued rabble-rouser on whom it might be wise not to place too much reliance. His previous service under the now deposed King of Oudh had not been entirely satisfactory—there had been ugly rumors concerning him, even one or two hints that he had betrayed his old master to the British in return for personal advancement.

Nothing had been proved, but . . . he had, of late, begun to exercise some influence over Azimullah and this the Nana was determined not to permit. Azimullah, although of humble origin and neither a Mahratta nor a Hindu, had become as indispensable to him as his own right hand and, at this critical juncture in his life, he had to have one man—apart from his two brothers—whose

13

undivided loyalty was beyond doubt. There was Tantia Topi, of course, the commander of his bodyguard, who had always served him well, but Tantia was a soldier, with a soldier's blunt honesty. He lacked Azimullah's shrewd wits, his political cunning, his knowledge of the British—acquired at firsthand in London and in the Crimea, as well as here in Cawnpore, when he had acted as *munshi* to General Wheeler's predecessor. Of the two, perhaps, Tantia was more to be trusted, yet . . . The Nana Sahib sighed.

"Well?" he challenged, as Azimullah reined in beside him. "What plots have you been hatching with the Moulvi?"

"We hatch no plots, Nana Sahib." The young man's tone was reproachful. "The Moulvi seeks only to serve you—as do I—and he offers two suggestions for your consideration."

The Nana's mouth tightened. His suspicions were far from being allayed; if anything they were increased. "And what, pray, does the fellow suggest?" he demanded coldly.

Azimullah gestured to the mob of looters with a disdainful hand. "He asks, Highness, whether you would not be well advised to keep this plunder for the sepoys when they return? They have been promised pay and this must come from *your* purse if these scum are permitted to carry off everything of value from the dwellings of the British. Shall I send in the bodyguard to drive them off?"

The Nana Sahib gave his assent a trifle sullenly, but the suggestion was a practical one which, had he not been so absorbed in thought, he might have considered without any prompting from the Moulvi. As his sowars went in with whoops of delight to wrest their prizes from the bazaar mob, he asked, still coldly, "And what is Ahmad Ullah's second suggestion? You said he had two to offer, did you not?"

Azimullah's dark eyes lit with a fugitive gleam of resentment. He had for so long enjoyed his master's favor that to be spoken to in this curt, disparaging manner roused him to indignation. His conscience was clear, Allah knew; what he had planned with the Moulvi was more for the Nana's gratification than his own, but the Moulvi had been most insistent that he should do all in his power to persuade his master to accede to the scheme, so he controlled himself.

"I had said, Highness, that when the sepoys swear allegiance to you it should be as Peishwa—that you should be proclaimed in your august father's title, with a twenty-one gun salute. Your brother and the Moulvi were in agreement with me but the Moulvi is of the opinion that the proclamation should be made here, when you lead your army back to the city, rather than at Kalianpore, before a few villagers. Also, so as to make the oaths binding on the men of both religions, he advises that we should plant two banners—one of Islam, for the Light Cavalry, and one for those of your Highness's faith, the banner of Hanuman. Thus it will be made clear to all who witness it that we are united in your service and that of Hind . . . and that the enemies we fight are the Christian British and their converts." The Nana was beaming on him, Azimullah saw and, his temper swiftly restored, he went into details of the proposed ceremony and then, recalling the promise he had made to Bala Bhat, he added, "At the same time, your Highness's brother, Bala Sahib, could be proclaimed Governor and Chief Magistrate of Cawnpore, to ensure that law and order are preserved in the city."

"Good, good. It is agreed, Azimullah. Arrange it so, you and Ahmad Ullah." The Nana laid a forgiving hand on his young aide's shoulder. "I shall proclaim myself Peishwa here, in the city, tomorrow morning. When it is done, I shall send a formal declaration of war to General Wheeler and we will launch an attack on his Fort of Despair immediately."

"That place will not hold out until nightfall, Highness! The heavy guns from the Magazine will demolish it, brick by brick, in a few hours," Azimullah declared scornfully.

"You will not need to dismount from your horse before you ride in to accept the old General's surrender!" He was smiling as he rode over to acquaint the Moulvi with his master's decision.

"Does he give his consent to the proclamation?" Ahmad Ullah asked, before he could speak.

"Yes . . . with much pleasure."

"And also to the manner of the oath-taking?"

"Also to that, Ahmad Ullah." Azimullah's smile widened. "Thou hast set great store by the oath-taking, hast thou not?"

The Moulvi did not smile but his dark, hawklike face revealed his relief at this news. "It is important," he answered gravely, "if we are to serve a Hindu prince—and a Mahratta—that the price of our subservience be settled in advance. We fight as equals and the rewards must be shared equally between us, with no discrimination against those of us who are True Believers. Thy master shall swear to this tomorrow, Azimullah . . . and Bala Bhat also, before he is made Governor."

"Yes, certainly," Azimullah confirmed. "They will raise no objections—least of all the Nana Sahib."

"See to it that he does not," the Moulvi ordered, his tone suddenly harsh. "They will rise now, throughout all Oudh and Northern India, the fighting men of the Bengal Army—thy master will have a great host under his command. But if he should break the promises he will make to us, remember that Wajid Ali—he who was once King of Oudh and a Believer—waits in enforced exile, eager to return."

"My master will keep his word," the Nana's young aide asserted stiffly.

"He has yet to prove himself," the Moulvi pointed out. "And the first thing he will have to prove is that he is no longer a friend to the British."

"Thou need'st have no fear on that account, Moulvi Sahib." Azimullah spoke with conviction. "The Nana's hatred for the British may have been hidden beneath the

16

cloak of soft words in the past but it is deeper than thine —and with reason. The British have humiliated him, times without number. They have taken from him greedily and given him nothing in return, save insults which have wounded him deeply. You will see what will happen when he gives free rein to the anger which burns in his heart— he will spare none of those who now cower behind their mud walls out on the plain, not even the women or the babes that cling to them! He will be as a tiger, thirsting for blood."

"Good!" The Moulvi's bearded lips curved at last into a smile. "Thy words have the ring of truth, Azimullah. Thou are a worthy son of the Prophet and we understand each other well. Stand thou at thy master's back and see to it always that he gives ear to thee for, when the winds of change blow, it is as easy to drag down a leader as it is to elevate him to leadership. The war we wage is a holy war and we shall be less tolerant than the British to any of our commanders who fail us." He shrugged contemptuously. "The British are fools to put their trust in the Company's gray-beard generals! Old General Hewitt, by his failure to act decisively in Meerut, has almost certainly lost India for them but what do they do? Demand his head, hang him . . . oh, no! They leave him in command at Meerut and put General Wilson—who behaved no better than he did—in command of the troops they send to attack Delhi. True, there is talk of an enquiry but . . ." He broke off, with a pleased exclamation, to point to a horseman in the French gray and silver of the Native Cavalry full dress, approaching them at a headlong gallop. "Allah be praised! It is the messenger from Kalianpore at last, with a summons for the new Peishwa to take command of his army. The hour strikes for him and for us also, Azimullah. . . . Come, my brother, let neither of us shrink from his destiny!"

"I shall glory in it." Azimullah unsheathed his *tulwar* and raised it exultantly above his turbaned head as he

17

rode forward to meet the messenger. "Before the sun sets tomorrow, my sword shall be red with the blood of the *feringhi*, I promise thee, Ahmad Ullah! I do not forget the haughty, highborn British ladies who received me in their London drawing rooms as if I were a pet lapdog . . . and laughed in my face when I sought to respond to their advances! I have waited a long time to take vengeance on them. As a boy, in their accursed Free School, I dreamed of slitting their white throats, even as I salaamed to them."

"I too." A gleam of remembered anger flared in the Moulvi's heavy-lidded eyes as he set spurs to his own horse. "There is one whom *I* would slay with my bare hands," he confessed. "He with the empty sleeve, to whom Sir Henry Lawrence entrusted certain letters, which he took secretly to Meerut. Had the Company's gray-beard Generals listened to him, the rising there might well have failed . . . but happily they did not."

"Colonel Sheridan, dost thou mean?" Azimullah questioned in some surprise. "He who was lately Commissioner in Adjodhabad and lost his swordarm in the Crimea? But he is in Lucknow, is he not, newly appointed to command of the Volunteer Cavalry?"

"That is who I mean—and he is *not* in Lucknow." The Moulvi laughed, in rare good humor. "Last night, to my joy, Allah delivered him into my hands. He rode across the Bridge of Boats from Lucknow and has remained in what you are pleased to call the Fort of Despair. His wife is here, I was told—doubtless it is on her account that he stayed."

"Yes, she is here—she gave birth to a child, a son, two weeks ago. And"—Azimullah chuckled maliciously—"the Nana Sahib, as was his custom, sent the child a silver loving cup. A loving cup! For all the good that whelp will have of it, he might have filled it with poison!"

They were both laughing when, breathless, they drew rein beside the messenger from Kalianpore. "What news?" the Moulvi demanded sharply, his laughter fading.

18

"It is as you wish, Moulvi Sahib," the native officer answered. "We do not march to Delhi."

"Allah is good," the Moulvi acknowledged softly. Raising his voice, he added, "Death to the *feringhi!* Not one shall escape from here!"

CHAPTER ONE

Soon after dawn on June 6th, the four mutinous regiments of the Cawnpore Brigade marched back to the city, bringing their artillery train with them. Within an hour of their arrival, a mounted messenger from the Nana Sahib presented himself at the entrance to the British entrenchment to deliver a written communication from his master. This, couched in arrogant terms and addressed to General Sir Hugh Wheeler, announced the Nana's intention to launch an attack on his position forthwith.

Such treachery on the part of the one Indian, above all others, in whose friendship and goodwill he had believed implicitly, left the old General stunned and heartbroken. For a long time he sat with his head buried in his thin, blue-veined hands, unable to speak coherently. Finally, at the urgent request of his second-in-command, Brigadier General Jack, he consented to call a conference of his officers and to permit the alarm bugle to be sounded, as a warning to any who had left the entrenchment to reenter it at once.

To the distant rumble of gunfire, the officers of the garrison made their way to the flat-roofed barrack block in which the General had set up his headquarters. All were aware of the significance of the gunfire, and the sight of smoke and flames once more ascending from the city and the civil and military cantonments afforded proof—if proof were needed—of the return of the mutineers from their overnight camp on the Delhi road.

To Alex Sheridan, abruptly roused from an exhausted sleep, the sepoys' return came as no surprise. Since his meeting with the Moulvi of Fyzabad the previous morning, he had known in his heart what to expect. Despite the fact that one was a Mohammedan and the other a Hindu of Brahmin caste, an unholy alliance between Moulvi and Mahratta had always been on the cards. Both men were ambitious and hungry for power and from the outset, he was certain, both had been involved with the plotters of sedition in Delhi and elsewhere. There could be no doubt that the Moulvi had been one of the active instigators of mutiny in Oudh—although the Nana had vacillated, at pains to remain on friendly terms with General Wheeler and his garrison lest, at the eleventh hour, the carefully planned sepoy rising should fail.

Alex hunched his shoulders despondently as he glanced across to the European hospital block where, last night, he had been compelled to part from his wife and newborn son. A few women were moving listlessly about the verandah, even at this early hour, but he could see no sign of Emmy. He was turning away when a tall, fair-haired officer in the scarlet shell jacket of the Queen's 32nd fell into step beside him and, following the direction of his gaze, observed wryly, "So near and yet so far, eh? I persuaded my wife to remove into that place, in the conviction that she and the children would be safer there than in a tent, and I've scarcely exchanged half a dozen words with her in private since her removal!"

His voice, with its hint of an Irish brogue, sounded familiar and Alex turned to look at him more closely, certain that they had met before but unable at first to recall where. The insignia he wore proclaimed him a captain; he was in his early thirties, tall and of powerful physique, with a humorous quirk to his mouth and the deeply tanned skin of one who evidently spent more time in the open than was usual for Queen's officers in India. A gleam of amusement lit his very blue eyes as he asked, in mock reproach, "Don't you remember me, Alex? Shame on you!"

"Good Lord!" Alex exclaimed, with genuine pleasure. "John Moore, by all that's wonderful! We last met at the Barrack Hospital in Scutari, did we not? You were with the Turkish contingent and I—"

"You were General Beatson's second-in-command and you were with him in Silestria in 'fifty-four. I'm delighted to renew your acquaintance, my dear fellow." They shook hands and Moore added, his smile fading, "Although I could wish that our reunion were taking place in happier circumstances. However . . ." He shrugged resignedly. "Surely you're a fairly recent addition to the garrison? I don't recall having seen you here before and I've been here for the past three months."

"I arrived yesterday morning from Lucknow—after the electric telegraph wires were cut—with a dispatch from Sir Henry Lawrence," Alex told him.

Captain Moore's fair brows rose in unconcealed astonishment. "And you stayed? Did you not realize the parlous state we're in? You would have been better off in Lucknow, my dear Alex."

"My wife and infant son are here. The baby was born prematurely less than three weeks ago. For his sake I dared not risk the journey."

"*Emmy* Sheridan—oh, yes, Caroline has spoken of her frequently. They've made friends but somehow I never connected her with you. Stupid of me but—I heard that you were seconded to the Political Service. Weren't you Commissioner for one of the Oudh districts?"

Alex nodded. "I was, yes. For Adjodhabad—where both the irregular cavalry and the native infantry have just mutinied, murdering most of their officers. But I had been relieved of my civil appointment before that happened." He did not go into details, and Moore, after a quick glance at his face, did not pursue the subject. "Why are *you* still here?" Alex asked curiously.

"It's not from choice, I assure you. I'm in command of our invalids—seventy-four men who weren't fit to move with the regiment to Lucknow—and I'm responsible for the wives and families, who were also left behind." John Moore spoke ruefully. "Would I were not! Frankly, Alex, I don't much relish the prospect of trying to defend *this* place against four regiments of Pandies—I take it we're about to be attacked by the mutineers, don't you? They appear to have abandoned the idea of marching to Delhi, more's the pity."

"Yes," Alex agreed. "They do, alas." They were passing one of the nine-pounder guns mounted on the north-western extremity of the entrenchment and he noticed, with shocked surprise, that no protection of any kind had been provided for either the gun or the team which manned it, apart from a few sandbags and a shallow trench which ran along inside the wall, and which appeared to be unfinished. No emplacement had been constructed and there was no shade; when the sun rose, the men would suffer acutely, and only a few uncovered buckets of water had been provided, from which they could slake their thirst. Again following the direction of his gaze, John Moore gave vent to a frustrated sigh.

"I know, I know," he acknowledged, as if Alex had spoken his thoughts aloud. "Our defenses are not completed and the coolies who were supposed to be working on the site have all disappeared. And—save for night alarms—the gunners have not been given permission to stand to arms in shirtsleeve order—none of us have. The General obviously was *not* expecting the mutineers to attack us but perhaps, now he's realized that they intend to, he'll agree to relax some of the regulations which are likely to hamper us." He tugged at the high white collar of his shell jacket with an impatient hand. "Have you been on a tour of our defenses yet?"

Alex shook his head. "No, not yet."

Moore repeated his sigh. "I'll take you when the conference is over. You'll find it alarming. Why in God's name the General didn't choose to defend the magazine I'll never know! We could have held out there for months, with little danger to the women and children . . . but old Wheeler insists that reinforcements are on their way and will reach us in less than a week. His main reason for choosing this site is, he says, because it's close to the Allahabad road and he doesn't want the reinforcements to have to fight their way through the city in order to reach us. He has a point, of course—*if* they reach us soon and in sufficient number. But if they don't . . ." He made a rueful grimace. "May God help the poor innocents we are pledged to protect!"

Remembering the message he had brought from Lucknow, warning of an unforeseen delay which had halted the relief column at Benares, Alex maintained a discreet silence. The delay might not be as serious as anticipated and it was, in any case, for General Wheeler to break this news to his officers—or not—as he saw fit. He and Moore entered the cramped, low-ceilinged room in which the General had established his administrative headquarters and, there being no chairs, they took up their positions by the wall on the far side of the room, where an open window admitted what air there was.

The room was already full but more officers came crowding in after them, all correctly uniformed and wearing swords and medals, as if for a peacetime inspection. None looked particularly happy and several were openly grumbling, with varying degrees of annoyance, at the sudden summons and the confined space in which they found themselves. One late arrival, a redbearded young giant in Native Infantry uniform, thrust a way through the press to join John Moore by the window and was introduced to Alex as Lieutenant Mowbray Thomson of the 56th.

"*Late* of the Fifty-Sixth," Thomson amended. He glanced with interest at Alex's uniform and his empty sleeve. "And you, sir, would seem to be late of the Third

Light Cavalry. May I respectfully inquire whether you were at Meerut when your regiment earned the doubtful distinction of being the first to betray its salt?" Alex stiffened involuntarily but the question was asked in an apologetic tone, clearly prompted by a desire for information and not intended to give offense and, after a slight hesitation, he answered it without rancor.

"Yes," he said quietly, "I had the misfortune to reach Meerut on the eve of the punishment parade which led to the outbreak and, I fear, precipitated it." He heard John Moore draw in his breath sharply and, conscious that both he and Thomson were eying him expectantly, shook his head, anticipating the next question that both wanted to ask but were reluctant to put into words. "I regret I cannot tell you why the Meerut mutineers were permitted to reach Delhi, without any attempt on the part of the British garrison to stop them. I—"

"Cannot—or will not, Alex?" John Moore challenged dryly.

"In all honesty, John, I cannot," Alex assured him, careful to control his voice as a wave of remembered anger welled up into his throat. He saw again in memory the obese figure of General Hewitt, slumped in what Colonel Jones of the 60th Rifles had scornfully called "his bloody bath chair," heard the voice of the Divisional Commander raised in petulant protest when he, and a dozen others, had pleaded to be allowed to go in pursuit of the mutineers. Such memories filled him with shame; he had endeavored to erase them from his mind but still they returned, like visions from a nightmare, to haunt his thoughts and torment his conscience. The Meerut garrison, barely a week ago, had fought the first gallant and successful action against the mutineers when, in overwhelming numbers and confident of victory, they had sought to bar the road to Delhi at the Hindan River bridge. Colonel Jones at the head of the Rifles, Charles Rosser with his two squadrons of Carabiniers, Henry Craigie, Hugh Gough and Melville Clark of his own regiment and even Brigadier Archdale Wilson had, it seemed, purged their memories of that night of failure and confusion in blood . . . whereas he, who had shared it with them, had only the consciousness of failure on which to look back. He had failed to reach Delhi with the warning Brigadier Wilson had eventually entrusted to him and, before that, he . . .

"You've nothing with which to reproach yourself, Alex," Moore said, breaking the brief silence that had fallen between them. "And you surely don't have to defend General Hewitt? For God's sake, everyone knows that he refused to allow any of his British troops to leave the station, even those who volunteered! *He's* to blame for the whole miserable affair, not the officers who were under his orders."

"I'd like to hear what really happened," young Mowbray Thomson persisted, his tone still apologetic. "From one who was there. That is, I—forgive me, sir, but there are so many rumors. One doesn't know what to believe. I've heard that General Hewitt is to be tried by court martial and . . ." he broke off as a staff officer called for silence and General Wheeler entered, with Brigadier Jack and an aide-de-camp at his heels.

The assembled officers came to attention and the General took a paper from his ADC with a visibly shaking hand. He was a small, spare man, with sparse white hair and of erect, soldierly bearing, whose boundless reserves of energy had hitherto belied his advancing years. In the past he had radiated a benign confidence but now, Alex thought as he watched him, white head bent, staring down at the paper in his hand, he seemed uncertain and hesitant, as if something—or someone—had dealt a mortal blow to his self-esteem.

Sir Hugh Massey Wheeler had a fine record of over fifty years' service with the Company's sepoy army, to which he had been posted as an ensign in 1805. He had seen action against Diraj Singh and in the Afghan War of 1839-40 and had fought with distinction as a brigade commander against the Sikhs. The only blot on his record had been his failure to act decisively when bringing up reinforcements prior to the Battle of Aliwal, for which he had incurred some criticism, but he had lived that down and his personal courage during the battle, in which he had been severely wounded, had finally been rewarded with a knighthood at the end of the Punjab campaign, when he had commanded the Jullundur Frontier Force.

He looked anything but a hero now, however, as he addressed his tensely listening audience in a voice that was at once querulous and charged with emotion. "I shall not keep you from your posts for long, gentlemen," he promised. "But I feel in honor bound to inform you personally that the native prince, whom I have trusted and regarded as a friend, has repaid my trust with the basest treachery." He paused, glancing about him as if expecting comment but no one spoke and he went on bitterly, "The Nana Sahib of Bithur, gentlemen, after repeatedly assuring me that the mutinous regiments would, if they rose, march to Delhi and do us no harm, has himself ridden after them and brought them back to the city. At dawn this morning I received from him what amounts to a declaration of war." The General's voice broke as he read from the paper he had been holding. " 'I am about to attack you,' he informs me and has the effrontery to sign himself Peishwa of the Mahrattas!"

At this there was a concerted murmur of outraged feeling which could not be contained and Mowbray Thomson exclaimed, with a shrug, "Well, what price the Magazine now!"

His voice carried and the General's pale cheeks were suffused with color. "I am aware," he said, as the indignant murmurs faded into disciplined silence, "that many of you considered me to be at fault in choosing to defend this site, instead of the Magazine, and I am forced to concede that our present position will not be easy to defend against overwhelming numbers and resolute attack. Most of you know why I chose this site—it is close to the road

27

from Allahabad, along which I believed and hoped that a relief column would come. I had intended, with the help of that column, to evacuate the women and children—of whom there are now three hundred and seventy-five—to Allahabad at the first possible opportunity. The last information I had from Calcutta, before the wires of the electric telegraph were cut, led me to believe that Colonel Neill was leading his regiment of European Fusiliers to our aid, and that we could expect his force within a week or, at most, ten days. However . . ." Again he paused, as if inviting comment and Alex, glancing at the faces of those about him, saw dismay mirrored in each one.

To endure hardship or to fight against overwhelming odds was, as he knew well, no new experience for most of the officers of this garrison, many of whom were veterans of the Sutlej and Punjab campaigns—but it was a very different matter when the lives of nearly four hundred helpless women and children were also at stake. Yet still no one voiced his dismay and General Wheeler sighed.

"The telegraph line between Lucknow and Calcutta is apparently still open," he went on wearily. "And yesterday, gentlemen, Sir Henry Lawrence sent one of his officers, Colonel Sheridan, to warn me that he had received news by telegraph that Colonel Neill's relief column has been delayed. The sepoy regiments at Benares have also broken out in mutiny and it is believed that a similar situation now exists at Allahabad and in the surrounding districts. We can expect no help from Colonel Neill until both these outbreaks have been dealt with, I regret to tell you. We are alone, gentlemen, and must defend ourselves as best we can, relying on our own resources. As many of you will already know, our position is rendered the more perilous because my order to blow up the powder reserves in the Magazine could not be carried out. Lieutenant Burnham, of the Oudh Artillery, the officer entrusted with this task, was fired on by the Nana's troops and, deserted by his native gunners, unhappily lost his life in a gallant attempt to enter the Magazine. As a result, the rebels will have at their disposal all our heavy guns and reserves of ammunition. . . ." He talked on, reminding them of the defensive plans they had already made and ordering others.

All able-bodied men, including civilians, were to be armed and given instruction in the use of their arms, should this be required; some of the infantrymen would have to be trained as artillerymen because the nine-pounder guns in the entrenchment would, almost certainly, have to be manned day and night.

"We have only sixty trained gunners of the Bengal Artillery and Lieutenant Ashe's half-battery has none at all, since the *golundazes* he brought with him have joined the mutineers," the General said, white brows meeting in an anxious frown. "This means that your invalids must be pressed into service, Captain Moore—any man who can stand on his feet must be asked to volunteer."

"They will, sir," John Moore answered confidently. To Alex he added grimly, lowering his voice, "Over a hundred of the women and children are of our regiment. If they have to crawl to their posts, my men will defend them."

There was no more talk of the Magazine; no one offered or even implied criticism of the entrenchment and, evidently heartened by this, the old General's face lost some of its wan pallor and, like the good commander he was, he put on a show of confidence once more, which had a marked effect on everyone present.

"We have provisions and supplies of ammunition for up to a month's siege, if necessary, gentlemen," he announced. "But please God, relief will reach us before they are exhausted. We have a good well but water must, of course, be rationed from now on, with priority for the women and children and the sick. We have adequate medical supplies, more surgeons than, I devoutly hope, we shall need, sufficient guns and muskets to hold the enemy at bay . . . and stout hearts. Trusting in the Divine Mercy

29

of Almighty God, we will do battle against this evil and not flinch from our duty. To your posts, if you please, gentlemen, and be ready should the alarm sound—unless any of you have questions or suggestions of a practical nature to offer, before we dismiss?"

A number of questions were asked, which included the request that shirtsleeve order should be permitted for those manning the guns and the perimeter wall, and then John Moore pressed forward as the General again moved to dismiss them.

"If you please, sir," he said. "There is one matter which I believe to be of some importance."

"Yes, Captain Moore?" The General's voice sounded tired but he waited courteously for the question.

"The unfinished barrack blocks, sir," Moore said. "Those which cross the southwest angle of our perimeter. I'm aware that we're to defend Numbers Five and Six, which command the entrenchment, but what of the others? I mean, sir, if the rebels occupy them or contrive to mount guns or mortars under their cover, they could constitute a serious danger to our defenses on that side. The well is within musket range of Number Four, sir. I know we have a gun trained on it but—"

"Are you suggesting that we should occupy Number Four?" Sir Hugh Wheeler spread his hands in a despairing gesture. "We haven't the men to spare, my dear boy—heaven knows, I wish we had! But as it is I am having to deppend on Mr. Heberden and his railway engineers to man the two blocks we *must* defend."

"Then ought we not to blow the rest up, sir?" Moore urged. "Or at least knock down the front brickwork of Numbers Four and Seven, to prevent the Pandies putting sharpshooters into them? Without cover, they—"

"I'll talk to the engineers, sir," Brigadier Jack put in, his tone impatient. "To see if they think Captain Moore's suggestion is a practical one."

"Very well," the General agreed. "Thank you, Captain Moore, for bringing the matter to my attention."

Moore met Alex's gaze and his shoulders rose in an expressive shrug. As they walked out together, he said resignedly, "I've already suggested that those buildings should be destroyed. At first I was told that no one had the required authority, then that compensation would have to be paid to the contractors who were putting them up and finally that it wasn't necessary, because there was no danger of attack from the sepoys! But come and look at the infernal things, will you, and see if I'm not right? If they're left as they are, the Pandies will get into them and we shan't be able to stop them." He led the way and Alex followed him, gratefully breathing in the fresh morning air. After the stifling atmosphere of the room they had just left, it was a relief to be out in the open although, once the sun rose, the flat expanse of rock-hard ground within the entrenchment would, he was only too well aware, become a furnace.

"At least," John Moore observed, as they passed a line of officers' tents which had been set up a short distance to the rear of the General's headquarters, "Eddie Vibart brought up the vexed question of our manning the defenses in shirtsleeve order, praise be! I'd intended, whatever was decided, to parade my men in hospital fatigue dress—some of the poor devils have been down with dysentery and various other fevers for weeks. I cannot, in all humanity, ask them to fight in skintight tunics and stocks which choke the breath out of them." He gestured to the tents. "Are you quartered in one of these, Alex?"

"Yes," Alex confirmed. "I was allotted a half-share in one with, I believe, a Native Infantry major by the name of Lindsay, whose wife, like yours, has just removed to one of the barracks. I haven't yet made his acquaintance —he was asleep when I took up my abode there and I, in turn, was sleeping when he left at some unearthly hour this morning."

"Willie Lindsay, the Assistant Adjutant General," Moore told him. "A charming fellow with a delightful wife. The whole Lindsay clan seem to be here—there's his

31

sister, who married a cousin and was widowed about eight or nine years ago. She came out here with her family—three very charming girls, the Misses Caroline, Fanny and Alice, and their young brother George, who's an ensign in the First Native Infantry. They all hail, as the name suggests, from Scotland. But I fear you'll be looking for other quarters, if the sepoys do attack us—a tent won't give you much protection."

"In view of which," Alex decided, halting in front of his shared tent, "I think I shall take the precaution of ridding myself of all this silver lace"—he gestured to his Light Cavalry tunic—"in exchange for the uniform Sir Henry Lawrence authorized for the mounted volunteers, if you will allow me a few minutes' grace." He smiled, indicating the rolled, knee-length *achkan* of dust-colored cloth which his orderly had laid out for him before returning to Lucknow. "I shall at least be less conspicuous, don't you think?"

"You damned well will," John Moore agreed. "It's what they call khaki, is it not, from the Persian word meaning dust?" He watched, his expression thoughtful, as Alex divested himself of his stable jacket and, with the deftness of long practice, donned the drab tunic, the right sleeve of which was already neatly pinned back to the elbow. "You've given me an idea. *Our* only alternatives are scarlet or white, but white could be dyed or, if that's impossible because of lack of water, rolled in the dust of the entrenchment. White's the most infernal color to fight in, particularly at night, and if the Pandies do put a few sharpshooters into those unfinished barrack blocks, they'll pick my fellows off like flies. But if you're ready, come and see for yourself."

"Yes, I'm ready." Alex exchanged a sun helmet for the tightfitting shako he had just discarded with relief and followed his guide towards the southwestern wall of the entrenchment.

"Well, there they are, Alex my friend." Halting to the right of one of the provision stores behind the main guard building, Moore pointed to a line of redbrick barrack blocks which stood outside and at right angles to the perimeter wall. A sentry and two men with field telescopes were posted on the roof of the nearest which, Alex saw, was about three hundred yards from where they stood.

"Number Six," his companion told him. "We've made that into quite a strong position, thanks to the ingenuity of the railway engineers. They're still working on Five."

"How many blocks are there?"

John Moore swore loudly and luridly. "There are nine of the infernal things altogether, but Numbers Eight and Nine can be disregarded—their walls are barely started. The rest are empty shells, most of them lacking floors but, as I'm sure you'll agree, they *do* constitute a very serious threat to all our defensive positions on this side—particularly Number Four." His finger stabbed angrily in the direction of the nearest of the unoccupied buildings. "They stand forty feet high, Alex, and the roofs are *pucca* tiling. True they're flat, but it only wants a few riflemen on top of them or even in the buildings themselves and we'll be pinned down too effectively for comfort. Besides, they could bring the well under fire. . . ." He went into details and Alex, following these with frowning concentration, was forced to the conclusion that he had not exaggerated the danger.

"Can we go across?" he asked. "I'd like to take a closer look at Number Four."

"I see no reason why not. The Pandies are still too busy burning and looting to worry about us." They both turned to look at the smoke cloud which hung like a pall over the city and Moore added, with feeling, "God, Alex, it's an appalling thought, is it not, that those devils will only have to walk into the magazine to help themselves to all the guns they can possibly require to pound this place into extinction? And ourselves and our women and children with it. That's what I find almost impossible to stomach . . . the fact that the women and children, *our* wives, *our* children, are in this place too." He bit back

33

a sigh. "Without them, we might have stood a chance of fighting our way to Allahabad or Lucknow, but with them . . ." He left the sentence uncompleted and Alex, sharing his bitterness and despair, could find no comfort to offer.

They left the entrenchment and crossed the intervening space to the fourth of the partly constructed barrack blocks, Moore pausing to point out the two guns mounted almost facing it, beyond which there was a strongly entrenched rifle pit, manned by two sentries of the Madras Fusiliers. A tall, darkhaired man in a shirt and white cavalry overalls stood on the parapet in front of the sentries, a spyglass to his eye.

"Eddie Vibart," Moore supplied, his habitual cheerfulness returning. "Of the Light Cavalry, Alex. He's the best of fellows and one very much after my own heart. He's called that post of his the Redan and he had a party of volunteers working all yesterday and part of the last night to build a *trou-de-loup* in the French style, to his left. You can't see it from here because he's had it covered in but he says it will stop a cavalry charge." He grinned. "Let us hope he's right! Well, this is Number Four. In my humble opinion, it's asking for trouble to leave it as it is—we ought either to occupy and defend it or blow it up."

Alex needed only the briefest of inspections to agree wholeheartedly with this assessment.

"It would not take a lot of explosive to bring the front down, John," he said thoughtfully. "I don't believe it would even require the services of the engineers—we could lay the charges ourselves in less than an hour."

"*If* we had permission," Moore pointed out. "Which we have not." He turned away with a resigned shrug. "Well, perhaps now that the matter has been brought to General Wheeler's attention, something will be done about it—my previous approaches on the subject were made, as I told you, to the Station Commander. And he, evidently sharing Wheeler's belief that the only attacks we should

34

have to ward off would be from the city riff-raff, wasn't anxious to destroy Company property. I'd like to see *all* the blocks we can't occupy laid flat and be damned to whose property they are! For God's sake, it scarcely matters now, does it? Half the city's gone up in flames already and the New Cantonment, of which everyone was so proud, is going up now by the look of it."

They reentered the entrenchment and Moore gestured to the smoke clouds rising sluggishly skywards from the direction of the river. "Everything we owned was in Number Twenty-Five The Mall, Alex," he said bleakly. "We had a garden with English roses blooming in it, and a summer house under a magnificent old banyan tree, which Caroline designed for the children to play and picnic in. We knew happiness there, perfect and complete. But neither of us ever dreamed that it would last for so short a time—or end like this."

The kind of happiness which he had known with Emmy. Alex thought, remembering Adjodhabad and the rambling, white-painted bungalow they had shared during his brief reign as District Comissioner. That house, too, was now a blackened, burnt-out skeleton; the garden Emmy had loved and watched over probably, but this time, indistinguishable from the jungle that hemmed it in and from which it had been wrested. He banished the thought from his mind, aware that to look back was to weaken and John Moore, evidently reacting as he had, said with an abrupt change of tone, "Have you been detailed to a sector, Alex?"

Alex nodded, recovering himself. "Yes—on the northeast face. Adjoining the Oudh Battery, I believe."

"Young St. George Ashe's—or what's left of it. Two brass nine-pounders and a couple of European sergeants," Moore supplied. "We'll head across there now, if you like. There isn't much more to show you, apart from a few more buildings we could well have done without. One stands due north of us, on the far side of the road from the city—can you see it?"

"Yes, I see it." Following the direction his companion had indicated, Alex studied the low, flat-roofed building with narrowed eyes. "What is it, pray? More Company property?"

"A riding school, my dear fellow, for the European cavalry we haven't got! Distance from our perimeter eleven hundred and fifty yards—an ideal site for a battery of eighteen- or twenty-four-pounders, don't you agree?" Moore laughed mirthlessly. "But, of course, no one anticipated that the Magazine would fall into the hands of the rebels. As the General explained this morning, he *ordered* it to be blown up. Young Ashe went to carry out that order at first light the day before yesterday, soon after the Light Cavalry mutinied and went on the rampage. He—"

"The day before yesterday!" Alex exclaimed. "I understood—"

"Hear me out, Alex," Moore put in. There was an angry glint in his blue eyes but his voice was carefully expressionless as he went on, "Ashe galloped his two guns to the Nawabgunge and unlimbered in front of the main gate of the Magazine. The sepoys of the First Native Infantry had joined the cavalry by that time but the two other regiments—still in their Lines—were wavering, and the Magazine guard found by the Fifty-Third were ready to admit Ashe, although they knew what he'd come to do."

"Then what went wrong, for God's sake?" Alex asked. "Did his gunners refuse their orders?"

Moore shook his head. "No, not then—their conduct was exemplary. The Fifty-Sixth were observed to be massing on their parade ground—their officers said afterwards that they were coming to our support in the entrenchment. But someone here panicked—I don't know for certain who it was—and Ashe was recalled, ordered to bring his guns round to the south of the entrenchment and open fire on the Fifty-Sixth. His, you understand, were our only mobile guns. The result was, of course, quite disastrous. With the exception of the native officers and a few loyal sepoys, the whole regiment marched off to join the mutineers and the Fifty-Third did the same. The unfortunate Astley Burnham, who was sent out with Ashe's half-battery a few hours later to blow up the powder in the Magazine, lost his guns and was cut to pieces when he attempted to do so. His sergeant was badly wounded but managed to get back. As the General said, the native gunners deserted them."

His words struck chill to Alex's heart. Why, he wondered, why in heaven's name had two lone Englishmen been sent, with native gunners—however exemplary their conduct might have seemed up till then—on so vital and dangerous a mission? Had the lesson still not been learned, even now? John Moore answered his unspoken question with a cynical, "Burnham volunteered, poor devil, and so did his gunners. They were the same men who had obeyed the order to fire on the Fifty-Sixth." He sighed. "Mowbray Thomson and Henry Delafosse offered to go with a party of unattached officers, in an eleventh hour attempt to reach the Magazine, but the General wouldn't hear of it, so . . . that's the situation, Alex my friend. And the reason why the continued presence of those barrack blocks and that infernal riding school is a constant source of anxiety to me. I've talked freely—too freely, perhaps—but I confess it's been a relief to get some of my anxieties off my chest. And at least you know what the situation is . . . I nearly said how bad it is, but that wouldn't do, would it?"

Alex forced a smile. "No, I don't think it would. But thank you for telling me, John. I'm grateful."

"And sorry that you didn't return to Lucknow, when the chance was there?" John Moore suggested shrewdly.

Conscious of a sick sensation in the pit of his stomach, Alex nodded. His fear for Emmy, rather than for himself, for Emmy and the little son he had wanted so much. But for them . . . His mouth tightened. "They will not have an easy time in Lucknow," he pointed out. "But they'll

37

fight and so shall we. How did the General put it? Relying on our own resources, and our resources include some pretty useful fighting men, if I'm any judge."

"They do," Moore agreed. He gestured to their left. "Over there, last but by no means least of our resources, is the only natural shade we possess—an attempt at a garden but alas, also left uncompleted. It was Lady Wheeler's idea, I believe. She thought it would be a playground for the children and . . ." His voice sharpened, in sudden alarm. "My God, Alex, there are some children there now, with their mothers, do you see? I think we ought to warn them to go back to the hospital and take cover, just in case. I can see no sign of an attack but it could come without much warning and if those children are caught there, I shudder to think what might happen."

He broke into a run and Alex followed him, sharing his concern. Smoke and flames still billowed up from the city and the cantonment area, and the flat plain which separated the wall of the entrenchment from the road was devoid of life, suggesting that the Nana's army was still occupied in arson and looting but . . . they had a regiment of cavalry. A mounted attack could be launched swiftly and with a minimum of warning; guns could be brought up, under cover of the trees. He experienced a moment of blind panic, imagining that he could see Emmy, with the child in her arms, strolling slowly along beside the low hedge by which the small, arid garden was surrounded. Then, as he drew nearer, he realized that he was mistaken—the woman with the baby wasn't Emmy, she had two other toddlers clinging to her skirts. Besides she was older, coarser-featured, and she did not move with Emmy's light, natural grace.

"We'd best not alarm them, John," he cautioned and they slowed their pace to a walk. The women watched their approach apprehensively, guessing what it portended, and they did not argue when John Moore delivered his warning, phrasing it as gently as he could.

"We just came out for a breath of air, sir," a handsome, darkhaired girl explained. "The kiddies were fractious, cooped up in that barrack room all night long, so we thought it might do them good if they could stretch their legs for a while. And they told us the sepoys had gone." She sighed, reaching for the hand of a small, pale boy in a grubby white sailor suit. "*Haven't* they gone, sir, after all?"

Moore shook his head. "They appear to have changed their minds, unhappily. But don't worry, Mrs. Widdowson—keep under cover, with the children. We'll drive them off, if they try to attack us." He smiled reassuringly from one to another, addressing several of them by name. "They're all Thirty-Second families," he told Alex, lowering his voice as the women started to move way. "The ones *I'm* responsible for, heaven help them! I wish we could have moved them to Lucknow with their husbands. Poor souls, it's no wonder the children are fractious—their quarters are appallingly hot and overcrowded. I suppose we might have left them to play for a little longer, so that—"

"I don't think we could," Alex interrupted. He pointed, his throat suddenly constricted. "Our time's run out, John. They're coming—cavalry and what looks like infantry, raising the dust on the Canal Road, do you see?"

Moore tensed. "Yes, I believe you're right. Damn their insolence, their drums and fifes are playing, aren't they? Pandies, marching to make war on us to the tune of *The British Grenadiers* . . . well, that's irony if you like! But I suppose we'd better get to our posts."

The alarm bugle sounded, shrill and clear, as they sprinted for the perimeter wall. They had scarcely reached it when the dry, sandy plain which lay between the entrenchment and the roads by which it was encircled—deserted a few moments before—was alive with mounted men in the French gray and silver of the Native Light Cavalry. Other horsemen, in the Nana's uniform, and two Horse Artillery teams, smartly handled, appeared from

39

the direction of the Nawabgunj to join them. The sunlight glinted on lance-tips and drawn sabers, as they maneuvered arrogantly in front of the watching British and, led by their band, the leading companies of a long column of infantry emerged, a solid wedge of scarlet and white, from beneath the clouds of dust kicked up by their marching feet.

There was a dull boom as a cannon within the entrenchment woke to life and then, heralded by a puff of white smoke rising above the feathery tops of the neem trees edging the Canal Road, a round-shot hurtled across the garden where the children had been at play, to tear a gaping hole through the half-grown hedge which bordered it. Bounding on, it scattered the team of a nine-pounder grouped about their gun on the north east face of the entrenchment, one of whom fell forward on to his face and did not rise again.

The siege of Cawnpore, Alex thought grimly, had begun.

CHAPTER TWO

Other shots followed the first in increasingly rapid succession, although at fairly long range, all but a few of which fell short of their target.

Alex, having ascertained that the section of trench for which he was responsible was fully manned, took up a position to the left of the line of riflemen, a field telescope to his eye. The enemy fire was becoming more accurate now and he saw, to his dismay, that the mutineers had contrived to mount two guns in the cavalry riding school, as John Moore had feared they would: both twenty-four-pounders. They were being well served and they quickly found the range, sending a hail of round-shot to thud against the flat-roofed building in which General Wheeler's recent conference had been held. He cursed under his breath, realizing that both guns must have been brought up under the cover of darkness the previous night, apparently unseen and unheard by anyone within the British entrenchment.

It had, of course, been madness to leave any buildings standing within gunshot range of the defenses, he thought wrathfully, understanding Moore's bitter outburst. It was true that, in Lucknow, Sir Henry Lawrence had refused to destroy the mosques and temples which, in places, overlooked the Residency defenses, on the grounds that they were holy . . . but General Wheeler had no such excuse. He must know that nine-pounder guns, however skillfully trained and worked, could do no appreciable damage to the riding school or to the unfinished barrack blocks which John Moore—and no doubt a number of other experienced officers—had urged him to demolish before an attack could be launched.

The barrack blocks might still be rendered harmless; they would require explosive charges to bring them down but little skill, surely, to place the charges in position . . . a few men should be able to manage it, without a great deal of risk. Devil take it, if the Pandies could use darkness and stealth as a cloak for their activities, that was a game both sides could play. With even half a dozen officers of John Moore's caliber, they . . . A shell screeched overhead, its fuse hissing, to burst with devastating effect amongst the cluster of officers' tents sixty yards behind him.

Alex swore, seeing out of the corner of his eye the tongues of flame which licked greedily at the tautly stretched canvas of one that might have been his own. He had brought only a bedding roll and a change of linen with him from Lucknow, in addition to his uniform, anticipating an immediate return, so he did not stand to lose much but . . . He turned, closing his glass. Obviously there would be no water to spare to extinguish the flames and, in consequence, some of the tents' owners would lose everything they possessed, unless the fire-party worked fast.

He watched six men and a sergeant go in, accompanied by a few reluctant native servants, but they had scarcely begun to haul down the blazing tents when two more shells, aimed with alarming accuracy, sent them diving for cover. One man, a servant by his garb, emitted a high-pitched scream of agony and rolled over in the dust, clutching his shattered leg.

After less than an hour's bombardment, the Cawnpore

garrison had suffered its second casualty. And this poor devil would not be the last, Alex reflected with bitterness, as the man's screams were drowned by the thunder of yet another heavy caliber gun, coming now from a new direction, to the west of the entrenchment. More round-shot struck the brickwork of the hospital building, shattering windows and bringing down a shower of beams and plaster, and a fresh salvo of shells whined high above his head, to find their mark amidst the smoldering tents. The rebels had established a battery of eighteen- or twenty-four-pounder guns behind the Native Cavalry Lines, his mind registered, and a mortar battery in or near the garrison church in the New Cantonment, due north of where he was standing. He ventured a glance over the top of the parapet, searching for it with his telescope. The mortar battery was well screened by trees and . . . He watched the hissing trail of the next shell. The battery was situated behind the church and closer, much closer than he had expected—no wonder they were so often on target. The range could not be much more than 800 yards!

"We trained them bastards too well, sir," a gray-haired corporal of the Queen's 84th observed wryly, as Alex ducked down beside him. He fingered his Enfield and swore, as a round-shot fell short and buried itself in the shallow ditch in front of the perimeter wall, sending mud and dust into both their faces in a choking shower. "If it had've been us out there, though, we'd have been at 'em with the bayonet by this time. I just wish them bloody Pandies would try it—but they've no guts, have they, sir?" He spat out dust. "I reckon they'll just carry on firing their guns at us until they've laid this place flat and killed or wounded all the fighting men. They aren't going to risk their perishing necks in no bayonet charge! It was always us that had to lead 'em against the Sikhs and we could drive the bastards out now, if the General would just give us the word."

There was truth in what he said, Alex was aware, but he was also aware that, with a scant two hundred trained soldiers—seventy-four of them invalids—and perhaps a hundred officers, with a like number of male civilians as yet untrained in the military use of arms, the garrison would be compelled to remain behind the crumbling walls of their ill-sited entrenchment. They had no alternative; they were hemmed in by a circle of heavy guns and by a force of nearly four thousand native troops, backed up by the Nana's army and the hostile population of the city. Even with the aid of the loyal sepoys—supposing they remained loyal—a bayonet charge would be suicidal. Whilst a small, resolute band might, by this means, succeed in fighting their way out, they could not bring the women and children with them and it was quite unthinkable to leave those defenseless ones, even for a few hours, by themselves. He thought of Emmy and his frail little son and shook his head regretfully.

"The General cannot give the word when there are women and children to protect, Corporal," he said and added, wishing that he could believe it himself, "Our time will come. When darkness falls, God willing, we'll find a way to silence some of those guns."

"You can count on me, sir," the corporal assured him, brightening a little. "Henegan's the name, sir, if you need a volunteer. I'm a single man, I don't mind chancing my arm, sir. Anything's better than lying here, letting the sun rot your insides or waiting for a ball with your name on it, like that poor sod of a gunner. The others, they saw it coming and dodged out of the way but McGuire just stood still and it took his legs off, sir."

"See that you dodge, then, Corporal Henegan," Alex returned. He moved on down the line of sweating, dust-covered defenders, offering what encouragement he could. Each man had an Enfield rifle to his shoulder, with five others, ready loaded, at his side but as yet they had been unable to fire a shot—even at the cavalry who, for all their arrogant wheeling this way and that across the plain, continued prudently to stay just out of range.

Like the grayhaired corporal, the men were chafing at

their enforced inaction, but it was evident that the sowars would not attack without infantry support and the infantry appeared to be driven by no sense of urgency. They were making for their old Lines, Alex saw, marching easy with muskets slung and drums and fifes playing them in, for all the world as if they were returning from a peacetime field exercise. The 1st were quartered in the former Dragoon Barracks north of the riding school and had left the column which, composed of the 53rd and the 56th, could be seen quite clearly as it swung along the road from the New Cantonment—also well out of range —and past the Artillery Hospital to the south of the entrenchment.

The Nana Sahib had warned of an immediate attack but in all probability, Alex thought, they would wait until dusk to attack in force, depending on the soaring temperature and the artillery bombardment to weaken the opposition they might expect to encounter and to keep the defenders pinned down. Already the heat was almost unbearable and it would get worse, he knew, as the day wore on. There was no shade for the soldiers manning the walls of the entrenchment; no relief, save for brief spells, which the men took in turn and spent crouching in the shallow trench at the foot of the wall, for it was death now to cross to the hospital block or enter the garden, on which the rebel gunners were keeping up an incessant fire.

From within the entrenchment, the British nine-pounders, outranged and throwing smaller shot, could make only occasional reply and even this seemed almost to have ceased when suddenly Alex heard the two guns to the right of his position open up a rapid fire. He turned to make his way towards them, conscious of a lifting of his spirits when he saw that both appeared to have found the range of the mortar battery which, from behind its screen of trees, had earlier wrought such havoc among the tents.

The officer in charge, a slim, pink-cheeked boy in the distinctive gold-laced blue shell jacket, with scarlet collar and cuffs, of the Bengal Horse Artillery, had contrived to mount his guns behind a protective embrasure of sand-bags and, by means of hand-spikes, was firing both at maximum elevation. In addition to his gunners, he had about twenty men—two of them officers, the rest private soldiers of the Queen's 32nd and 84th—under instruction and, as Alex neared the group, the young artillery officer ordered his own men to "take a breather" and put his trainees to serve both guns.

On his advice, they stripped to shirts and trousers and he worked them hard, pacing up and down between the two gun positions to check each gun before permitting it to be fired. The infantrymen were slow and clumsy at first but began to improve under his painstaking coaching. A gray-whiskered Engineer captain was sponging the muzzle of the nearest gun, a lieutenant of Native Infantry and a portly sergeant of the same regiment were acting as ammunition numbers, while four hefty young privates of the 84th—all Irishmen, from their voices—manned the drag-ropes and hand-spikes and served as ventsman and firing number.

The sweat was pouring off them but, responding to their instructor's enthusiasm and ready praise for their efforts, they did everything he demanded of them without complaint and they raised a lusty cheer when an explosion, followed by a sheet of flame, sent some of the mutineer gunners running in panic from the shelter of their screening trees. The rain of shells from the mortar battery abruptly ceased and when, a little later, the whole battery was seen to be withdrawing to the rear, the artillery lieutenant gave vent to a delighted "View Hulloo!" and flung his forage cap high into the air.

"Well done, my boys, well done!" he shouted at them, and the smoke-grimed faces of his newly-initiated gun teams split into answering grins. Seeing Alex, the boy recovered his cap and, cramming it on to his head again, came across to join him.

"That was damned fine shooting," Alex told him, as the men in his own sector took up the cheering. "And it

46

has provided a much needed boost to morale. You're Lieutenant Ashe, I take it?" He introduced himself and Ashe came respectfully to attention.

"It wasn't bad for amateurs, sir, was it? We were firing shrapnel, at four percent elevation, and I must admit it was a lucky chance that enabled us to hit one of their ammunition limbers." He called out to his battery to cease fire and when the two officers came to take leave of him, mopping their heated faces, he introduced them. "Captain George Kempland, sir, Fifty-Sixth and Lieutenant Henry Delafosse, Fifty-Third . . . Colonel Sheridan, gentlemen, Third Cavalry. We'll make gunners of them yet, I truly believe . . . and of you, too, sir, if you'd like to try your hand. The General's given me carte blanche to train up as many unattached officers as I . . ." He noticed Alex's empty sleeve and broke off. "I'm sorry, Colonel, I didn't realize."

"Do not concern yourself, Mr. Ashe," Alex besought him. "You could perhaps use me as a firing number, if the worst comes to the worst."

"Which it well may," Captain Kempland stated gravely. He passed a powder-blackened hand through his thinning hair and slowly resumed his jacket. "I'm sorry to sound so despondent a note, gentlemen, but—" He jerked his head to the guns. "With our puny firepower, what the devil can we do? Wheeler has left the entire contents of the Magazine to the Pandies. They're free to help themselves to all the ordnance they need in order to crush us— eighteen- and twenty-pounders, whilst we . . ." He spread his hands helplessly. "Oh, I'm not decrying your efforts, Ashe, my dear boy. You'll keep those popguns of yours firing till they burst their barrels, I don't for one moment doubt. But what's to happen to us when they do?"

No one answered him but they all exchanged uneasy glances and Kempland said, with controlled bitterness, "God forgive General Wheeler for his decision to abandon the Magazine—I confess *I* never shall as long as I live. We could have held out there for three months—six, even—don't you agree, Colonel Sheridan?"

Sharing his regret and his misgivings, Alex inclined his head in unhappy silence. Young St. George Ashe returned with Lieutenant Delafosse to his guns, to begin instructing a second batch of infantrymen and, as he did so, the mortar battery opened up again from a new position and at considerably longer range. But it was soon on target. The fourth wave of shells whined high over the puny barrier of the entrenchment wall, with the all too familiar sound of hissing fuses and, of a group of men attempting to draw water from the well, only one escaped unscathed, to fling himself dazedly into the shelter of the hospital veranda. The half-filled bucket of water he had been carrying slipped from his grasp, to spill its precious contents over the wooden floor.

A stretcher party, choosing theilr moment carefully, ran across the intervening space but, after a brief inspection of the bodies scattered in the vicinity of the well, went back to the hospital with their *doolie* empty, leaving the dead where they lay.

George Kempland said nothing but his expression spoke volumes, as he looked up into the shimmering heat haze above his head in mute, reproachful anger.

"All right, lads," he bade the men who had been with him on the gun. "Dismiss for an hour and get some food inside you, while you've got the chance. But watch your step, Sergeant Maywood— you saw what happened just now at the well. Don't attempt to march your men. Let them double across to the cookhouse when they see an opportunity. And have a care yourself—we can't afford to lose a trained loader!" To Alex he said, as the men obediently moved in the direction of the cookhouse in ones and twos, "One begins to wonder whether one is justified in permitting them to risk their lives for the chance of filling their bellies but . . . a man fights better on a full stomach, there's no doubt of that. In such circumstances as these, at any rate . . . and the poor fellows

48

will *have* to fight. God alone knows how, when half of the Thirty-Second can hardly walk and some, according to the surgeons, shouldn't be on their feet at all. But now we've got them working guns!" He shrugged disgustedly. "I suppose the Pandies will attack us with everything they've got once the sun goes down, don't you agree, Colonel?"

"Yes, I'd expect them to," Alex agreed. "They're bound to try for a quick victory. The Nana knows our resources down to the last man and the last cartridge case and he won't anticipate that we shall put up much of a resistance." He frowned and added thoughtfully, "I hope they do attack us this evening."

"You *hope* they do? In heaven's name why?"

"Because we're more than ready for them and it will give us all more heart if we can hit back and inflict casualties on them at this early stage. Morale is dangerously low, even among the officers."

"True," the grayhaired Kempland admitted wryly, "my own has touched rock-bottom, as you've observed, but I can make no apology for it. On the even of Chilianwala I was more hopeful of the outcome than I am now. You were also in the Punjab campaign, were you not, Colonel?"

"Yes," Alex confirmed. "And I was at Chilianwala."

"Then you know how I feel."

"Yes, perhaps I do, but—"

"I've seen commanders commit costly errors before," the older man put in. "But in the whole of my career, never so disastrous an error as Wheeler has made in refusing to occupy and defend the Magazine. *This* place is indefensible. Damn it, there are over three thousand rebels out there, well armed, well fed and almost certainly well doped with *bhang*. Do you really believe that we can hold them off, if they launch a full scale attack on us this evening?"

"Yes, I am confident that we can." Alex eyed his questioner searchingly, seeing anger in his face but no fear. George Kempland was a tough, experienced soldier, whose regiment had suffered heavy casualties at the Battle of Chilianwala; he was not the type to adopt a defeatist attitude or yield to panic. "Our Enfields against muskets, nine-pounders, well served and at close range against infantry—British soldiers against sepoys! They will not stand a chance if they attack us with infantry. *My* fear is that they won't." Remembering the corporal's glum prophecy, he added reluctantly, "Because if they really know what they're about, they'll simply continue their bombardment until they've reduced every building we possess to dust."

"Heaven forbid!" Captain Kempland exclaimed. He shivered, despite the heat. "God spare us that, with all those women and children trying to find shelter. It is infinitely worse for them than it is for us. I . . . have you a family here, Colonel?"

"I have my wife and son," Alex said, feeling his throat tighten. Kempland's eyes met his in sympathetic understanding.

"I have a wife and three children," he managed huskily. "May God have mercy on them all!"

They separated and Alex went back to his sector. He sent his men, a few at a time, to the cookhouse for a meal, but there was no relief for them. As soon as they had eaten, they had to return to their posts to enable others to be released.

All day the cannonade continued with unabated fury, as the sun rose to its zenith in a brazen sky and, long before sunset, several men had collapsed from heatstroke, their faces blackened and the breath strangled in their throats. Most of them had exhausted the contents of their water bottles, however sparingly they sipped at the tepid water in an effort to make it last throughout the endless day, and there was little to be done for those who collapsed, until a *doolie* party from the hospital could brave the perils of the fire-raked compound and remove them.

With the help of an Engineer officer, Francis Whiting,

and a party of young Company's officers, Alex salvaged a number of the burnt-out tents and contrived a shelter at either end of his sector, slinging the charred canvas on planks over a shallow trench. The labor of digging even a few feet into the rock-hard ground was considerable but a succession of volunteers, working in relays, managed it at last and both shelters were soon in constant use, serving as a temporary resting place for stretcher cases from his own and Lieutenant Ashe's sectors.

Ashe was seemingly indefatigable; his guns, their barrels too hot to touch with the bare hand, kept up a steady fire on any target within their range. When they fell silent, Alex could hear his voice, hoarse with the strain of shouting, as he lectured his trainee teams on the essentials of gun drill, driving them mercilessly but himself harder still. He had lost his senior sergeant, he told Alex sadly when they met during one of the few respites he allowed himself—blinded by a shell splinter, the man had died half an hour later. There were tears in the youngster's eyes as he recounted the manner of his loss but, within the next few hours, it was doubled and then trebled, when the battery in the riding school sent a deadly salvo of round-shot into a group of his gunners. Dryeyed and grimly determined, Ashe brought up more ammunition, a line of sweating, straining men dragging the tumbril from another sector of the line and, with a mixed team of amateur gunners, subjected the riding school to a withering and vengeful fire. Only when the gun carriage cracked under the pressure imposed on it at a maximum elevation did he regretfully discontinue his efforts and the eighteen-pounder sited behind the riding school went on with its relentless pounding.

"If only those devils would come at us!" Corporal Henegan of the 84th muttered angrily. "If only they'd show themselves! Gutless bastards, why don't they attack? They've had all day, haven't they?"

He was expressing the thoughts of almost every man crouched behind the mud walls of the entrenchment, Alex

51

knew, not to mention his own. The order for the defenders to stand to arms—in force since 10:30 that morning—had not been countermanded although, apart from gun and mortar fire, the enemy had made no hostile demonstration. Since noon, the infantry had remained in their Lines and, well before that, the cavalry had withdrawn from the plain. Did they intend to attack? he wondered anxiously. Would they attempt to carry the British position by assault this evening? Or had the Nana, with the inherent cunning of his race, decided to play a waiting game? That he might delay, leaving his guns to do the work for him, was not beyond the bounds of possibility, although there would be pressure on him, of course. Hotheads like Azimullah Khan, the onetime *munshi*, who had no military experience—even the Moulvi of Fyzabad, to whom the political advantage of a swift victory would be all-important . . . both of them would undoubtedly urge their leader to take the risk. But would he listen to their counsel, unless the mutineers themselves also urged it?

The sun was sinking now, like a ball of molten fire behind the feathery tops of the shadetrees lining the edge of the racecourse, but there was only a slight breeze and this brought more dust than relief with it, and the faint yet unmistakable stench of putrefaction from the bodies scattered about the compound. Animals as well as humans had died under the pounding of the guns, Alex realized. An officer's charger lay near the quarter-guard building, still saddled, its entrails spilling out over the silver-crested sabretache, its blood-soaked tongue hideously lolling and, seventy or eighty yards beyond, the commissariat cattle enclosure was a shambles . . . but, until the guns stopped firing, no one could move the bodies, save at the risk of life and limb.

He sighed and turned, rubbing eyes weary and swollen from the glare, to look with shocked dismay at the battered walls of the hospital behind him. Emmy was inside that building, he knew; Emmy and his son and with

52

them other women and children, the wounded and the dying ... dear heaven, what must they have had to endure, with fear allied to the stifling heat and overcrowded conditions? All day he had forced himself to concentrate solely on the duties of his command, the needs of the men in his sector and the prospects of coming to grips with the enemy. He had not dared to let himself think of anything else and least of all of Emmy, but he thought of her now as two more heavy round-shot buried themselves in the wall of her refuge, and felt sick with despair.

Fool that he had been to allow her to stay here, he reproached himself savagely. Thrice-damned, witless idiot, to imagine that the perils of the journey to Lucknow for their sickly child would be greater than those to which both the child and his mother were now exposed behind the honeycombed brickwork of the hospital! Why had he listened to Emmy's pleas, why had he taken heed of her concern for the child? God in heaven, what was the life of the child compared with Emmy's safety, her precious life? His only excuse was that he had not realized how inadequate Wheeler's defenses were, had not seen them until this morning. He had taken it for granted that, because Lawrence in Lucknow had prepared so well for a siege, Wheeler had prepared equally well. True, he had seen the first part of the entrenchment being built before he had left Cawnpore for Meerut, but it had not then been completed and it had not occurred to him that so experienced a campaigner as Sir Hugh Wheeler would fall so far short of the standard a civilian had set in Lucknow. Now, like George Kempland, he ...

"Alex!" John Moore halted breathlessly beside him, his face red and blistered from the sun. Hopefully, Alex gripped his arm, buoyed up by the thought of action.

"Are we to blow up those barrack blocks?"

Moore shook his head. "No," he said harshly. "I've just seen the Station Commander. No one is to leave the entrenchment—the General's orders. No one, that is to say, except the out-pickets and a burial party, after dark. There'll be no burials, of course, that's out of the question. The bodies will be"—there was a catch in his voice—"*disposed* of in the disused well, between Numbers Five and Six of the barrack blocks. Edward Montcrieff, the chaplain, will go with them."

They were both silent for a moment. Then Alex said flatly, "Yes, I see. Well, ours not to reason why but . . . suppose the Pandies occupy Number Four Barrack? It's within musket range, they could make things devilish hot for us—but you pointed that out, I imagine? If our drink-well comes under musket fire, there will be hell to pay and—"

"I used every argument, Alex, and Francis Whiting backed me up. The Brigadier wouldn't listen. The railway gentlemen are in occupation of Numbers Five and Six, and he told me to leave it to Heberden and Latouche, who have apparently said they can hold both without military aid. The General has agreed to leave the barrack blocks to them, so . . ." Moore rolled down the sleeves of his filthy, bloodstained shirt, his face expressionless. "I must get back to my post. Four of my poor invalids are back in hospital with sunstroke. I saw your wife and mine, for a few minutes, when I helped to carry the men across. They're both bearing up bravely and your Emmy sent you her love."

"Thanks, I . . . I'm glad to have news."

"I thought you would be. Well"—Moore braced himself—"I'll be on my way. Brigadier Jack thinks they'll attack us before nightfall but I'm not so sure."

Alex found himself praying as he stood behind the mud wall, watching the light fade and listening to the weary curses of his men—a brief, almost blasphemous prayer that the mutineers would indeed launch an attack now, before it was too late. He knew that his prayer had been answered when Corporal Henegan called to him in a voice tense with eagerness, "They're coming, sir, I think—the sepoys are coming!"

They came, in the last of the fading light, in two lines,

with the cavalry to the left and skirmishers, in extended order, spread out as a screen across their front. They came steadily, making no attempt at concealment, their native officers at their head, keeping them in well disciplined alignment. Each maneuver was executed with parade ground precision; the scarlet-clad ranks wheeled and re-formed, obedient to British bugle calls and orders shouted in English as, from either flank, a field-gun battery moved smartly forward, unlimbered and opened fire with case and grape.

Behind their shell-scarred ramparts, the British defenders waited in grim silence, broken only by the frightened chattering of some native Christian bandboys who squatted behind the riflemen, ready to reload their weapons when the need for this should arise. Alex's line had been augmented by half a dozen officers and two Madras Fusiliers, he saw, as he cautioned them to hold their fire, and he recognized Captain Whiting running past him, bent double, to take his place with one of two reserve gun teams which Ashe had collected in the trench behind his guns. The grayhaired Kempland hurried after him, red of face and breathless after doubling across the compound.

"Steady, my boys!" she shouted hoarsely. "Hold your fire till I give you the word. We've got to make every shot count—so let 'em come at us!"

A bugle shrilled above the roar of the field-guns. The skirmishers took ground to right and left and the front line of the advancing infantry discharged their first volley in well drilled unison ... but too soon, Alex noted with relief, hearing the bullets spatter into the ground well short of their target. Still the British defenders made no answer. Another thirty yards, he thought, assessing the range. The field-guns were blazing away with creditable speed but their gunners were merely wasting ammunition—they were too far back for their fire to be effective. He put his telescope to his eye, focused it on the right-hand battery and saw, as he had expected, that they

55

were limbering up, preparatory to moving forward in support of the infantry.

So far it had been a perfectly executed movement, straight out of the textbook; a trifle cautious, perhaps but ... Suddenly, to his bewilderment, he realized that the line of red-coated sepoys had halted. Peering out between the sandbags of his observation post to ascertain the reason, he was astonished to see a body of horsemen, led by some of the Nana's gaudily uniformed irregulars, start to surge forward across the infantry's line of advance. A resplendent figure on a white Arab rode at their head, with *tulwar* drawn, urging them on and, guessing that it was Azimullah, the Nana's impulsive young aide, Alex called out a warning to Ashe.

"Action front—cavalry!" the artillery officer yelled at the pitch of his lungs. He stood waiting, his arm raised high above his head and, as the cavalry broke into a gallop, he brought it down smartly. "Fire!"

The thud of hooves on the hard-baked sand was drowned by the crash of guns from within the entrenchment and Ashe's nine-pounders, double-shotted with grape, did swift and terrible execution amongst men and horses. The sowars, who had clearly expected to dash straight into the entrenchment without meeting more than a token resistance, unable to slacken speed, could only close their ranks and come on. Ashe's guns, quickly reloaded, got off two more rounds before they wheeled in confusion, to head for the triangular sector on the north face of the perimeter—the Redan—commanded by Major Vibart. There a blaze of artillery and small-arms fire, delivered at point-blank range, finally scattered them and they vanished into the smoke, beyond the line of Alex's vision. When he glimpsed them again, they were galloping back towards their own Lines in little semblance of order and, he thought exultantly, too badly mauled to be capable of rallying.

Their charge had been a bad tactical error and their precipitate retreat had thrown the right flank of the in-

56

fantry into a confusion which momentarily matched their own but whoever was commanding the infantry did not lose his head. The sepoys dressed ranks and, once more in impeccable alignment, resumed their advance. Their second volley was delivered from much closer range and, as musket-balls whined above his head like a swarm of angry bees, Alex bawled the order to his men to return fire.

The Enfields spoke and spoke again with scarcely a pause and, with the range rapidly shortening, few missed their target. The bandboys scrambled pluckily for the discarded rifles, loading and ramming like veterans, and the men behind the parapet, their weariness forgotten, used their weapons with deadly effect. The front line of sepoys faltered, as man after man went down under the raking fire of lead. It reformed briefly to advance a few more yards and then broke, and Alex, recklessly mounting the parapet, emptied his Adams pistol into their fleeing backs. His own men were cheering now and the second line of attackers, after getting off a ragged volley, hesitated and then joined their comrades in headlong and undisciplined retreat.

"No guts! What did I tell you, lads, the beggars have no guts!" Corporal Henegan shouted derisively. A native officer, as if to challenge this accusation, put spurs to his horse and rode straight at him, with saber raised and lips drawn back in the ferocious parody of a smile. The corporal took aim coolly and shot him down within thirty feet of the parapet. His foot caught in the stirrup iron and his horse, bearing a charmed life, dragged him the length of Ashe's sector before following the sepoys in their retreat.

Darkness fell with the habitual suddenness of the East and firing from the entrenchment petered out, cheers for their victory spasmodic and swiftly silenced as the exhausted defenders let their weapons fall and started grimly to count the cost of it.

"Sure, now 'twas a rare trouncing we gave them, was

it not, Seamus me boy?" a husky Irish private of the Madras Rusiliers exulted. "Seamus . . ." He got stiffly to his feet, glancing anxiously about him. "Seamus O'Neill, are ye there? Corporal, have yez seen me pal O'Neill? He's a little feller, so he is and a Blue Cap the loike o' meself. Six-seven-two O'Neill and—"

A voice from the darkness of the trench answered him. "He's here, lad, what's left of him. Took a round-shot in the chest . . . and there are two more poor fellows with him that won't see another dawn. *Doolie*-bearers . . . over here! We've two for you!"

The butcher's bill, Alex thought, as the wounded men were carried away, the bearers running over the rough, shell-pitted ground with scant regard for the moans of those to whom such jolting was unbearable agony. Always the butcher's bill had to be paid. The Pandies' was, no doubt, heavier than their own—as the big Irish Blue Cap had put it, the rebels had been given "a rare trouncing" but . . . He moved slowly down the line, sickened by what he saw.

There were nearly four thousand Pandies and more, probably, would join them from outlying stations like Fategarh and Adjodhabad, recently the scenes of mutiny. Their losses could be replaced but every British soldier killed or wounded or falling sick within the entrenchment would place an intolerable burden on the few who were left to defend it—a burden they must contrive somehow to shoulder, if the women and children were to have any chance of survival.

Alex sighed and stood back to allow a burial party to pass him. His sector had come off comparatively lightly, he realized, as he exchanged news with other officers—two killed and seven wounded, but only three of these seriously. Ashe had lost six of his gunners in the space of as many minutes, and Edward Vibart, at the Redan on the north face, had been compelled to depend on semitrained volunteers to man the guns with which he had so successfully completed the rout of the charging cavalry. And he had prayed—he had actually *prayed* for the mutineers to launch an attack, in the belief that it would raise morale! Well, perhaps it had, but there was a bitter taste in Alex's mouth as he looked down at the body of Fusilier O'Neill lying mutilated at his feet.

"They're after puttin' them down a well, they say, sorr, not buryin' them." O'Neill's comrade was on his knees beside the body, his voice flat and controlled but, for all that, he sounded shocked. "With your permission, sorr, I'd loike to put him there meself. O'Neill was me front-rank man, ye see and he'd have done as much for me, God rest his soul." He rose and came awkwardly to attention, white-faced, his control slipping a little. "I'm two-seven-three Sullivan, Madras Europeans, sorr."

"All right, Sullivan," Alex assented. "You can take him with the next party. On your way back, collect a man to help you and go to the comissariat godown by the quarter-guard. Ask whoever's in charge for the rum ration for this sector and bring it up here. I'll sign the authority as soon as I'm relieved."

He was on his way to the comissariat warehouse with Whiting and Ashe, ten minutes later, when the sudden crackle of musketry, coming with uncanny accuracy from their right, sent all three of them running for cover. The shooting continued and, directed now at the well, it scattered a party of men who, by the light of hurricane lamps, were endeavoring to draw water.

The three officers looked at each other in shocked dismay.

"The unfinished barrack block next to Number Five," Francis Whiting said. "Those devils must have slipped in unobserved, while the attack was being repulsed! If they keep the well under fire day *and* night, it'll be all up with us."

"Unless we can dislodge them." Ashe moved to the corner of the warehouse and stood listening to the steady discharge of musketry, which was now being answered by the British defenders in Number Five Block, as well as by those on the southwest side of the entrenchment. "I don't think, by the sound of it, that there can be many of them. Not more than half a company, anyway, but they're spread out the whole length of the building and keeping under cover of the walls." He hesitated, frowning. "God, what I'd give for the howitzer we had to leave behind us in Lucknow! Or even a couple of mortars but . . . if we brought Depster's gun from behind the *pucca* roofed barrack and mounted it to the right of Number Five, we might be able to shift them."

Alex shook his head. "I doubt if you could. Those half-finished blocks may not have floors but they're roofed and they stand forty feet high. The Pandies would put men up there to fire down on you while you were moving the gun—and even if you got it in position, you'd make little impression on walls as thick as those. It's going to take cold steel to shift the swine, I'm afraid."

"Cold steel, sir?" Ashe stared at him. "Do you mean a raiding party?"

"Yes, that's what I mean. Captain Moore and I discussed the possibility of either blowing in the front of the block, to prevent the Pandies occupying it, or else occupying it ourselves. But that was this morning . . . whatever we do now will be a bit late, alas." Alex joined the artillery officer at his point of vantage and stood for a moment, counting the musket-flashes which came from the newly captured building. "You're right, Ashe— there aren't very many of them. I fancy a raiding party could work its way across from the rear of Number Five without being seen. In fact, I'm sure it could . . . and with the railway gents to provide covering fire and a few of your shells used as hand grenades and lobbed in through the windows, we could probably get rid of most of them."

"The General's orders are that only burial parties are to leave the entrenchment," Captain Whiting reminded him apologetically. "Don't misunderstand me, Colonel—

I'm as anxious as you are to drive the Pandies out. But how is it to be done when—"

"It has *got* to be done, with or without orders," Alex returned impatiently. "Number Four should have been provisioned and occupied this morning, dammit! That well is our lifeline—the women and children cannot hope to survive if their water supply is cut off. Poor souls, they must be suffering enough already without lack of water to add to their discomfort!"

He was suddenly angry as the memories of Meerut, searing and bitter, came flooding back into his mind. The tragic loss of so many innocent lives, which had been the result of General Hewitt's refusal to take action, or to permit any of his subordinates to do so, was the most painful memory of all and it still ate into him like a canker. He recalled the impotent fury he had felt when Brigadier Wilson had hesitated, compelled to delay making the vital decision which might have saved Delhi, because the orders of his superior—whether right or wrong—had to be obeyed without question. One of General Hewitt's orders had been that he was not to be disturbed after he had retired to compose his report . . . and Archdale Wilson had not even questioned that, although Meerut was going up in flames and the mutinous sowars of the Light Cavalry had already started on their way to Delhi.

God in heaven, was it all to happen again? Was the disgraceful story of Meerut to be repeated here, because the Company's generals—the gray-beard generals, as the Moulvi of Fyzabad had so contemptuously called them— were too old, too set in their peacetime ways to be able to adjust to a crisis situation which demanded swift, courageous action? And because . . . Alex felt the sweat break out on his brow and cheeks . . . because no subordinate officer dared question the orders they gave or the decisions they made, lest he jeopardize his own career. It was the system, the stern military code which was the very basis of discipline and he had lived most of his adult life believing it. General Hewitt had used it to cover his own deficiencies but Sir Hugh Wheeler, despite his seventy years, was surely made of sterner stuff than the obese and senile Hewitt.

Wheeler's record spoke for itself: he was a fine soldier. His decision to defend this entrenchment, in preference to the Magazine, might well prove to be a costly error, perhaps even a disastrous one, as Captain Kempland feared, but at least he intended to go down fighting. At this morning's conference, he had shown himself bitterly disillusioned by the Nana's betrayal but he had not attempted to shrink from his responsibilities. He had given the reasons for his decision to defend the entrenchment and had admitted the possibility of error with courageous frankness—and he had shown himself to be approachable, to be willing to listen to suggestions from his juniors. Indeed, he had invited them, so that the chances were that he would listen now.

"Well, sir?" Whiting prompted wearily.

"I'm going to the General," Alex told him. "To request him to rescind that order."

"Now, sir? He may be asleep," Ashe warned uncertainly.

Alex smiled. "Not if he's the man I think he is, Mr. Ashe." He looked at Francis Whiting. "Are you with me?"

They both nodded. When they entered the headquarter block, they found John Moore and Mowbray Thomson already there and the General, fully dressed and wakeful, talking to them.

"You, I take it, have come on the same errand as these two gentlemen, Colonel Sheridan?" Sir Hugh Wheeler smiled briefly but there was an approving gleam in his faded blue eyes as he added, "I applaud your zeal and, needless to tell you, I appreciate the urgency of the matter to which you have drawn my attention. That block *must* be cleared and—if we cannot destroy it—then we must occupy and defend it, if necessary at the expense of Number Five. Mr. Heberden's party can be transferred in daylight and our out-pickets can assume responsibility for Number Five. I've given permission, at the request of Captain Moore, for a small party of volunteers to go out now, under his orders, to endeavor to clear Number Four. But I did specify that the party should consist of unattached *junior* officers and men who can be spared from their posts. That excludes Mr. Ashe, I fear, who must remain with his guns . . . and it should exclude you, Colonel Sheridan, should it not?"

"I'm unattached, sir," Alex assured him. "And have just been relieved of my post by Colonel Ewart of the Thirty-Fourth. My rank is a brevet one only, sir, which I would willingly relinquish to serve under Captain Moore's command."

The General's smile returned. "I wish *I* could relinquish mine, for the same purpose! Very well, Colonel Sheridan—I will not deprive you of this opportunity to serve the garrison. May God go with you, gentlemen!"

The raid, skillfully planned by John Moore and gallantly carried out by his small party of volunteers, succeeded beyond even its leader's expectations. Choosing their moment carefully, when the moon was obscured by cloud, the fifteen officers and men slipped silently from behind the sheltering wall of Number Five Block and, as the defenders engaged the enemy's attention, they made their way in twos and threes to the rear of their objective. Alex and the red-bearded Mowbray Thomson lobbed their grenades, with fuses hissing through the open windows and the sepoys fled in terror, few of them waiting to do battle with their unexpected assailants. Those who did stand their ground were driven out at the point of the bayonet by seven men of the 84th, led by Corporal Henegan.

No attempt was made by the mutineers to retake the disputed barrack and, well before the first light, the railway engineers, under the big, cheerful Michael Heberden, were transferred there, together with their arms and a large reserve of ammunition. The raiding party's final task was to place two kegs of powder against the outer wall of the vacated block. This done and the fuses lit, under the expert supervision of Francis Whiting, the whole party withdrew, having suffered only a few minor casualties. On the credit side, Number Four Block had been occupied and made reasonably secure; six mutineers had been killed and an estimated ten or eleven wounded and, with gaping holes blown in its roof and outer wall, Number Five Block would, in the immediate future, offer no concealment worthy of the name to the enemy's marksmen. Seven was covered by two guns inside the entrenchment.

Elated but unutterably weary, Alex went to the hospital in search of Emmy. The veranda, where she had slept since first coming to take up her abode in the entrenchment, had become untenable under the pounding of the rebel guns and he found her in a hot, airless room, so crowded with sobbing children and their helpless, terrified mothers that he recoiled from it in something akin to horror. But Emmy, although she looked pale and exhausted, smilingly shook her head to his anxious inquiries.

"I'm all right, Alex . . . and William, too. Lucy—that is Lucy Chalmers—is helping me to look after him. She's still very shocked, you know, and doesn't speak. Except to William, she speaks to him, sings to him sometimes and I think it is doing her good to have him with her. You see, I—"

"You're looking worn out, darling," Alex put in.

"We don't get much sleep," Emmy answered wryly. "And I've been helping Dr. Harris and some of the others to care for the wounded. It's better to keep busy, I believe—one has less time to worry and feel afraid. And it's not like Scutari." Her voice held no conscious irony. "The surgeons have their hands so full, they're grateful for any assistance any of us can offer, despite the fact that we're women. I told them I'd nursed cholera cases in the Crimea and worked under Miss Nightingale, so they welcomed me and I hope I've been useful." Her eyes were tender as they rested on his face. "Oh, Alex my dearest love, it's wonderful to see you—to know that you're safe! The mutineers attacked yesterday evening, did they not?"

"Yes," he confirmed flatly. "But we repulsed them."

"Will they attack again?" she asked.

"I don't know, darling. I hardly think they'll be in a hurry to—we gave them a hotter reception than they had bargained for." He heard the guns open again and expelled his breath in a long-drawn sigh. "They've got heavy guns and plenty of ammunition, so I'm afraid they're likely to keep *that* up for most of the day. Is it very bad here, Emmy, when the guns are firing?"

"It's frightening," Emmy admitted. "That's why I prefer to have something to do. I couldn't bear just to sit here and listen to the guns and to the children crying and asking questions—I should go out of my mind. I . . . Alex, I'm thankful that William isn't old enough to ask questions. How can you explain to a child what is happening? No British child can understand why the sepoys should want to kill us and I don't suppose any of them have ever been under gunfire in their lives. They simply can't be made to understand why no one must stir from this building in daylight or why, when they are thirsty, they must make do with only a few sips of water. They—"

"Are you short of water?" Alex asked sharply.

She shook her head. "No, not yet. But it's rationed. Two men were killed drawing water from the well yesterday and five or six wounded last night. Now Mr. McKillop, the Deputy Magistrate—the one with the limp—has taken charge of the well and promised that he'll see we get a regular supply. But . . ." Emmy hesitated. "Alex, it's very serious, our situation here, is it not?"

"It's serious but not hopeless, darling," Alex answered.

She met his gaze gravely. "*Not* hopeless, Alex?"

He held her to him, regardless of their lack of privacy. "Darling, the General is confident that reinforcements will reach us very soon. Colonel Neill is at Benares with a relief column. We may have to hold out here for a week, even two, but"—Alex forced a cheerful note into his voice—"he'll get to us, never fear. And there will be more troops on their way from Calcutta. Our plight is known and—" A round-shot struck the rear wall of the hospital, bringing down a choking shower of brick-dust on their heads and causing the whole building to shake. A woman screamed and went on screaming in mindless terror and the children's shrill cries and shrieks were redoubled, sounding so unnaturally loud in that confined space that, for a few moments, they blotted out the sound of the guns.

Alex felt his wife's slim body tremble against him. She said, her voice not quite steady, "I'm not afraid for myself, Alex. Only for you . . . and for William. He's so small, you see, and he feels the heat so terribly. He'll die if—if the relief column doesn't reach us soon."

"Yes, my love, I know. But it will come. Neill won't let anything stand in his way, he'll get here as fast as he can—and we'll hold our own until he does, believe me." He had no other comfort to offer and she lifted her head to smile up at him, although her eyes were filled with tears.

"I do believe you, Alex. It's just that I . . . take care of yourself, darling, for my sake. If anything happened to you, I couldn't bear it."

"We're all in God's hands, Emmy," he reminded her gently. "I'm in no more danger than anyone else."

"No, of course you're not." Bravely she bit back the tears. "But you look ready to drop. Can you stay for a little while? There's not much room here but I could find you some where to rest."

Alex shook his head, thankful that he could not. The open compound and the parapet were bad enough but this . . . the frightened, unwashed faces of the children, the screaming woman and the noiseome heat of the crowded room were suddenly more than he could stomach. Ashamed of his own weakness, he repeated his head-shake. "No, I must get something to eat and then report to my post. Our mess is still functioning after a fashion but . . . Emmy, are *you* getting enough to eat? They feed you, don't they?"

"Oh, yes," she assured him. "And I have Mohammed Bux. Dear, loyal old man! He hasn't run away, as so many of the other servants have, and he sees to it that I have more than enough. Truly I'm all right, Alex. You must not worry . . . just come back, when you can, even for a few minutes." She raised her lips to his and he kissed her hungrily, conscious of a pride and a pity no words could express. Emmy clung to him for a moment and then let him go.

Reaching the corridor, he turned for a last glimpse of her and saw that she had gone to kneel beside the woman who had been screaming. The screams ceased; Emmy waved her hand to him and smiled and, oddly moved by that smile, Alex went out into the pitiless sunlight of the entrenchment to begin another day.

It was Sunday but he did not realize this until the Garrison Chaplain, Edward Montcrieff, came bravely across the shell-torn compound, in cassock and surplice, bearing his Communion vessels. Aided by two native Christian bandboys, he held his customary morning service of prayer with each group of men separately and it was well past noon before he had done.

CHAPTER THREE

After six days and nights of almost continuous bombardment, with the noon temperature rising to 130°, the defenders of the Cawnpore entrenchment still held out against every attack that was launched against them.

Death was no stranger to them now. To a few of the fighting men it came swiftly and cleanly at the parapet, but to most of the wounded and to all too many of the sick, it came slowly and without dignity, often as the only relief from unendurable pain. Men were blinded by shell splinters; their rifles exploded in their faces from the heat; 24-pounder round-shot left them mangled and mutilated, yet still alive . . . and the surgeons were hard put to it to deal with the shattered limbs and the broken bodies which were brought to them, in increasing numbers, at all hours of the day and night.

In Number Four Barrack, after a heroic defense against night raids and incessant sniping, Michael Heberden and his railway platelayers and engineers were all killed or wounded. On the evening of the third day, Mowbray Thomson, with eight men of the Madras Fusilers and four civilians, took over responsibility for the barracks, assisted by three young ensigns. Heberden himself, shot through both thighs when drawing water from the drinking well, lay on his face in the hospital, slowly dying.

John Moore, to Alex's distress, took a musket-ball in the shoulder but, with his right arm in a sling, he carried on, making a wry joke of their two "useless members." Sniping became almost as great a peril as the pounding of the big guns; the mutineers dug trenches among the ruined bungalows of the New Cantonment and in front of the burnt-out Garrison Church, from which their infantry kept up a ceaseless volley of musketry from a range of 350 yards. They picked off so many of Ashe's gunners that two out of three of his guns were manned solely by volunteer officers and convalescent men of the 32nd.

The dead posed an appalling problem for the living. During the hours of daylight, when seven batteries of guns and mortars and upwards of a thousand muskets subjected the entrenchment to a merciless hail of shot and shell, the bodies of the dead could not be taken for burial in the well outside the perimeter. They had to be left, mostly unshrouded, on the veranda in front of the hospital or where they had fallen behind the crumbling mud walls or in the compound. Sometimes a woman's body or that of a little girl in crumpled muslin was laid beside the legless corpse of a soldier, his unshaven face burnt black by the sun, and those who must walk past them did so with averted eyes, steeling their hearts to pity.

At nightfall there was usually a two-hour respite from the firing while the sepoys took their evening meal, and the dead were hurriedly dragged out of the entrenchment and lowered, with ceremony, into the dried-up well that was to be their last and only resting place. No mourners went with them—it was too dangerous, for the burial parties had frequently to ward off attacks by prowling sepoys, who slipped past Number Four Block in the darkness, hoping to take them unawares. But, even after the last body had gone, the awful stench of putrefaction lingered on in the nostrils of the weary defenders, mingled with other no less unpleasant odors from which, waking or sleeping, there was no escape.

Emmy's hours of work in the wards increased as casualties mounted, and those who worked with her collapsed under the strain. She saw little of Alex, who spent most of his waking hours at the parapet, or with John Moore and Mowbray Thomson, with whom he took part in numerous raids on the partially constructed barrack blocks to the north of Number Four. He visited her when he could but usually only for a few brief minutes and she could seldom rely on his coming at regular times. She worried about him constantly and sent their faithful old bearer, Mohammed Bux, to look after him, sacrificing his services gladly in return for the news he brought her of her husband's continued safety.

By the end of the first week of the siege, life in the thatched-roof barracks had taken on a strange, nightmare quality, of wich Emmy—working to the point of exhaustion—was only dimly aware.

The women were silent now. They no longer cried out in terror when round-shot thudded against the frail walls of their refuge. Familiarity had dulled their fear and the whole facade of the building was so riddled with holes that none dared guess for how much longer it would afford them their precarious shelter. To cry out was to waste precious energy; instead they prayed, sometimes alone but more often together, in small groups and in whispers, so that the children might not hear and sense the growing despair with which they begged their God for deliverance.

The children, too, were unnaturally quiet. Sinking into apathy from the heat and discouraged by their elders' manifest inability to make reply, most of them had long since ceased to ask questions or plead for permission to go out into the compound to play. They had seen death there and had lost the childish desire for play. Many were ill; dysentery or attacks of vomiting and fever struck them down and they lay in pitiful rows on quilts or ragged scraps of carpet, too weak and dispirited even for tears. Their mothers tended them as best they could, until they themselves fell victims to the prevailing malaise and had, in turn, to be tended by others, who somehow remained immune to both infection and fatigue.

Ironically, it was often the strong and the apparently healthy who died, Emmy learnt, the weak and puny—like her own tiny William—who miraculously survived. Lucy Chalmers, still too shocked by what she had experienced in Adjodhabad to be able to carry on a coherent conversation with anyone except her mother, nevertheless nursed William with devoted care, so as to leave Emmy free to work all day with the surgeons. It was she who kept vigil each night beside the child's cot, insisting that Emmy must rest, and her mother, gaunt-faced and prematurely aged, who took her place when even Lucy flagged.

As day followed day, social barriers which had at first been jealously preserved became part of another, half-forgotten existence, shattered by the wretchedness that was common to all and by the enforced proximity of officers' ladies to soldiers' wives. Privacy, like sleep, had become a luxury enjoyed by few and there could, in any case, be little social distinction between the lowly and the gently born when two privies had to meet the needs of everyone in the crowded building, and when sickness and diarrhea afflicted them all with complete impartiality. Cleanliness was impossible when a bucket of water might cost the man who drew it his life. Each night men did risk their lives to haul water from the well with block and tackle—some for money and others, like the Deputy Magistrate, John McKillop, out of selfless pity—but there was seldom enough to drink for any of them. Although many gave up their own small ration to a wounded husband or a sickly child, the ravages of thirst were added to the torment suffered by those lying helpless in the grip of fever or enduring the agony of a newly amputated limb.

There were, inevitably, some who complained, some

71

who yielded to grief, and one or two who held themselves aloof from the tasks which the rest shared. There was some bickering and even an occasional bitter quarrel among them, yet somehow—none of the women could have said how—they contrived to meet the trials and tribulations of each day as it came. They adjusted themselves to new perils and faced bereavement bravely; they accepted the need for fresh sacrifices and bore their anxiety for husbands and children, together with the heat, the stench and the flies, with a fortitude at which Emmy could only marvel, unaware that her own was of the same high caliber.

Always when morale sank, the courage of a few shone like a beacon of hope amidst the general misery. The wife of a private of the Queen's 32nd, Bridget Widdowson—who confessed that she could neither read nor write—kept the children entertained and happy for hours on end with the droll Irish stories she made up for them. Later, armed with an officer's sword, she coolly stood guard over an intruder found with matches in his possession on the thatched roof of the building, while the fire he had started was extinguished.

Mrs. Hillersdon, whose husband was Collector and Chief Magistrate of Cawnpore, although desperately weak from fever and mourning the death of her elder child from the same cause, gave an eloquent rendering of the Twenty-third Psalm each evening at candlelight. She continued until both her strength and her beautiful voice failed her ... but only her silence at the accustomed hour on the evening of June 9th, revealed that she had herself entered the Valley of the Shadow and would not return.

Other heroines emerged; women who refused to give in to despair or to lower the standards of behavior in which they had been brought up to believe. Griefstricken mothers, learning that they had been widowed, said no word of their loss to their children; others, who had watched their husbands or their sons die, returned from the wards to perform once more the chores allotted to

72

them, hiding their heartbreak with a smile. Two—one the wife of an officer who was in Lucknow—reaching their time, were compelled to give birth in the crowded room and stifled the cries that were wrung from them by biting on leather straps until the agonies were over.

Squalor, in such conditions, could not be avoided; brick-dust, from the pounding of the guns, was everywhere, often inches deep on the floors; glass from shattered windows, fallen beams and masonry, human excreta —all had to be cleared away, perhaps a score of times each day, but it was done. Gently nurtured girls, officers' ladies, like Caroline Moore and Grace Kempland who all their lives had been accustomed to be waited on by a host of native servants, now uncomplainingly performed such menial tasks, cleaning, scouring and even cooking, for there was no one else to do it. The native servants— bearers, *ayahs*, sweepers and cooks—had begun to flee the entrenchment as the siege went on, sensing defeat and anxious to save their own skins. Those who were left were needed to prepare food for the men defending the perimeter, who could not be spared from their posts, and the women had, perforce, to fend for themselves.

They made *chapattis* and lentil stew and pease puddings from the uncooked rations they received. All too often, however, if they were unable to obtain the use of an oven or reach the cooking-fires in daylight, even these meager supplies had to be eaten raw, washed down by sips of rum or—incongruously—champagne, with which they had been issued at the beginning of the siege. Tea, coffee and milk were unheard-of luxuries; the most that could be managed were a few grains of sugar, carefully dissolved in a little of their precious water, which was given to the sick and the younger children. William—since Emmy, to her distress, was no longer able to suckle him —existed on this, with the addition of a drop or two of brandy.

After the first five days there was no meat, except when the soldiers on out-picket or burial duty contrived to shoot a stray horse or cow, and the few jars of preserved herring, jam and pickles, which had been doled out with the champagne, were soon used up or were kept in reserve for the children. Virtually everything was shared, the needs of the wounded and the sick taking precedence ovr all others. Women who had had the foresight to bring a stock of clothing with them, intended for their own use, cut up dresses and petticoats from which to make bandages, resisting, with one or two exceptions, the temptation to indulge themselves in the luxury of clean linen. They went bare-legged when an urgent request came from Lieutenant Ashe for all the stockings they could provide. His request was answered at once and later became the subject of wry laughter when the owners heard that the young Artillery officer required them in order to replenish his dwindling supply of cartridge cases.

There was, heaven knew, little cause for levity, as day followed endless day and no word of the promised reinforcements reached them from Allahabad or Lucknow. Yet, against all reason, a brave spirit of optimism prevailed: even, Emmy observed with wonder, amongst the wounded, many of whom voluntarily returned to duty with bandaged heads and arms in slings, scarcely able to walk.

The mutineers had increased their number to an estimated eight or nine thousand, with the addition of revolted sepoy regiments from Jhansi, Saugor and Nowgong. It was also reported, by native spies, that they had seized two boatloads of munitions, sent upriver from Benares and intended for the Cawnpore garrison, but despite their vast superiority in arms and manpower and despite the ceaseless bombardment, they had failed to break down the British resistance.

Every attack, whether by day or night, had been beaten off; the Pandies had not succeeded in entering the entrenchment, save as prisoners, and all their attempts to occupy the unfinished barracks blocks to the north of Number Four were thwarted by Captain Moore's raiding parties. If British casualties were high, those of the enemy were invariably higher. True, the worn-out guns in the entrenchment could no longer be relied on, ammunition was running short and the defenders were unwashed, sweating scarecrows, almost blinded by the glare of the sun, their bodies burnt raw, their strength sapped by the relentless heat . . . but they could still fight, and they gave proof of it daily.

By the sixth day the rebel attacks had dwindled and become more cautious and, at times, even cowardly. The cavalry sowars seldom showed themselves; the sepoys allowed a dozen half-starved British soldiers and civilians to put ten times their number to flight with scarcely a shot fired, and prisoners, taken on raids, admitted that their leaders were losing heart. Still the heavy guns continued their pounding, with red-hot grapeshot added to the screeching mortar shells and the volleys of musketry. When the bombardment was at its height, as many as 300 missiles an hour rained down on the parched ground of the entrenchment, and the men behind the parapet dared not move from their posts, taking what rest they could leaning, rifles always to hand, against the bullet-pitted mud wall or in the shallow trenches behind it.

But they were not defeated; they could hold out, Alex declared, when Emmy ventured to question him. They could hold out until Neill's relief column reached them; Allahabad was, after all, no more than 120 miles distant. Six days' march, eight at the outside—they could defend the entrenchment for another eight days, and there was always the hope that aid might be sent from Lucknow.

Another eight days of this living hell, Emmy thought miserably. Eight more days of slaughter, of heat and squalor, of raging, unquenchable thirst and of racking anxiety for friends and loved ones—oh, no, dear, merciful God, no! Already Alex looked like a ghost, filthy, blistered, unshaven, his clothes hanging on his emaciated frame like rags—how could he imagine that they could hold out for another eight days? But she had learnt the

75

value of silence; she did not dispute his claim, did not voice her own fears—he had enough to bear without that. If he and the other ragged ghosts who haunted the ramparts like sleepwalkers could keep the enemy at bay, then the battle was not lost. She brushed his stubble-grown cheek with her lips and they parted as they had done so many times in the past week, he with a quick smile and she with a prayer in her heart that she would see him again.

There was, as he had said, always the hope that aid would come from Sir Henry Lawrence. Lucknow, as far as anyone in the entrenchment knew, was not yet under siege and, although communication by normal channels was clearly impossible, it was rumored that General Wheeler intended to try to send a message through the sepoy lines. Emmy, uncertain whether or not to believe this rumor, found it unexpectedly confirmed when Brigadier Jack was brought into the hospital. He was suffering from heatstroke and very ill but, in one of his lucid moments, he was able to tell her that a trusted native had offered to attempt the perilous journey to Lucknow for the payment of a hundred pounds. The General was sending an appeal to Sir Henry Lawrence for aid—any aid— and felt sure that Lawrence, once made aware of their desperate plight, would respond to it if he could.

This news, when she imparted it to the women in the barrack-room on her return there, just before sunset, revived their sorely tried spirits. Haggard faces broke into smiles; eyes swollen and redrimmed from weeping lit with new hope, and voices rose in excited chorus as those who had not heard Emmy's announcement clustered round her, begging her to repeat it. A thin woman, whose name she did not know, hugged her.

"Oh, but that's wonderful, Mrs. Sheridan! Let us pray God that the messenger gets safely through!"

"Sir Henry Lawrence will not fail us," Grace Kempland said. "When he realizes how great our need has

76

become, he will do all in his power to help us, I am sure of that."

"Please God he will send the Thirty-Second!" a corporal's wife exclaimed. "Oh, please God, let him send our men to save us! *They* will get through, if anyone can!"

Her words were echoed eagerly by the rest. "Even two hundred men of the Thirty-Second—two companies would be enough," Agnes Johnson, the Sergeant Major's wife, asserted. "My husband said, only this morning, that if we had two hundred fit trained soldiers, we could fight our way to Lucknow. He says the Pandies are so demoralized by their failure to defeat us that now they would not dare stand in our way."

"Lucknow is only fifty-three miles from us, isn't it?" Mary White looked up from the task of suckling her twin babies, her pale, tired face lit with a flush of excitement. "The messenger could get there in a day and a night, couldn't he, if he bestirs himself?"

"He will be on foot, Mary," another private's wife reminded her. "And the roads will be guarded."

"All right, two days, then. If the troops start at once, they could be here in another two or three days, surely."

"In less than a week—Holy Mother of God!"

"If only they'll come—if only they'll hurry!"

"They'll come, as sure as God they'll come! It is not their wives and bairns who will die if they do not?"

The eagerness with which they had seized on the glimmer of hope her news had offered them alarmed Emmy and, as she listened, she found herself wondering whether she would have been wiser to keep her own counsel, as she had with Alex. She exchanged an anxious glance with Caroline Moore, who said regretfully, "We cannot depend on aid from Lucknow. Sir Henry Lawrence has his own problems there—he is responsible for thousands of lives, compared with our few hundred, we have to remember that. The native inhabitants of Lucknow number close on five hundred thousand and Sir Henry has only the Thirty-Second with which to hold them at bay. I doubt

77

whether he will dare to send them here, even if our messenger reaches him."

An unhappy silence followed her words.

"Not even a company, Mrs. Moore?" the Sergeant Major's wife asked gravely.

Caroline Moore shook her head sadly. "Captain Moore does not think he can afford to take the risk, Agnes."

"Then we are lost," a soft Irish voice whispered. "Sweet Mother in Heaven, we are lost entirely!" Little Mary Kelly held her two-year-old daughter to her and wept. They were the first tears she had shed since the siege began and now she abandoned herself to grief and, although both Emmy and Caroline Moore went to her and endeavored to console her, she would not be comforted. Rising suddenly to her feet, she ran with the child to the corridor and, before any of them could guess her intention or attempt to dissuade her, she was running across the open compound, screaming hysterically to the mutineers to put an end to her suffering. Musket-balls peppered the ground about her, as if in answer to her cries, but none struck her, and a young private of the 84th, with his arm in a sling, bravely went after her and brought her, with the child, safely back to the hospital—all three of them miraculously unscathed.

"We must not give up hoping," Caroline Moore said, when the girl and her daughter were settled at last. "I might be wrong—perhaps Sir Henry Lawrence *will* be able to send help to us, after all. And there is the relief column, there is Coloned Neill's regiment—we've been promised that it's on its way to us, with more British regiments following on from Calcutta. They won't forget or desert us in our hour of need—they are our countrymen. We must have faith in God, trusting in His mercy to deliver us."

There were nods and a few tremulous smiles but the hope had gone, Emmy realized, once again regretting her premature attempt to rekindle it. Yet the hope of relief was all they had left now, all they had to live for—without it, they were lost. They would turn their faces to the wall, as Mrs. Williams had done, following the death of her husband, the commanding officer of the 56th, and simply die of grief. Or, like Mary Kelly, they would deliberately court death by running out to meet the sepoy's bullets. She thought of Alex and repeated what he had told her about the coming of Colonel Neill's relief column, with more conviction than she had felt when she had listened to him.

"If the men who are defending us say that *they* can hold out for perhaps another eight days, than we can," she added. "We know that they will never permit the Pandies to enter the entrenchment while any of them are left alive and that, surely, is the worst we have to fear. If God will give us strength, we can endure anything else."

Caroline Moore smiled her agreement. "We'll dole out the rations, shall we?" she suggested, with forced cheerfulness. "One of the soldiers has promised to bring us some meat broth for the children and the guns will stop soon—it's almost candlelight and . . . " She broke off, the last remnants of color draining from her wan cheeks. "Dear heaven, what was that?"

From the other side of the building they heard a reverberating crash and the sound of running feet. "Fire!" A panic-stricken voice shrieked the warning they all dreaded. "The roof is on fire! Save yourselves!"

This time there was no doubt of the seriousness of the warning. The intruder who had previously crept in with matches had succeeded only in igniting a few strands of thatch, which they had had little difficulty in containing. Now, however, they realized that a carcass—or fireball, composed of sulphur, resin and tallow—from one of the rebel batteries must have been aimed at the hospital roof, with the intention of setting it on fire. The missile had struck the north side of the roof—where the tiling which General Wheeler had ordered as protection was incomplete—and within minutes the whole thatch was alight and the rooms below filled with suffocating smoke.

As the women, frantic with terror, sought to drag or carry their children from the building and others struggled to assist the sick to their feet, some of the roof-rafters fell in and the north wall collapsed, unloosing a cascade of smoldering debris, beneath which many of the helpless were buried.

For the first few terrible minutes, panic reigned and no attempt at organized rescue was possible. The women milled in the corridors, running this way and that, blinded by the smoke and losing all sense of direction. With the sobbing, terrified children and a few dazed wounded from the wards, they blocked the exits, seeking to escape from the flames and the falling masonry, yet afraid to face the danger of the open compound outside. Every enemy gun seemed to be concentrating its fire on the blazing hospital and, from their trenches in front of the New Cantonment, the sepoys poured volley after volley of musketry into the open space at the rear, to which some of the fugitives had managed to run and where they presented an easy target, silhouetted against the glow of the flames. The running children were ruthlessly mown down, as were the soldiers who dashed from the parapet in valiant attempts to guide them to safety.

Emmy lost sight of Lucy Chalmers in the awful confusion and then glimpsed her again, with her mother beside her and William clasped in her arms, crouching behind the bathhouse. She attempted to follow them but the shrieks of those still left in the building and their agonized cries for help rang in her ears, louder and more compelling than the thunder of the guns. She turned back, groping blindly for the entrance to the ward where, less than an hour before, there had been men whose wounds she had dressed and to whom she had held out hope of survival. The gallant, stoically uncomplaining Michael Heberden, with his terrible injuries; the eighteen-year-old Ensign Dawson, whose prayers were never for himself but for his mother, safely at home in England; the stouthearted old Artillery pensioner Cox, with both legs amputated, who could still laugh at his own jokes; the brother of Brigadier Jack, a civilian on a visit from his sheep station in Australia, whose right leg had been carried away by a round-shot; the Brigadier himself . . . their faces and a score of others swam before her tear-filled eyes.

If only she could get help for them, if only she could reach them . . . some of them, surely, must be still alive. A party of soldiers, who had come in from outside to give what assistance they could, appeared suddenly through the smoke.

"Get out while there's still time, lady!" one of them urged her breathlessly, but she shook her head and stayed with them, pointing mutely in the direction of the ward. They managed to haul some of the wounded out before the flames beat them back, grabbing any they could see by the legs and even the hair, shutting their ears to the sufferers' moans. A big, bearded Fusilier seized Emmy in strong arms and, ignoring her protests, carried her out and across the now mercifully darkened compound to one of the godowns at the rear of the Main Guard.

"We can't do no more, ma'am," he told her bitterly. "Them bastards—begging your pardon, but that's what they are—they've finished the hospital. There ain't no one left alive in there now. And not that many got out alive—firing at little children, they was, filthy black swine! And then they attacked us at the perimeter, thinking they could sneak in because it was left unguarded. That was why we couldn't come right away. The Colonel, he ordered us to drive them off first and then he let us go. But he was right—if we'd all left our posts, they'd have been into the entrenchment and that would have been the end of us."

'The . . . Colonel?" Emmy queried faintly. "Which Colonel do you mean?"

"Colonel Sheridan," the Blue Cap told her. "Him with one arm." He sat her down gently and grinned, mopping at his sweat-streaked face. "Do you know him, ma'am?"

81

"Yes," Emmy said. "Yes, I know him." She swayed, conscious of nausea, and he put an arm round her, holding her upright.

"Better let me help you inside, ma'am. You need to lie down and rest. This is where most of the women and children have ben taken." He indicated the door of the godown. "Poor souls! It's a poor enough shelter for them but there ain't nowhere else, now the hospital's gone."

Emmy thanked him and let him lead her into the dark, airless confines of the provision store. A single candle gleamed at its far end, and the sound of weeping assailed her ears as she stumbled inside. It was a hopeless, defeated sound, which tore at her heart as she looked about her and saw, when her eyes became accustomed to the dimness, that the room was already crowded to capacity with blackened shapes, scarcely recognizable as women.

"Please," she requested the Fusilier. "When you go back to your post, would you tell Colonel Sheridan that his wife is . . . is safe."

He stared at her uncomprehendingly for a moment and then drew himself to attention. "I'll tell him, Mrs. Sheridan ma'am, don't you worry. Here . . . " He divested himself of his torn and filthy jacket and, finding a space, spread the garment out for her. "Just you lie down now and try to sleep. I'll tell the Colonel where you are . . . and I'll tell him something else, too. They don't come no braver than his lady and that's the gospel truth—he's a right to be proud of what you did back there in the hospital, ma'am, if any man ever had."

He left her and Emmy sank down in the space he had cleared for her, so numb from shock and exhaustion that she fell instantly into unconsciousness, incapable of inquiring for William and lacking even the strength to attempt to identify the women huddled on either side of her. Twice during the night the crash of guns from within the entrenchment wakened her, as it wakened her neighbors, but no one spoke and she drifted back into sleep, too spent in mind and body to lift her head from its malodor ous pillow.

It was not until the following morning that she learned, from a sobbing and barely coherent Lucy, that her little son was dead. He had died quietly, without pain and almost unnoticed, Lucy whispered brokenly, in the early hours of the morning. She had been wakened by the gunfire and had realized that he was no longer breathing.

Emmy comforted the unhappy girl, herself feeling no grief, only a strange, cold numbness of the spirit that did not admit of pain. She wrapped the tiny limp body in its ragged shawl, looked for the last time on her child's still face and laid him, with the rest of the night's dead, to await the burial party.

There were a great many dead but they were not all there. Forty-two sick and wounded men had perished in the blackened ruins of the hospital, Mrs. Chalmers told her, and their bodies would have to be left where they were, for it was impossible to remove them until the heat subsided. The surgeons had lost all save one small medicine chest, which one of them had risked his life to snatch from the flames. Their instruments, the bandages which the women had provided at such sacrifice, their precious reserves of water and a week's rations had also been lost.

As yet, it had not been possible to call a roll of the women and children; they were scattered throughout the entrenchment, wherever shelter could be found for them, but a number were known to have been wounded or injured or to have succumbed to sickness.

"I think," Mrs. Chalmers said, a catch in her voice, as she looked down at Lucy's bent head and despondently bowed shoulders, "I truly think that I envy your little William, Mrs. Sheridan. At least he is at peace and nothing can hurt him now. The dead cannot hear those guns and for that I envy them. I thought my faith was strong but when I look about me, when I see the terrible change all this has wrought in Lucy, I find myself wondering if

83

there *is* a God watching over us. I feel . . ." She sighed. "But here is Mr. Montcrieff, good, kind man that he is, come to help us to renew our faith. I'd forgotten it was Sunday. Well, we can pray, I suppose, and hope that Almighty God will hear our prayers and send us deliverance."

The chaplain came limping in, white with fatigue, his once spotless surplice torn and bloodstained. Alex was with him, Emmy saw, and a dark-faced Eurasian drummer bearing the Communion vessels—now only a symbol, for both were empty.

Alex crossed to her side and Emmy's heart lifted at the sight of him, losing a little of its frozen numbness.

"William . . . " she began. "Oh, Alex, William is . . . "

Gently he stopped her, "I know, my love, they told me. That's why I've come. I'll dig a grave for him in the garden, where the Hillersdon children are buried." He took her hand in his and they knelt together, as the women gathered round and the chaplain's tired voice started to intone the Lord's Prayer.

"Our Father which art in heaven, hallowed be Thy Name . . ."

They said the familiar words after him, as spent and weary as he, some kneeling but many lacking the strength to rise to their knees, their voices scarcely audible above the unremitting thunder of the guns and the high-pitched, hissing screech of approaching shells. Blistered hands trembling the Rev. Edward Montcrieff turned the pages of his prayer book. *"Almighty God, King of all Kings and Governor of all things, whose power no creature is able to resist, to whom it belongeth justly to punish sinners, and to be merciful to them that truly repent. Save and deliver us, we humbly beseech Thee, from the hands of our enemies; abate their perils, assuage their malice and confound their devices; that we, being armed with Thy defense, may be preserved evermore from all perils, to glorify Thee, who art the only giver of all victory, through the merits of Thine only Son, Jesus Christ our Lord."*

"Amen," Alex said. His fingers tightened about Emmy's hand and she let her head rest against his shoulder, feeling his strength flowing into her to renew her own.

CHAPTER FOUR

That evening—Sunday, 14th June—General Wheeler composed his appeal for help to Sir Henry Lawrence. Aware that it would have to be brief, since at his own request the missive was to be inserted into the messenger's ear by a surgeon, the old General wrote: *"We have been besieged since the sixth by the Nana Sahib, joined by the whole of the native troops, who broke out on the morning of the fourth. The enemy have two twenty-four and several eighteen-pounder guns—we have only eight nine-pounders. Our defense has been noble and wonderful, our losses heavy and cruel. All our carriages are more or less disabled, ammunition short; we have no instruments, no medicine; the British spiritual one remains but it cannot last forever."* He paused, deep in thought, and then his pen stabbed at the coarse, native-made paper as he added, underscoring the last three words: *"We want aid, aid, aid!"*

Two hundred men would, he knew suffice to raise the siege, but he had to leave it to Lawrence to decide what troops he could spare. . . . "It is ready, Dr. Newenham," he announced. The surgeon of the 1st Native Infantry took the paper and, without glancing at its contents, screwed it deftly into a thin spill.

"Very good, sir," he said. "I'll attend to the matter immediately."

Accompanied by the General's son, Godfrey, an Ensign in the same regiment, he left the room and the old man leaned back in his chair, his heavy lids falling. He was tired, he thought, dear God how tired he was! Even to write a letter in this heat exhausted him and he longed for sleep. His wife was lying on the only bed the small room possessed—a string *charpoy*—but he hesitated, loath to disturb her or his two young daughters who lay, their arms clasped about each other as if for mutual reassurance, on quilts spread out on the opposite side of the room. Poor girls, this was a terrible ordeal for them, as it was for all the women and children . . . and worse might be in store for them if Lawrence did not send aid and send it soon.

Was it true, he wondered uneasily, the story the messenger had told him a few minutes ago, when he had paid him the agreed sum in gold for taking his letter to Lucknow . . . could it possibly be true? Was the Nana Sahib, who had been his friend, capable of such merciless cruelty? He stifled a sigh. The messenger, Ungud, was a reliable man, who had been useful as a spy many times in the past few months and his information was, as a rule, accurate. He had reported growing lawlessness among the Nana's troops, quarrels between their leaders and brutal treatment of civilians, Bengali clerks and Eurasian Christians who had remained in hiding in the city —all of which had the ring of truth about them. But this last story must surely have been exaggerated, perhaps because the fellow wanted to justify the high price he had demanded for undertaking the journey to Lucknow . . . although it had been very detailed, even to the naming of names.

According to his account, two boatloads of fugitives from Fategarh, numbering a hundred and twenty-six in all—the majority women, children and civilians—had been seized by a detachment of the 2nd Native Cavalry

87

at Bithur. Having, unhappily, no idea that Cawnpore was itself under siege, the Fategarh party had been on their way to seek refuge from a threatened mutiny of their own native troops. Although lightly armed, they had not expected to be attacked when almost within sight of their goal and they had put up little resistance, even when the troops they had supposed to be friendly had opened fire on them from the bank of the river. Taken in open carts to the Nana's camp at Savada, deprived of food and water and subjected to the grossest abuse and humiliation, the wretched captives had been kept all day in the sun, bound tightly together.

Finally, by the Nana's orders, they had been savagely hacked to pieces in his presence by Muslim troopers of the 2nd Cavalry, who had spared none of them.

"I did not witness this foul deed, General Sahib," the messenger had admitted. "But I was told of it by one who did—Nerput, the opium agent, who was at the camp on business. He said that the bodies were cast into the river and many, who saw them there, spoke of it to me. It is said that one child, a girl, survived and that she has been taken by a *golandaz* to his home to be cared for."

The General shivered as he visualized the ghastly scene. He did not want to believe the horrors which Ungud had described. The Nana had betrayed his friendship, it was true, but he was a civilized man, a Hindu Mahratta of the highest caste. It was inconceivable that he should have had women and innocent, defenseless children barbarously tortured and done to death by Rampoorie Muslims of the 2nd Cavalry . . . unless, of course, the other rumors were true and he had failed to maintain discipline in his mutinous regiments. If he had lost control of them or delegated authority to his degenerate brother, Bala Bhat, and to Azimullah and the Moulvi of Fyzabad, then anything was possible. Even this . . . The old man slumped further back in his chair, willing himself to sleep, to shut out the vision of mutilated bodies, of women pleading for mercy and violated by their pitiless killers before being

88

put to the sword. It could not be true . . . the Nana Sahib would never permit such license. Azimullah and Bala Bhat were his creatures, they . . .

"Sir—" It was his son Godfrey, punctiliously carrying out the duties of aide-de-camp, and the General sat up, blinking in the light of the lantern the boy had brought with him.

"Yes?" he invited, shrugging off his weariness.

"The messenger is on his way, sir. Captain Williamson has undertaken to see him through our pickets. And Captain Moore is here, requesting to speak to you."

"Moore?" John Moore was a splendid officer, possessed of outstanding courage and powers of leadership, who had already proved himself one of the heroes of the defense but—he was so devilishly tired, the old General thought. "What does he want, Godfrey, do you know? Can it not wait till morning?"

His son shook his head, "No, sir, I don't think it can. He and Colonel Sheridan want your permission to make a raid tonight—a morale-raiser, they call it, to show the Pandies that we're not giving up just because they managed to burn down the hospital. Captain Moore would like to take fifty men and spike the twenty-four-pounders in the East battery—the one in the Church compound, sir —and—"

"Fifty men!" the General exclaimed, shocked out of his desire for sleep. "But that would leave the ramparts seriously undermanned!"

"He can't do it with less, Father," Godfrey Wheeler pointed out. "And it would give a tremendous boost to morale if he could put that battery out of action—it's done us more hurt than any of the others."

"No doubt it would," his father said dryly. *"If* it succeeds and if the party don't suffer any casualties. We cannot afford to tose a single man, Godfrey—you know that —still less can we afford to risk fifty lives in what, by any standard, is a most hazardous undertaking. Where does Moore think he can find fifty fit men?"

"Colonel Sheridan has picked them, sir. He—"

"Officers, I suppose?"

"A proportion, of course," the boy admitted. "As you say, they've got to be fit. Those who volunteered for the raid and weren't considered up to it are to man the defense. . . ." He talked on enthusiastically and his father listened, conscious of the stirring of a spirit he had imagined long since dead. Damn it, the old General told himself, the idea was one after his own heart. To attack, when your enemy imagined you were beaten; to come out fighting, when you should have been licking your wounds; to show defiance instead of fear. . . . He had said, in his appeal to Lawrence, that the defense had been noble and wonderful and, for all the risk it involved, this proposed raid was in the true British spirit. He *had* to permit them to make it, if for no other reason than because Ungud's story of the massacre of the Fategarh fugitives might be true.

"Very well," he said, his mind made up. "You may tell Captain Moore that he has my permission. I'd better see him, I suppose. I'll come with you, I don't want to disturb your mother and the girls." He rose stiffly to his feet. "On you go, Godfrey. I'll follow you."

Godfrey held his ground. "There's just one other request I'd like to make, sir," he said formally. "May I go with the raiding party?"

The General stared at him in shocked surprise. He had not expected the request and it had caught him off guard. The boy was so young; unwashed and unshaven, as they all were, he was still a fine-looking boy, with all the makings of a first-rate officer. It would break his heart if anything happened to this son of his, and as for the boy's mother . . . He glanced across at the *charpoy*, willing his wife to waken, to open her eyes and add her plea to the excuses he was about to offer. But she remained silent, oblivious to what Godfrey was asking of him and he turned back to meet the boy's gaze uneasily.

"You're my ADC, Godfrey," he began. "I don't feel, in the circumstances, that—"

"I am also an officer of this garrison, Father," Godfrey reminded him. "And I hold a Company's commission. I'm not a child. Please, sir, I beg you to let me go. I'm fit—unlike Colonel Sheridan and Captain Moore, I have the use of both my arms."

Sir Hugh Wheeler hesitated, unable to restrain the unmanly tears which pricked at his eyes. He had no justification for refusing his son's request, he knew. If he permitted other officers to risk their lives, he must also allow his son the same privilege. He bowed his white head and said gruffly, "All right, my dear boy, go if you wish. I . . . you can see Captain Moore for me. He doesn't need me to plan his raid for him—he knows what to do, better than I do. Ask him not to take the Artillery officers, if he can do without them, that's all."

"Yes, of course, sir." Godfrey's blue eyes held a glow of excitement. "Good night, sir, and . . . thank you. I'm most grateful to you, believe me."

Grateful . . . dear heaven! The General expelled his breath in a longdrawn sigh. "Good luck," he said, still gruffly, and, when the boy had gone, eager as a puppy, he sank back once more into his chair and closed his eyes. But now they were closed in prayer; for all his weariness, he knew that he would not sleep this night. . . .

II

The raiding party gathered on the northeast corner of the entrenchment, behind Ashe's guns, their faces blackened, looking more like the company of a pirate ship than soldiers. The officers had pistols thrust into the waistbands of their trousers and most of them, like the men, had Enfields, to which, in response to a whispered order, bayonets were silently fixed. They had all been told what was expected of them and they were grinning, in high spirits, eager to hit back at the enemy now that at last the chance had come.

Alex, waiting with Francis Whiting and Henry Delafosse, listened to John Moore, as he issued last minute instructions to the men who had been selected to spike the guns. By common consent, command of these raids was Moore's responsibility; he had been on all of them and knew the ground so intimately that he could have found his way blindfolded to any point he wished to reach. He and Lieutenant Saunders of the 84th were to disable the guns, backed up by two sergeants and half a dozen men of the two Queen's regiments, and they carried handspikes, sponge-staffs and a supply of powder for this purpose, in addition to pistols.

"We want to blow up those guns if we can," John Moore reminded them. "But if we can't, then they must be well and truly spiked. Kill any Pandies you see; we can't take prisoners. Mr. Delafosse's party will go in first, to deal with sentries and gunners—with the bayonet, Henry, if you possibly can. Don't use firearms unless you must. They keep a pretty poor lookout but we don't want to alert them too soon. As soon as the job's done, I'll give you a 'tally-ho bike'—and then it's back to the entrenchment as fast as you know how, except for the rearguard. If any man's hit, he should try to get back under his own steam and if he can't, then the rearguard will pick him up. If they come after us in any number, both advance and rear parties wil cover our withdrawal. If not, leave it to Colonel Sheridan's party. Understood? Right, Henry, off you go—and good luck!"

Delafosse and Godfrey Wheeler, who were leading the advance party, slipped over the parapet with scarcely a sound. The moon was obscured and they vanished swiftly from sight. Alex and Francis Whiting, the rear-guard commanders, led their men into position and crouched behind the wall, listening intently. There was no sound, save for the men's heavy breathing and the occasional cry of a sentry from the other side of the entrenchment.

Ashe's gunners stood to their worn-out nine-pounders, ready to give covering fire should it be required, all of them peering anxiously into the semidarkness.

The advance party had, seemingly, met with neither challenge nor opposition and Moore, clasping a sponge-staff, vaulted on to the top of the parapet and down into the ditch below, his men at his heels. Alex and his party followed, well spread out on either side of them. They covered the seven hundred yards of flat, shell-scarred ground at a rapid jog trot, guided by the red glow of the enemy's cooking fires, and reached their objective without being challenged. The trenches were empty and the first gun, an 18-pounder, was surrounded by dead *golandazes* —proof that the advance party had done its work well.

John Moore's men wasted no time in preparing to put it out of action. A double charge of powder and a wad, rammed well down, and then the gun muzzle plugged and depressed, and a lighted fuse left smoldering at the touch-hole. . . . They ran on, to serve the next in the same manner. Both burst with a dull roar and, as the spiking party headed for the 24-pounders, mounted on top of a steep bank, Alex and his rearguard divided, to take post to left and right of the slope.

The noise of the explosion aroused several sleeping sentries but, realizing that they were outnumbered, they let off their muskets without pausing to take aim and fled in panic, making no attempt to protect their threatened battery. The camp was alerted, however, and about sixty or seventy infantry sepoys came pouring out of a building on the left, which was evidently their mess house. Delafosse's men fired a telling volley into them from the top of the bank and Alex, with a wildly yelling Corporal Henegan bidding fair to outstrip him, led a bayonet charge into them before they could form ranks.

"No bleeding guts, sir!" Henegan shouted, flashing him a grin as the rebels made a concerted rush for the shelter they had so recently left. He impaled a white-clad sepoy on his bayonet and dexterously withdrew it, swearing horribly when the second of his intended victims eluded him and ran screaming to safety. "Yellow livered swine! They c'n shoot down women and little children but they never could stand and face our bayonets, none of 'em. Shall we clear the bastards out of there, sir? Why should they fill their perishing bellies when we can't?"

Bugles were sounding the alarm now in the old Dragoon Barracks to the north, where the 1st Native Infantry were quartered and in the Foot Artillery Barracks on River Road, and lights were flickering through the trees as, from the Riding School and the Cavalry Lines, the hitherto silent guns woke to life once more, to send a hail of shot into the entrenchment. They had been taken by surprise and, for the moment, all was confusion in the enemy camp, but this would not last for long, Alex was aware, and he shook his head regretfully to Henegan's suggestion. The raid had been planned as a swift sally, for the sole purpose of disabling the battery in the New Cantonment, and John Moore's party, once they had achieved what they had set out to do, would be preparing to withdraw. His orders were to cover them as they retired and pick up wounded.

"No," he said, hearing the shout of "tally-ho bike" which had been the agreed signal to begin the withdrawal. "I'm sorry to disappoint you, Henegan, but it's time for us to leave." He raised his voice. "Rearguard, rally on me! That's it, boys—tally-ho bike!"

The men fanned out, taking up their prearranged positions, and Francis Whiting said, a pleased note in his voice as he ducked down beside Alex, "They did it, by God—they knocked out four guns! Henry's on his way back now, I've just seen him. Two men slightly wounded, he says, but we needn't worry about them—they'll make it back with the advance party. Godfrey Wheeler was hit in the arm but he says it was a spent musket-ball and he's all right. Not bad, eh? We certainly caught the swine napping! Henry said that all the sentries were sleep."

"They've woken up now," Alex observed. "I've never

heard so many bugle calls coming from so many different directions! Keep your eye on that mess hall, Sergeant Maywood. If a Pandy shows his face in the doorway, let him have it."

A few desultory shots were coming from windows on the near side of the building but none of the occupants ventured outside it and Corporal Henegan, his finger on the trigger of his Enfield, gave vent to a few choice oaths as he waited, squinting along his sights with barely controlled impatience.

A voice called "Tally-ho bike!" from the darkness and John Moore's small party slithered down the slope and passed through the rearguard, shadowy figures in the dim light, dragging two boxes with them.

"A few items we've been short of lately, such as percussion caps and shell-cases," Moore explained, answering Alex's unspoken question. "And some nine-pounder cartridges, as a small token of my esteem for Georgie Ashe!" He grinned, completely in his element and in high good humor, like a boy released from school, the shocks and setbacks of the past ten days forgotten in the excitement of the moment. "I killed a fellow back there with my sponge-staff—he took a potshot at me and I just spotted him in time. God, Alex, it's good to hit back at them, isn't it, instead of cowering behind a mud wall being slowly roasted to death! I feel like a new man."

He looked like one, too, Alex thought, and echoed his grin. Quite apart from its tactical success, this raid had been a tonic to them all and, after last night's disaster, a much-needed boost to morale, as he had hoped it would be.

"My chaps enjoyed their bayonet charge," he said, remembering Henegan. "Are you ready to withdraw now, John?"

Moore nodded. "The proverbial hornet's nest is about to erupt, alas, so we'll have to. Give us a couple of minutes, if you will, and then fall back. Oh, by the way, we left a little surprise firework display for the Pandies—a

95

slow-match set to blow up a couple of their ammunition dumps in approximately seven or eight minutes from now. We thought it might provide a useful distraction, should any of them pluck up enough courage to come after us."

"They won't," Francis Whiting asserted. "Cowardly devils! We've got about fifty or sixty of them penned up in there"—he pointed to the mess house—"and there's hardly been a cheep out of them."

"Fifty or sixty, you say?" Moore frowned. "They might recover their nerve when we pull out and we can't afford casualties. I think perhaps I should—"

"Rearguard's privilege, John," Alex put in, guessing his intention. "If you have the means to clear them out, oblige me, please. You mentioned shells and—"

Moore laughed. "Help yourself," he invited. "There are a couple in my pouch. Best homemade variety—matches, too, if you need them." He divested himself of the pouch and straightened up. "Right, then, I'll be on my way. Retire as soon as you're ready. We'll be watching for you."

He was gone and Alex picked up the pouch, listening to the subdued hum of voices coming from the mess house and to the still distant crackle of musketry. They had time, he thought—not much, but enough. The advancing infantry were firing at shadows, in no hurry to reach the scene of action. . . . He issued crisp orders and, as his party obediently prepared to retire, Francis Whiting held out his hand for the pouch.

"My job, I think, Colonel."

"I think not, Francis. Able-bodied officers can't be spared, least of all trained gun commanders. But"—Alex gave him the box of lucifers—"oblige me by lighting the fuses. I have just the man for this job—Henegan!"

Corporal Henegan was beside him, eyes gleaming in his blackened face and his rifle already slung. He took the first of the crudely made missiles from Whiting and blew on its smouldering fuse.

"Left-hand window," Alex told him. "I'll take the right —now!" They ran forward together, both bent low, and separated, Henegan going left-handed. Shots whined above their heads as watchers in the mess house saw them coming and fired an ill-aimed, hurried volley. Alex reached his objective a second or so before the corporal and, rising to his full height, lobbed the hissing grenade in through the open window, turned and ran back. The blast from two successive explosions knocked him flat and, when Henegan crawled over to him, the whole building was ablaze. About ten or eleven sepoys made their escape by the door and a few more by the rear windows but they were unarmed, running in blind panic from the flames as, Alex thought, the women and children had run from the barrack hospital the previous night. He left his pistol in its holster, making no attempt to fire on the terrified fugitives, and waited for Henegan to tell him that they had no guts. To his surprise, the man was silent, and turning to look at him, Alex saw that his face was contorted with pain.

"Where are you hit, Henegan?" he asked.

"In the . . . lungs, sir. In the . . . bleeding lungs."

"We'll get you back," Alex promised. "We'll—" he broke off, glimpsing the ghastly wound. The ball must have entered his chest at pointblank range to have done such hideous damage: the poor devil was spewing up blood with every breath—there was not the smallest chance of getting him back to the entrenchment alive.

"I'm . . . done for," Henegan gasped, guessing his thoughts. "Arcn't I, sir?" He did not wait for an answer, aware of what it would be, but summoned a lopsided smile. "It was . . . worth it, to take . . . some of those blasted . . . black sods . . . with me. Don't you . . . wait, Colonel, sir. Leg it . . . back while . . . you've got the chance. The lads . . . Captain Whiting . . . they won't go without you. No sense in us all . . . and you . . . have a wife, sir."

The rearguard, under Francis Whiting, had obeyed his order to retire but, Alex saw by the light of the burning mess house, they had not got far. They were going through the correct, drill-book motions, the front rank covering the rear rank's withdrawal and then reversing the process, but they were not under fire and they were moving with a deliberate lack of urgency—obviously waiting for him, as Henegan had suggested. He cursed them silently. Devil take it, he could not leave Henegan to the mercy of the Pandies! The poor fellow might take some time to die and if they got their hands on him, the possibilities did not bear thinking about.

"No," he said tersely. "I'm taking you in. Give me your hand, lad, so that I can get you on to my back. Come on, I—" The thunderous crash of an explosion swallowed up his words, as the first of John Moore's promised firework displays lit up the night sky behind them. It was followed, almost simultaneously, by a second and more powerful explosion, which tore at Alex's eardrums, momentarily deafening him. A shower of shell fragments, splintered timber from gun carriages and munition tumbrils and shapeless particles of metal from the guns themselves hurtled into the air, briefly illuminated by the red glow of the ignited powder. This faded and a dense cloud of black smoke billowed skywards, to hang like some harbinger of doom over the scene of devastation it had left in its wake. It was, no doubt, more spectacular than effective, but seen from the entrenchment . . . and those guns, at least, would never fire on them again.

"Holy Mother of God!" Henegan was suddenly on his feet, eluding Alex's groping hand, the rifle unslung and held across his chest. He ran forward, his long bayonet gleaming dully in the glow of the burning mess house as, with practiced skill, he thrust it into the ranks of an unseen and wholly imaginary foe. "Come on, boys!" he shouted. "At 'em with the bayonet! Never could stand up to us when we charged 'em, not even the sods of Sikhs! Never could . . ." The hoarse voice hiccoughed into silence and Corporal Henegan fell forward, clutching at his chest. When Alex reached and turned him over, he

98

was dead, blood-flecked lips parted and an expression of savage joy on his grimy, stubble-darkened face.

Whatever else the Pandies had done, they had not defeated Henegan, Alex thought, picking up the Enfield and slinging it awkwardly over his right shoulder. True, they had killed him, but he had died like the good soldier he was, taking quite a few of the enemy with him, as he himself had claimed—which, in these circumstances, was all any soldier could hope to achieve. He would not have to watch the sun rise tomorrow, would not have to—how had John Moore put it? He would not have to cower behind a mud wall, being slowly roasted to death; neither would he have to watch his wife suffer nor bury his firstborn in a nameless grave, scooped out of contaminated ground with his bare hands. Henegan had given his life in defense of the Cawnpore entrenchment but he had been spared these torments; perhaps, of the two of them, he was the more fortunate.

Alex left him and rejoined the rearguard. They came under some random musketry fire from infantry but the range was too great for this to be accurate. The infantry, for all their frantic bugle calls, made no attempt to attack them and the cavalry did not appear, although from the gun and mortar batteries to north and south of the entrenchment, the rebel gunners kept up a rapid and vengeful cannonade for what remained of the night.

"Does this not prove that we could fight our way out?" Francis Whiting asked bitterly, as he and Alex returned to their posts behind the parapet. "If we had only two companies—two trained companies of fit British soldiers —I swear we could reach Lucknow, even burdened by the women and children. If we made the attempt now— as we stand, without waiting for help that may or may not come—I'm beginning to think it would be preferable to staying here."

"We should be compelled to leave the sick and wounded behind," Alex reminded him, "if we were to have the slightest chance of success."

99

"But most of them will die in any case, if we're not relieved soon," Whiting argued. "Damn it, Alex, we shall all of us rot here! We're getting weaker with every day that passes and more of us are being wounded or falling sick. This infernal place is virtually indefensible *now* and if the rains come before help reaches us, we shan't only lack food and ammunition—we'll have no blasted mud wall to defend, it'll be washed away! Our only hope is to break out at once, in my view, but I suppose the General won't hear of it." He sighed in frustration. "Pray God his messenger manages to get to Lucknow and Lawrence sends us two companies of the Thirty-Second . . . although frankly, I don't think he's in a position to send us even one."

"There's Neill—"

"Yes, but *when?* With the road to Allahabad swarming with Pandies and the river heavily guarded, it's impossible to get word out to him, to tell him the straits we're in. He'll take his time, mopping up as he goes—in addition to which, he'll have a battle on his hands before he can get to us, won't he?"

"Yes," Alex had to concede, "I fear so." He knew of the unsuccessful efforts which had been made to send an appeal for help to Allahabad. One man—George Kempland's Eurasian servant, assisted by some loyal sepoys—had made the attempt by river, but he had been caught and murdered, perhaps betrayed by the men who had accompanied him, no one could be sure. The native officer who had tried to get through by road had returned after a few hours, with the information that all roads were closed and patrolled by cavalry and that no native, whatever his rank or calling, was permitted to leave Cawnpore without a written pass, signed by the Nana Sahib. A number of others, native servants or Eurasian Christians, had left the entrenchment—some escaping without permission, others sent by the garrison to bring back information—but few had returned. Those who had spoke of the im-

100

possibility of eluding the Nana's vigilance and of the tortures inflicted on any who were caught.

Several officers, including himself, had at various times, volunteered to try to make contact with Neill's column; the General—probably rightly—had refused to give his consent. They had no horses; on foot and alone, no European would stand a chance of eluding the rebel patrols, for the Nana's men were proving all too expert at penetrating disguises. Had he still had his orderly, Partap Singh, or *Daffadar* Ghulam Rasul, Alex reflected, he might have stood an even chance of getting through in their company, but . . . he had sent them both to Lucknow, before the seige began.

"As I said," Francis Whiting went on despondently, "tonight's sally has proved that the Pandies won't stand up to us if we carry our attack to them. I honestly believe that we'll all be done for if we stay here much longer, Alex."

"The alternative is unthinkable," Alex said regretfully. "And you know it, as well as I do. We cannot abandon the wounded . . . and we can't fight our way to Lucknow —fifty miles, Francis—with women and children in our midst, half of whom would have to be carried after a few miles."

"Then Lawrence is our only hope."

"Yes. And perhaps James Neill, whether or not we get word to him . . . he'll have a fair idea of what we're up against."

Whiting bowed his head. "I wish I could still believe in the power of prayer . . . because it will take a miracle to save us."

As the next week crawled by, Alex, too, found his faith shaken. The entrenchment was under continuous bombardment—the guns they had destroyed with such a feeling of triumph quickly replaced by others from the Magazine—and attacks at night became more frequent, particularly on the out-picket in Number Four Block. The defenders were at their posts day and night, with little relief and less sleep, and there was no shelter for them, except in the trenches. The burnt-out hospital block retained its heat for three days and was impossible to enter, and the women and children who had previously been accommodated there had either to crowd into the stifling, airless storerooms behind the Main Guard or find what shelter they could, with their menfolk, behind the parapet. The men dug shallow holes and trenches for them and erected crude awnings in an attempt to shield them from the sun but inevitably deaths mounted, both from wounds and disease. The surgeons, suffering casualties themselves, did what they could, but, without instruments and with a rapidly diminishing stock of medicines, this was little enough. Men—and frequently women also—died from gangrene, after suffering quite minor wounds, because amputation was no longer possible.

The Main Guard became a hospital for the most seriously wounded and Emmy worked there, sometimes for twelve or fourteen hours without relief, reduced to a shadow of the lovely, vivacious young woman she had once been. Her long hair was shorn since it could not be washed, her clothing was in tatters and, with each day that passed, her dark eyes seemed to sink deeper into her lined, emaciated face. Alex found the sight of her unbearably painful and when she came to him at night, utterly spent and stumbling over the uneven ground like a sleepwalker, oblivious to the pitiless rain of shells and musket-balls, he was hard put to it not to cry his agony aloud. They would have a few moments together, talking in whispers, and then she would sink exhausted into the small pit he had lined for her with some scraps of canvas, and sleep the sleep of the dead until the glare of the sun brought her reluctantly back to what passed for life in the entrenchment.

Usually, when they talked, they spoke of the past, but sometimes Emmy would tell him sadly of the losses sustained since their last meeting. The gallant, black-bearded Fusilier Sullivan, who had carried her from the blazing barrack hospital on the night of the fire, whose Enfield had exploded in his face from heat and overuse; John Mc-Killop, the limping, self-appointed "Captain of the Well," struck down by a charge of grape when in the act of hauling up a bucket of water, his conscience troubled, even as he died, because the woman for whom he had drawn the water had been deprived of it. . . . There were so many losses now, all of them heartbreaking.

Apart from young St. George Ashe, all the Artillery officers and fifty-nine gunners were dead or wounded or victims of fever. Colonel Larkin had been one of the early cases of enteric, which had taken his wife and two small children; Lieutenant Dempster and Eckford had both been killed by round-shot in the entrenchment. Now the guns, their muzzles buckled, the bores warped, were served by teams of infantrymen and civilians, captained by Henry Delafosse, Francis Whiting, Edward Vibart and the sickly George Kempland. They fired only when certain targets presented themselves, for there was no ammunition to spare. Delafosse had risked his life and been badly burnt when an enemy shell had fallen among his ammunition wagons. Lying full length underneath it, with the fire of two rebel batteries fiercely concentrated on the remaining wagons, he had torn at blazing splinters with his bare hands and flung handfuls of earth onto the flames, aided by two privates, who had sacrificed two buckets of precious drinking water before the danger to their last reserves of ammunition was finally averted.

Yet, in spite of the relentless drain on their manpower and resources, the defenders continued to put up an obstinate resistance. John Moore, although in pain from his wounded arm, which had turned septic, continued to organize sallies, but now these had to be restricted to parties of six or eight and, of necessity, aimed only at clearing snipers from the unfinished barrack blocks to the west of the entrenchment. Mobray Thomson, bearing a charmed life, clung tenaciously to his battered stronghold in Number Four but had, almost daily, to request replacements for his wounded which the other sectors could ill afford to do without.

Alex now held his line with twelve officers and men, where before there had been three times that number, and two of his section were pensioned drummers, whom almost incessant practice had transformed into marksmen as deadly as the rest. In the exposed Redan, Edward Vibart suffered acutely from the fire of mutineers, who had advanced a sap to within a scant 250 yards of his position, whence they picked off any man who showed his head about the parapet. Women acted as loaders when there were no men free to undertake the task and George Kempland, fighting his single worn-out gun in the southeast corner of the entrenchment, was reduced to tears of impotent fury and distress when four of his gallant female volunteers were killed by round-shot in the space of an hour.

Physically all were in pitiful condition. The food rations, even for the fighting men, were reduced and then reduced again, until the most that any of them could count on was two or three handfuls of parched grain—originally stored as horse fodder—soaked in water or rum. It kept them from starvation but that was all and many of the men could hardly stand. Their bodies broke out in suppurating sores and they leaned against the crumbling mud walls as much for support as for protection, firing when ordered to and sleeping, in brief catnaps, whenever they could. The children became living skeletons, prematurely aged and solemn, too weak to stir from the scooped-out holes in the ground in which their mothers placed them, and in which most of them lay from dawn to dusk in terrible, uncaring apathy.

The heat induced apathy but rumors kept their fading hopes alive. A relief column was said to be within a few miles of the Bridge of Boats on the Lucknow road, and a body of marching men, approaching from the south, was for a long time believed to be Neill's column—until telescopes revealed the dark faces beneath the shakos and it was borne on the anxious watchers that these reinforcements were not for them but for the enemy.

On the morning of June 21st, the arrival of a solitary British officer in their midst caused feverish excitement among the garrison. It was claimed that he had come from Lucknow, slipping unobserved through the Nana's camp in darkness to bring them word that help was on the way, and even the sick roused themselves, eyes brightening in the belief that their ordeal might be nearing its end.

But the officer had come alone, seeking refuge from a peril more immediate than theirs. He had ridden overnight on the open plain and at dawn, wounded and in the last stages of exhaustion, had leapt his horse over the mud wall of the entrenchment, being fired on by two of the defenders, who took him for an enemy *sowar*. He proved to be the sole survivor of a party of officers sent, with a detachment of the 7th Light Cavalry and the 48th Native Infantry, from Lucknow ten days before, to endeavor to keep open the road between Fategarh and Cawnpore.

"My name's Bolton, Seventh Light Cavalry," he said, looking in shocked astonishment at the scarecrow figures who surrounded him. "The sepoys of the Forty-Eighth mutinied yesterday morning—they turned on us, without warning, and murdered their own officers. Major Staples and I were the only ones who got away from them but some of our *sowars* pursued us. Poor Staples was shot down and they cut him to pieces before I could lift a hand to help him. After that, I was on my own. They followed me for about sixteen miles before I managed to lose them in a wood. I decided to make for Cawnpore because I thought—that is I was given to understand that you . . ." He broke off in embarrassment.

"You thought that we were defending ourselves against the Nana Sahib," Ashe finished for him, his tone cynical. "Well, we are, my friend, we are . . . all that are left of us. And waiting, in vain it would seem, for a relief column to reach us."

"From the south—from Allahabad or Benares?" Bolton asked, still puzzled.

"Or from Lucknow," several voices informed him and Alex, standing silently by, saw a look of dismay spread across the newcomer's bloodstained face. He hesitated and then said bleakly, "Gentlemen, I—I fear that no help can be sent from Lucknow. When I left, the situation there was such that . . ." Again he hesitated, ducking involuntarily as a shell whined overhead and added, as if reluctant to shatter such hopes as they might cherish, "I do not know, of course. Sir Henry Lawrence might find a way. I . . . if you are hungry and on short rations, as you appear to be, my horse is wounded. Shoot it, if you wish, and put me to work. My wound isn't serious, just a saber cut on the cheek. I'll gladly help in any way I can."

"I need a loader for one of my guns," Henry Delafosse told him and summoned a grin. "And the horse will be a welcome addition to our diet, believe me. We've been living on cattle fodder for the past week." He put one of his blistered arms round the boy's shoulders and led him away.

That evening, Ungud returned from Lucknow, bearing a reply from Sir Henry Lawrence, and Alex, who admitted the messenger to the entrenchment, took him first to a surgeon and then to General Wheeler. The General was alone in the small, bare room which served him as an office and he stared at both his visitors without recognition for a long moment, having to make an effort to rouse himself before he could take in the reason for their sudden appearance.

"I had asked that I should not be disturbed," he said querulously. "I have had a shock, I . . . that is, I have suffered an irreparable loss and I wanted to be alone, for a little while, with my grief." His thin, bony hands clenched and unclenched themselves, as if he were fighting for control of his emotions. "But of course if . . . well, what is it, Colonel Sheridan? Why did you wish to see me?"

"The reply to your message to Sir Henry Lawrence, sir," Alex answered, holding the spill of paper out to him. "This man has just arrived from Lucknow and I thought you would want to be informed at once."

The old General's hand was visibly trembling as he took the paper and, with slow clumsiness, unfolded it. He read its contents two or three times, his gaunt face expressionless; then, his voice flat and controlled, he dismissed Ungud, with the promise that he would see and reward him next morning. When the man had gone, he passed the letter to Alex. "Read this," he invited. "And then acquaint the senior officers with Sir Henry's decision. I . . . I cannot face them tonight, Sheridan. I am not myself and this . . . this is the final blow."

Alex moved closer to the single flickering lamp. Lawrence had written, with heartbroken regret, that it was impossible for him to spare a detachment from the weak force which was all he had for the protection of his own people. Cholera had broken out among his garrison; the native police had risen in revolt and he had been compelled to dispense with the services of all save four hundred of his native troops, due to doubts concerning their loyalty. Apart from his Sikhs, he had only the 32nd Foot, fifty men of the 84th and the 40-strong Volunteer Horse; with over twelve hundred noncombatants to protect—half of them women and children—he dared not weaken his garrison by a single European soldier. To send native troops, in the present circumstances, would be worse than useless.

It was what he had feared, Alex thought—what he had expected, after talking to Lieutenant Bolton. Knowing Henry Lawrence, he could guess what this refusal must have cost that good and kindly man; yet, in his place, he knew that he would have been compelled to reply, as Lawrence had, that no aid could be sent to Cawnpore. Lawrence's first concern had to be Lucknow; Lucknow was his responsibility, his charge. To lose the capital of Oudh, at this critical time, might prove as disastrous to the British cause as the loss of Delhi had been, and Lawrence was a statesman, who looked to the future and would not allow himself to be blinded by past or present. With the fate of all India in the balance, he had made the only possible decision . . . even if, by that decision, he had sealed the fate of Cawnpore and of every man, woman and child who remained there.

His own fate and Emmy's, Alex thought. The stubborn defense, the privations they had endured, the tragic losses they had suffered would all be in vain, unless Neill could reach them—and God only knew when that would be. He felt the bitter taste of bile rising in his throat and swallowed it, sickened. Had Francis Whiting been right after all—ought they to have abandoned the wounded after the burning of the hospital and endeavored to fight their way to Lucknow? A handful of them might have won through if they had taken the gamble then but the cost, surely, would have been too high—the cost to conscience, the cost in human suffering. And now it was too late; there were not enough fit fighting men even to make the attempt. Bolton was the only one who had eaten normally since the siege began; the rest of them were . . . He glimpsed his own image in a cracked square of mirror behind the General's chair and sighed despairingly. The dirty, bearded apparition, with its hollow cheeks and skin burnt to the color of teak needed only a few daubs of gypsum and vermillion, of sandalwood and ash to pass for a *sadhu*, one of the beggar tribe of itinerant holy men who traveled the Indian roads. In fact . . . Suddenly excited, Alex moved towards the mirror, subjecting his reflection to a closer scrutiny. He spoke the language well enough and his missing right arm would add to the credibility of such a disguise . . . By heaven, it was worth a try! Even the Nana's men would hesitate before they arrested a holy man, fearing his curse.

He stepped back, confronting the General. "Sir," he began, a note of urgency in his voice. "Would you give me permission to endeavor to make contact with Colonel

108

Neill? I believe that I . . ." Meeting the General's blank, unseeing stare, he realized that the old man was lost in his own unhappy thoughts and had not heard him.

"So we are to be deserted, left to die like rats in a trap—even by Lawrence!" The tired old voice was bitter in its disillusionment. "He will save his people but I have brought mine to *this*. After a lifetime of service—honorable service—I am left with no alternative. I must either capitulate to the Nana or condemn my valiant garrison to death."

"Sir," Alex besought him. "Listen to me, if you please, sir. You—"

Sir Hugh Wheeler ignored him, seemingly deaf to any voice save his own. "Did you know that my son Godfrey was killed whilst they watched! He was lying on his mother's *charpoy*—he had been slightly wounded and my wife was about to change the dressing for him. A roundshot entered through the archway of the veranda and took the boy's head off. His blood and brains are spread across the wall of the room . . . the room in which all of us must try to sleep."

"I'm sorry, sir, deeply sorry," Alex managed, with genuine grief.

"He was a fine boy, Sheridan. Although I was his father, I . . . but it's of no importance now, is it? He's dead and tonight, when darkness falls, they will take his body and cast it into the well with all the others. Over two hundred others, they tell me . . . two hundred poor, brave souls who trusted me to defend and protect them, to preserve their lives. But I failed them." Tears were streaming down the General's emaciated cheeks and he made no attempt to stem them. "I'm a broken man," he went on sadly. "I no longer have the will to fight, I . . . I must relinquish my command, place it in more capable hands." He looked at Alex then, as if seeing him for the first time. "You will have to take over, Sheridan—you and Captain Moore. You are the only officer of Lieutenant Colonel's rank alive and unwounded, are you not?"

Alex stared at him in dismay. "Mine is only a brevet rank, sir, and I'm here as a supernumary—my command is in Lucknow. Captain Moore is the only senior officer with a command here and—"

The old General sighed. "Then it will have to be Moore. He's a good officer, he . . . The Brigadier is dead, of course. And poor Colonel Williams. Ewart is badly wounded, they tell me, and Wiggins down with fever. There's Major Vibart, of course, who is a splendid officer, but like you, he has no command here. I will hand over to Moore tomorrow, I . . . you had better warn him, perhaps. And give him your support, you and Vibart."

"Yes, sir, of course. But"—Alex studied his face with concerned eyes—"will you not give the matter more thought, sir? The garrison has every confidence in you and, whilst I feel sure that Captain Moore will be most willing to relieve you of some of your responsibilities, I hardly think that he will be anxious to take over command from you, sir. Will you not speak to him about it? I could send him to you now, if you wish."

But the bloodshot eyes had resumed their blank, uncomprehending stare and once again the old man lapsed into deafness. "Leave me alone," he said plaintively. "I said I was not to be disturbed. I have lost my son—may I not be permitted to mourn him?"

Alex left him. He took Lawrence's brief note to John Moore and told him what the General had said.

"I thought I'd become inured to shocks, Alex," Moore confessed wryly. "But evidently I have not because this has shocked me. Being offered the command, I mean—I had more than half expected that Lawrence would have to refuse our appeal." He shrugged, wincing as a spasm of pain shot through his injured arm. "I think the General will change his mind, though, when he's had time to get over his son's death, so we'd better just wait and see. However"—he looked up suddenly, his blue eyes blazing

—"if I *do* assume command, I know exactly what I shall do."

"And what is that?"

Moore sighed. "I shall lead every man who is capable of following me in one last night raid. We'll take possession of every one of those blasted enemy batteries or die in the attempt. That's what they all want, Alex, both officers and men . . . if they've got to die, they want to die like soldiers and so do I. In fact, I intended to put the proposal to General Wheeler, as soon as . . . that is, when it becomes evident that our position is hopeless."

"And the women?" Alex challenged. "The women and children?"

John Moore eyed him somberly. "You know the answer to that question, my friend. There'll be enough of us left to . . . to do what is necessary. Obviously they can't be allowed to fall into the Nana's hands. Well . . ." He repeated his sigh. "The swine have mounted a six-pounder behind Number One Block and I'm just collecting a party to spike it. Are you coming with us?"

Alex inclined his head. It was not the moment to speak of his own plan to contact the Allahabad force, he decided; that, too, could wait until tomorrow. He felt for his pistol, glanced over to where Emmy was sleeping, and then fell into step beside Moore.

"I want to take a prisoner tonight, Alex," the Irishman added. "There are a few things we'll have to know about those gun positions. Will you attend to it?"

Alex nodded again. A few minutes later they slipped silently out of the entrenchment, with five men of the 32nd.

CHAPTER FIVE

The prisoner taken duing the aid—whom Alex selected because he was a *jemadar*—proved an unexpectedly valuable and willing source of information. Dragged unceremoniously into Number Four Block for interrogation, he recognized Mowbray Thomson of his old regiment and begged, with tears in his eyes, to be permitted to return to the British service.

He gave his name as Ram Gupta and admitted that he had been one of the native officers who had joined the garrison in the entrenchment at the beginning of the siege and subsequently deserted. Unlike most of the mutineers captured on earlier raids, he expressed regret for his infidelity and seemed anxious to talk, replying readily to questions and even volunteering information on his own account. Alex and Mowbray Thomson interpreted his replies for the benefit of John Moore, who spoke little Hindustani and, after finding out most of what they wanted to know about the gun positions and the slack watch that was kept on most of them, Moore was jubilant.

"What did I tell you, Alex old man?" he demanded. "We *could* take those guns, if only the General will give his consent. I'm going to see him at first light and insist that it's our only hope. If necessary, I'll damned well

Micronite filter.
Mild, smooth taste.
For all the right reasons.
Kent.

© Lorillard 1973

America's quality cigarette.
King Size or Deluxe 100's.

Collect the Kent "Collectables."

Take advantage of this special Kent offer. Order these attractive items for your family and friends.

 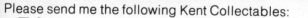

accept the command . . . at any rate for long enough to put my plan into operation."

"Let us hear what else this man can tell us," Alex cautioned. "They may have heard rumors about Neill's column that we haven't." He turned again to the *jemadar* but the man shook his head. No reports had come in from the Nana's patrols on the Allahabad road but a British column was believed to be in the city.

"A small, weak force only, Sahib," he added. "The native garrison is said to be engaged against it and the whole area is in revolt."

"You see?" Moore's tone was impatient. "We cannot depend on outside aid reaching us, perhaps for weeks. Ask him about things here—morale, for instance."

On this subject, Ram Gupta spoke freely and bitterly, needing little prompting. The British defense had astonished and angered the mutineers' leaders, he told them, and morale amongst the rebel troops was at a low ebb.

"Every day more regiments join us—we have close on eight thousand men of all arm, yet you defy us. You beat off every attack, causing such heavy losses to us, it is believed that you have a minefield girdling your ramparts. Some have asked that a herd of asses be stampeded across the plain to explode these mines but the Nana Sahib will not hear of it. He has issued orders for a great attack to be launched against you, which must succeed or every man must die in the attempt to breach your walls."

The officers exchanged wry glances, when Alex translated this statement. "When, Ram Gupta?" he asked quietly. "When is this great attack on us to be launched?"

The *jemadar* shrugged. "Soon, Sahib, very soon. In two days, perhaps, or three—I am not sure. There is a reluctance amongst our soldiers. Many care more for plunder than for fighting and do not want to risk their lives when they believe that the guns will do their work for them. When the rains come, they say you will have no rampart and will be compelled to yield. But the Nana Sahib is impatient—he will not wait. He demands victory."

He talked on, his tongue now loosened. From what he said, he appeared to have been disillusioned by the poor discipline maintained by the native officers promoted to high rank by the Nana and, in particular, by the arrogance of the cavalry and the excesses they committed, usually without incurring punishment.

"They are dogs of Moslems, Sahib," he said resentfully. "Cowards and killers of the helpless, who like nothing better than to seek out Christians who have hidden themselves in the city. These they murder and rob, without mercy. They slaughter cows in our holy places and hold even the Nana Sahib in contempt when he bids them cease. Teeka Singh, he who was *Rissaldar* Major of the Second Light Cavalry, was made General over us, but now his own *sowars* demand his arrest because he has amassed more than his fair share of plunder. Instead of acceding to their request, the Nana has rewarded him with many *khilluts,* including an elephant and many gold bangles, as a mark of his favor. The men of my regiment are angry. They weary of the siege and of attacks in which they die but the Cavalry take no part. The *golandazes* are also weary, for they must serve their guns all day long in this heat and suffer raids when, in the hours of darkness, they would rest. They say that the Cavalry should protect them and they do not."

Alex smiled as he translated this lengthy statement, word for word, to John Moore, who noted it gleefully.

"We could succeed with a bold sally, I swear! They are thoroughly demoralized, for God's sake . . . they'll run, the instant they catch sight of our bayonets. They—" He was interrupted by a shouted warning from Lieutenant Stirling, who was posted on what the defenders of Number Four Block termed their "crow's nest," a loopholed edifice built of discarded bricks twenty feet above the roof. A fusillade of shots from the picket swiftly dispersed the threatened attack and Stirling called down matter-of-factly, "Six, boys. Not bad but we've done better. All clear now."

Ram Gupta looked from one to another of them, his jaw dropping in ludicrous surprise. "Truly the gods are with you, Sahib," he told Mowbray Thomson. "You are so few . . . we had believed that fifty Sahibs held this building. Indeed, it is said that without supernatural aid, you must long since have been overpowered by our number and by the heat . . . yet you fight on! You have little water and no food, whereas our bellies are full, yet you defeat all our efforts, you and your memsahibs also. We had supposed all the memsahibs and the white children dead, but it is not so, is it? You saved them, even when *Subadar* Riaz Ali set fire to the thatched roof of the hospital."

Again the officers exchanged wary glances and Mowbray Thomson nodded. "You will not defeat us, *Jemadar-ji*," he returned with quiet confidence, "however many fires you start."

The *jemadar* bowed his head. "This I believe now, Sahib, for you are gods, not men—and I would return to fight at your side. Like many others of my paltan, I had no wish to betray my salt. Truly, it was the *hawa*, the devil's wind, that caused us to break faith with the Company and now we regret it. Our hearts are sickened by the manner in which the Nana Sahib rules and by the favor he shows to the pigs of Moslems."

Alex's interest quickened, as the significance of the native officer's words sank in. "Are there many others who feel thus, Ram Gupta?" he asked.

The man met his gaze squarely. "*Ji-han*, Sahib, there are very many in the infantry *paltans*. Those of my Faith . . ." He hesitated and then went on, with an earnestness which, of itself, carried conviction, "I think that if they were promised pardon and, perhaps, some reward by the General Sahib, they would return to the Company's service. There has been talk that we should leave for Delhi but that would be silenced were such an offer to be made. In truth, Sahib, we do not trust the

115

Nana. He is of our Faith but . . . he is a Mahratta. Let me return to my men with an offer of pardon."

"And that," Alex told John Moore, when he had translated the *jemadar's* suggestion, "is something else for the General's ear, is it not?"

"Yes, perhaps it is," Moore conceded, a trifle reluctantly. "If you think this fellow can be trusted."

"He had an exemplary record in the regiment, John," Mowbray Thomson observed.

"But he betrayed us—not once but twice! He deserted from the entrenchment."

"And appears to have learnt his lesson." Thomson spoke without heat. "We've surely nothing to lose if we send him back with an offer—such as he suggests—to his men. He can bring us their answer and—"

"*If* the General is willing to pardon them, Tommy."

"Why should he not be willing? We're in desperate straits—surely any gamble is worth taking?"

Moore frowned, still not entirely convinced. He said, with a hint of irritation, "Your Company's officers are always so ready to trust the blasted sepoys, aren't you? But . . ." he controlled himself and looked across at Alex. "What's your opinion, Alex? By virtue of your brevet, you are the senior—what should we do?"

"Take Ram Gupta to the General," Alex answered, without hesitation. "If he *is* prepared to pardon any mutineers who renounce their allegiance to the Nana and return to us, then this man can be sent back with the offer. As Tommy says, we've nothing to lose by making it . . . and perhaps everything to gain." He lowered his voice. "We all know we can't hold out much longer."

"I still believe we can fight our way out but . . . so be it. I'll take him to General Wheeler." Moore scratched at the unsightly stubble on his chin, his frown deepening. "Just one point, though. You don't propose that we should admit any ex-mutineers to the entrenchment, simply relying on *their* word that they are returning to fight for us, do you?"

116

Alex shook his head, restraining the impulse to reply sharply. They were all tired, he thought, so tired that tempers were easily frayed. "No, naturally not. But as a Company's officer, my dear John, I'd rely on their word to the extent of being willing to lead them in a raid on the battery in the Cavalry Lines . . . does that satisfy you?"

Moore's expression relaxed. "That's good enough for me—I hope I live to see you do it! And I have the greatest admiration for all the Company's officers I've had the honor to serve with here, I assure you." He laid a hand briefly on Alex's shoulder and rose from his crosslegged position on the earthen floor of the barrack, to stretch his cramped limbs wearily. "Well, we'd better try to get a little sleep, I suppose, in case your *jemadar* was telling the truth about the do-or-die attack the Nana is planning. We—"

"I think," Alex warned him, "that—in case he is—you would be wise to postpone *your* plans for a final sally. We'd have a better chance of taking those guns if we defeat the worst they can throw at us before we try it, don't you agree?"

"Then you *do* believe the fellow's story?"

"Yes, I do—on that score, at all events." Several of the others nodded their agreement and Alex added thoughtfully, "Knowing the Nana, I'm surprised he's waited so long to order a full scale attack, because he needs a victory—and needs it badly—if he's to retain power. He's losing prestige with every day we resist him. Besides, idle troops are lawless troops—his best chance of enforcing discipline is by making them fight. I'm quite sure they'll attack us and very soon."

The attack came sooner even than Alex had anticipated. At dawn on 23rd June—the anniversary of Plassey—a great mass of troops was seen to be collecting on all sides of the entrenchment. Although still some distance away, it could be seen that they no longer resembled regular corps, for most of the sepoys had discarded

117

their scarlet Company uniforms and, whilst a few wore jackets and shakos, the majority were in undress white uniforms of the type worn by recruits. The cavalry, too, presented a strangely unmilitary appearance, the French gray and silver of the 2nd Native Cavalry worn only by a few officers, and their ranks augmented by several regiments of irregular horse, whose colorful costumes and brightly hued turbans were reminiscent of bygone frontier wars. But telescopes revealed that they were well armed and being kept sternly in hand by their officers, wheeling into line of regiments with disciplined precision, so as to provide protection for the horse artillery troops which accompanied them.

The gun batteries surrounding the entrenchment opened the heaviest cannonade the defenders had yet experienced, causing them some discomfort and a number of casualties, as the women and children were hastily crowded into the godowns and the flat-roofed barrack, which, although honeycombed with holes, now offered the only shelter available for the helpless. A few found precarious sanctuary behind the blackened, crumbling walls of the burned-out hospital, while others, caught in the open and unable to reach any of the buildings, crouched in the drain or the shallow trench behind it.

Alex, having escorted Emmy to the main guard, was forced to leave her there, with the most cursory of farewells, when the general alarm sounded. With Captain Athill Turner, of the 1st Native Infantry, and a young cavalry officer, Charles Quinn, who had recently joined his sector, he ran to the parapet and took his place at the loopholed observation post, telescope to his eye, expecting to have to ward off an attack. But the alarm appeared to have been somewhat premature and he put the glass down, in order to ascertain whether he had his full complement or whether it would be necessary to reorganize the vulnerable parts of his line.

There were no absentees; every man who could fire a rifle had answered the call, some having to be helped

118

across the compound by their comrades and others contriving to hobble along unaided, using their rifles as crutches. They looked more like scarecrows than British soldiers, Alex reflected wryly, many of them wounded or ravaged by dysentery and fever, all of them on the verge of starvation and suffering acutely from the pangs of prolonged thirst. Their uniforms hung on them in unrecognizable, filthy rags, their emaciated bodies were burned and blistered by constant exposure to the sun, and their limbs were grossly swollen and covered in sores—an inevitable result of the diet of parched, uncooked gram and dried peas to which they had been reduced. All were in the same state, officers and common soldiers alike; it was impossible to tell the difference between them, save by their voices and the oaths they used.

But they were in better spirits than they had been for days past and there was no fear in the haggard, unwashed faces lining the parapet. They had all suffered so much, seen death in its most hideous forms so often that it held no terror for them now—some, indeed, might welcome it as a friend. But they would fight and they would sell their lives dearly, Alex knew, conscious of a feeling of intense pride in their toughness, for these were the survivors of the long battle against impossible odds. They had lost wives, beloved children, comrades and friends, and had not yielded; now they had come to defend their tiny, indefensible fortress for perhaps the last time, sensing that the attack for which they waited would be the ultimate test of their courage and endurance.

If they failed now, it would be the end, and most of them were aware of it . . . yet they managed to joke among themselves. Men who had breath to speak swore, grumbled and laughed, and swore again; they cursed the heat, the stench and the flies and then made lewd, foulmouthed jokes even of these. Edward Montcrieff, the garrison chaplain, came to them, making his dogged, dutiful rounds and, out of respect for him, the swearing instantly ceased. The men bowed their heads in prayer but, when

119

he had gone, they wiled away the tedium of waiting by betting on the destination and effect of the round-shot which crashed into the entrenchment and Alex heard one wager offered, the result of which depended on whether or not the chaplain would manage to complete his round unscathed.

To his right, ammunition wagons were dragged into position and he saw young Ashe, stripped to the waist and with a motley team of gunners, working to load his battered guns with double charges of grape. Ashe grinned and waved, with the irrepressible cheerfulness he always displayed when an attack of some kind was imminent. He gestured to one of his loaders, his grin widening, and Alex recognized *Jemadar* Ram Gupta, who was toiling as hard as the rest. The General, he knew, from what John Moore had told him of their interview, had refused to commit himself on the question of a pardon but was keeping the *jemadar* in the entrenchment, pending his final decision. He had also postponed his decision concerning the sally on which Moore had set his heart and Moore, in consequence, was on tenterhooks and uncharacteristically irritable.

Well, perhaps if they could inflict one more humiliating reverse on the Nana's troops this morning, both questions would resolve themselves, Alex thought philosophically, but his heart sank when, picking up his telescope again, he saw the force which the enemy was ranging against them.

The flat plain to the northwest was thick with horsemen; there must be nearly two thousand of them already, and more were crossing the Canal Road—irregulars, judging by their formation and the caliber of their horses. There was also considerable activity among the infantry in the New Cantonment, he saw, taking a sweep with his glass. The trenches were packed and there was a mortar battery to the rear of the Church compound, which was keeping up an accurate and rapid fire on Henry Delafosse's position—evidently in the hope of repeating their earlier success and exploding his reserve ammunition. But Delafosse was equal to the challenge. A tremendous roar—young Henry must have treble-shotted his gun, Alex decided—came from the southeast corner of the entrenchment and the rain of screeching, hissing shells abruptly ceased. His spirits rose but, as he was trying to ascertain whether Delafosse's sorely-tried ninepounder had been damaged, his attention was distracted by the sound of very heavy musketry fire, which appeared to be coming from the row of unfinished barrack blocks to the west.

Minutes later, John Moore came running breathlessly across, to ask for as many men as he could spare from the parapet.

"The devils are swarming into all the unoccupied blocks," Moore told him. "They're threatening Mowbray Thomson's position in Number Four. We're sunk if they once get control there and he's only got fifteen men, so we'll have to help him. I told Eddie Vibart that we'd try to clear them out and, if it can be managed, that we'd drive them into One and Two. He has a gun laid on both blocks so, if we can get them there, he'll be able to rout them with a few rounds of canister. But I'll need at least twenty-five able-bodied men, Alex. I can't take any from the Redan, they're pushed as it is, and the cavalry attack will probably be concentrated on them. Can you let me have ten of your fellows and come yourself? It's best to stick to our usual team and it shouldn't take long—you'll be back here before the main attack develops, with any luck."

Alex complied with his request, recognizing its urgency. To lose control of Numbers Four and Six Blocks would, he was only too well aware, render the west side of the entrenchment untenable. Number Four, in particular, *had* to be held. He caught the pouch of homemade grenades Moore tossed to him and handed over command of his sector of Athill Turner.

"Sorry to leave you in the lurch, Athill. We'll be back as soon as we can."

Turner nodded, relieving him of the glass with a tight-lipped grin. "Don't hurry—*they* won't, cowardly swine! They're probably consulting the oracle to see which of 'em have to face us first."

With two Native Cavalry officers, Quinn and Wren, and Sergeant Maywood of the 32nd, Alex completed his small party by selecting five men of the 84th and two Fusiliers—the choice virtually made for him, since few others in the sector could lay claim to being able-bodied. They joined Moore, Francis Whiting and the rest of the men and, without the need for orders—since all were veterans of innumerable sallies into the disputed barrack blocks—slipped out of the entrenchment. In ones and twos, bent low and steering a zig-zag course, they ran the gauntlet of the rebels' musketry, to fling themselves down under cover of Number Four Block to regain their breath.

When all had crossed, Moore led one party to the left, Alex the others to the right and, with Thomson's marksmen providing them with covering fire, they set about clearing the blocks in methodical fashion. They had been compelled to do it so often before that they now worked to a well-tried routine; first the grenades, lobbed in through the unglazed window spaces; a pause, then a few shots from accurate Enfields, followed by a bayonet charge and, with the rebels as always in full retreat, on to the next. It was an exhausting task in the daytime heat for half-starved, parched and weary men, few of whom had had more than an hour's sleep but somehow, calling upon reserves of strength they had not realized they possessed, it was accomplished and the threat averted. Some of Thomson's picket made a dash to support the forward parties and cover their withdrawal and then, in response to their signal, Vibart's well-sited guns on the north face sent a shower of grape into the end pair of the line of barrack blocks, known to the defenders as One and Two.

Limping, barely able to walk, the men of the raiding

122

parties reformed on Number Four. They had sustained casualties; Charles Quinn was hit in the leg; Moore himself had been creased by a musket-ball which had laid the right side of his scalp bare for almost four inches; the valiant Maywood was carried back by two of Thomson's men with a severe wound in the chest, and two men of the 84th, although unwounded, collapsed from heatstroke.

"We'll leave our casualties with you, Tommy," Moore said, when he could get his breath. "And get a surgeon to come across. They'll be better off here—at least the poor devils will be out of the sun and they can be moved tonight, if they're in your way. In the meantime, do what you can for them, will you? Because we've got to go back."

"There's been no attack yet, John," Mowbray Thomson told him. "Andy Stirling's been keeping a lookout." He added cynically, "They're depending on a prolonged and heavy bombardment to soften us up, like the French in the Crimea, but I don't think it will be a conspicuous success for them either, unless they're prepared to come at us with infantry."

"I think they'll try that," Alex said. "They must." He had been kneeling at Sergeant Maywood's side, holding a water bottle to the wounded man's lips and he rose reluctantly to his feet. "I'll have to go back." It was an effort to move, an effort even to speak; he felt nauseated and lightheaded, unable to focus his gaze or see clearly, and Mowbray Thomson said, with concern, "Rest for a few minutes, Alex. You'll never make it if you don't."

Francis Whiting took his arm. "I'll come across with you. We can take it slowly—there aren't any snipers, thank God. At least we gave them a pasting."

They returned to the entrenchment together, with the slow, uncertain gait of old men, pausing often to regain their breath and managing somehow to avoid the bouncing round-shot which added to the perils of their three-hundred-yard journey. The three men of the 84th and the two Fusiliers who returned with them were in no better

123

shape and Whiting said despondently, "I fear John will have to abandon his plan for a sortie, Alex. We're none of us fit to undertake it. All we're capable of now is the defense of this godforsaken entrenchment . . . if that."

"We've *got* to hold the entrenchment," Alex answered. "It's do or die for us, as well as for them. If they do launch a full scale attack this morning—as I'm convinced they will—our fate will be decided, one way or the other. The Nana's, too, perhaps." He sighed. "This is our last stand, Francis. If we make it a good one, it might even become a victory."

"Pray God you're right," Francis Whiting said. "Pray God you are!"

Alex said no more but he, too, was praying as he went from man to man, offering what encouragement he could and conscious of a pang when he saw that six or seven women had joined his depleted line in order to pass ammunition and load for their husbands. Minutes later, Athill Turner called out a hoarse warning and, returning to his observation post, he saw that a number of field batteries, with six- and nine-pounder guns drawn by horses and bullocks, were advancing on the north and northeast faces of the entrenchment. They came boldly, with a cavalry escort and unlimbered within four hundred yards but, choosing their moment with the skill of long practice, Ashe and Delafosse opened a withering fire on those within their range and forced them to withdraw.

They had scarcely done so when skirmishers began to deploy from the trenches in front of the New Cantonment. Under cover of bales of cotton, which they rolled in front of them, they kept up a brisk fire with their muskets as they advanced in extended lines, making difficult targets, even for practiced riflemen.

"Steady!" Alex cautioned, watching them, glass to his eye. "Hold your fire—let the guns deal with them!" His vision had cleared now and his telescope revealed a great mass of infantry issuing from the trees and buildings which had given them concealment. The sun glinted on their bayonets and on the drawn sword of a tall, powerfully built *Subadar* Major, who was leading them, and they raised a concerted shout, deep-throated and savage, as they cleared the trenches and began to swarm across the Cantonment Road.

Ashe's guns poured grape and canister into the cotton bales, their staccato thunder echoed by Delafosse's to the east and Kempland's to the southeast of the entrenchment, followed by the crack of rifle fire from the Redan on the north face. The enemy were closing in from all sides, Alex's mind registered, and in such overwhelming numbers that, if they pressed home their attack with sufficient resolution, they could not fail to take their objective. In previous attacks, they had lacked resolution but— He swung his glass round, anxious to ascertain the movements of the cavalry, of which he had lost sight in the dust and smoke. They were over to the left of the Riding School and had wheeled into four close-packed lines, preparatory to making a charge—their objective, as John Moore had forecast, almost certainly the Redan, which jutted out in a semicircle to the rear of the flat-roofed barrack, defended by two guns and twenty riflemen.

A trumpet sounded, shrill and clear above the mutter of light-caliber guns—the 24-pounders had ceased fire now, in anticipation of the attack—and the horsemen started to move forward in a cloud of reddish-brown dust, slowly at first, but each line gathering momentum as the sowars kicked their horses into a gallop. They made an awesome spectacle, the 2nd Light Cavalry with lances couched, the Oudh irregulars with *tulwars* drawn, thundering across the flat expanse of sun-bright sand, their banners and the green, blue and yellow *achkans* and turbans weaving intricate patterns of rippling color among the white-clad ranks. As they broke into a gallop, they shouted their battle cries, two thousand voices raised in a bloodchilling chorus of vengeance and hate calculated to strike terror into the stoutest heart.

"Din! Din! For the Faith—kill for the Faith! Death to the feringhi! *Maro! Maro!"*

The speed of their charge and the sheer volume of sound which accompanied it made them seem invincible; to many of the anxiously watching defenders it appeared that only minutes stood between them and annihilation. But they obediently held their fire, although the first wave of infantry, led by the giant *Subadar* Major, was advancing from the Cantonment Road. The front rank fired a volley, without evoking any response and beside him, Alex heard a young private draw in his breath in a sobbing gasp. The infantry came swarming across the intervening space, yelling their heads off and trampling over the discarded cotton bales as if they, too, scented victory. But the cavalry had begun their charge too soon; in the blazing noonday sun, their horses were winded, losing impetus and alignment, failing to close their ranks.

Ashe's guns crashed out again and again—in the din, Alex could hear no others—and the cavalry charge was checked. Horses fell, others were plunging, flinging their riders headlong to the ground, to be trampled, screaming, by those who came behind. Then they were past, still heading for the Redan but in confusion, and Vibart's defenders met them with a wall of fire. Alex raised his arm and his line of scarecrow soldiers fired almost as one man, fear, exhaustion, hunger forgotten or overcome, the rifles burning their blistered hands, as they loosed volley after volley at the oncoming infantry. Now a line of dead and dying mutineers lay between the mud wall of the entrenchment and the oncoming swarm; they faltered but their *Subadar* stood, his sword raised, urging them on and the young private who had sobbed fixed him in his sights and, with cool deliberation, cut him down.

Still the following waves continued their advance; Ashe turned his guns on them and only a few reached the ditch in front of the entrenchment; fewer still survived to hurl themselves at the parapet, to be met by British bayonets. They might, by sheer weight of numbers, have carried

126

the northeast face but the sight of the cavalry in full retreat unnerved them. They wavered and, lacking resolute
leadership, broke and fled, tearing through the ranks of
their own oncoming support troops which, in turn, were
thrown into confusion and fell back. One of Ashe's hard-
used guns blew up, its barrel shattered, but they had
served their turn and gradually the fire from the entrenchment slackened.

No cheers saluted their victory; it had been won at too
great a cost and the men lining the parapet leaned against
it with closed eyes or collapsed into the trenches behind
it, spent and gasping for breath. It was the women who
came out to do what they could for those who were
wounded and Alex, sitting dazedly with his back against
the ruins of his observation post, his empty pistol in his
hand, found Emmy beside him, holding a cup of water to
his parched and blistered lips. He could not speak but he
drank gratefully and then, the cup almost drained, he
turned to her shamefaced, offering her what was left.

"I . . . I'm sorry, I didn't think, darling. Dear God, I've
taken it all."

She smiled, shaking her head. "You needed it, Alex.
Rest now, won't you? They're beaten off, there's no more
firing . . . surely you have earned a rest?"

He dragged himself up. "That water saved my life,
Emmy. Bless you for it. I . . . I'll rest in a minute. I have
to see to my men, I—"

"We're doing what can be done. There'll be water—a
party is drawing it now." She gestured towards the well.
"The General is wounded, did you hear? In the leg, I
believe. The gallant old man joined them in the Redan.
They suffered badly there, I'm afraid. Three young officers, all boys, were killed by round-shot before the cavalry charged. Poor young Ensign Supple was one of them.
He was such a nice young man—he used to visit his
friend, Tom Forman, in the hospital. He helped me often,
when I . . ." Emmy's voice broke. "Oh, Alex, is it never

going to end, this terrible killing? Will they go on attacking until we are all dead?"

Would they? Alex wondered, unable to answer her . . . or would this morning's attack have convinced even the Nana that his opponents would yield only to death? He must have lost hundreds of men today and he had seen his cavalry vanquished and humiliated—but would this be enough to give him pause? Would it be enough to induce the sepoys of the 53rd and the 56th to desert him and return to their old allegiance, as *Jemadar* Ram Gupta believed they might?

Alex sighed, forcing his tired brain to consider the possibilities. After this morning, the advantage lay—if only fleetingly—with the defenders, but they would have to act now, at once, or it would be too late. He looked at the men who had held his sector of the perimeter so valiantly and repeated his sigh. They could not hold it for much longer; by this evening, if they had to endure another day in the hot sun and the continued pounding of the rebel guns, half of them would be in a state of collapse. For God's sake, Ram Gupta *must* be sent back to his regiment! He might fail but his suggestion was worth trying. A pardon—even the promise of reward— if the sepoys of the 56th agreed to return to the Company's service was surely not too high a price to pay if it would end the siege or enable them to fight their way to Lucknow. The women, his own beloved Emmy, had suffered more than any women ought to be called upon to suffer—if the price of their lives was a pardon for one or two regiments of mutineers, it was certainly not too high . . . and the General must be made to see it.

There was also his own, half-formed plan to disguise himself as a *sadhu* and attempt to contact Neill in Allahabad; that, too, might be a chance worth taking, however long the odds against it. Alternatively, he . . .

"Poor Mr. Haycock died the other day," Emmy was saying. There were tears in her eyes and she moved away from him, smoothing the folds of her ragged and filthy

128

dress. "It was a merciful release for him, poor soul—he was quite out of his mind with sunstroke and fever for several days. But I'm sorry for his mother. She's old and frail and she nursed him so devotedly, day and night. Even when he ran out into the compound naked, saying that he was going to pray with the sepoys, she brought him back and soothed him. And poor Mary White—the one who has twins . . . oh, Alex, did you hear what happened to her? A single musket-ball broke both her arms and killed her husband, with whom she was walking under cover of the godown wall, as well as wounding one of the twins. Now she must suckle them lying on her back and—"

"Emmy, my love . . ." Alex gently interrupted her. "You said the General was wounded, did you not?"

"Yes—in the Redan this morning. He was hit in the leg and—"

"Is he badly wounded?"

Emmy shook her head. "I don't think so. It was only a graze from a shell splinter, someone told me. But like Mrs. Haycock, he is old and frail. Wounds turn to gangrene in this heat, Alex, and we've no medicines and hardly any clean dressings. The surgeons—"

"I must see him, darling," Alex said, again having to cut her short. She spent all her waking hours in the makeshift hospital in the main guard building and the deaths, he realized, were beginning to prey on her mind. Poor child, there were so many of them now, it was small wonder. "I must see the General at once," he repeated. "Where was he taken, do you know?"

Emmy eyed him apprehensively. "To his own quarters, I believe. His wife and daughters are caring for him but . . . why, Alex? Why must you see him at once?"

He told her the truth and saw fear dawn in her eyes. "You mean that *you* will offer to take a message to Allahabad? Oh, Alex, no! You won't stand a chance, truly you won't! They say that all the roads are guarded, the river too—you'd never get through. You—"

"I think I might. For heaven's sake, darling—look at me! I'd pass for a native easily, my skin's burnt black, and I speak the language fluently." He hesitated, reaching for her hand. "Darling, *someone* has to try to reach Neill—we can't just stay here waiting until . . . Emmy, I won't volunteer if you don't want me to, my love. But I believe I'd have as good a chance as anyone."

She did not look at him. "If you want to go, I won't stand in your way, Alex. But I am afraid for you . . . every minute of every day, I am afraid for you. Each time they bring a wounded man to us, my heart stops beating for fear that it will be you."

Alex drew her to him. "My dearest Emmy, it will be me, it will be all of us if Neill's column does not reach us very soon."

She hid her ravaged face against his chest and he felt her trembling. "I know," she whispered huskily. "I know. Go if you must, Alex, but I . . . I cannot bear to . . . to bid you farewell, I . . ." She left him and went, a thin, pitifully limping figure, back across the reeking dust of the compound to the main guard building She had scarcely gained its shelter when the rebel guns opened once more and a round-shot scattered those who were endeavoring to draw water from the well.

Alex braced himself. He dismissed all the men of his sector except the sentries, sent a man to draw the rum ration and told the others to get what rest they could in the trenches and shallow, scooped-out holes behind their mud wall. Then, handing over command to Athill Turner, he went to seek audience with the General.

The old man was lying on a mattress in one corner of his small room, with Dr. Harris, the Civil Surgeon, and Dr. Boyes, surgeon to the 2nd Cavalry, attending him. He looked very ill but insisted that his injuries were slight and, when the surgeons had gone, he sat up and listened attentively to all that Alex had to say. His wife and two daughters, hovering anxiously in the background, listened also but did not speak until the General expressed reluctance to come to any decision without time to consider the implications of Alex's proposals.

"I cannot, in all conscience, pardon or reward sepoys who have been untrue to their salt, Sheridan," he said uneasily. "Nor can I lightly send you to almost certain death. Truly I—"

"Are we not all of us facing almost certain death, Papa?" his elder daughter put in harshly. "Unless Colonel Neill is informed of our plight and urged to relieve us with all possible speed?" She was a tall, thin girl of about twenty who, Alex thought, seeing her consciously for the first time, must once have been handsome, even beautiful. Now, like all the rest on whom the nineteen-day siege had set its mark, she was pale and gaunt, her long hair cropped, her face and hands begrimed with dirt. But her courage had not deserted her; she stood up to her father, arguing forcefully with him and ignoring her mother's somewhat hesitant attempts to interrupt her.

"I'd come with you, gladly, Colonel Sheridan," she added. "If it would be of the smallest help . . . I, too, would pass as a native, I believe." She smiled, her tone defiant. "As to whether you can reconcile your conscience to offering a pardon to mutineers, Papa, I do not think you have much choice. They could save us if they came to our aid—even one regiment of them—but they will *not* come unless they are promised pardon and a reward, will they?"

"That's enough, Amelia," her mother chided. "This is a matter for your papa to decide. He is ill, he has been wounded . . . he needs time to think over what Colonel Sheridan has said and—"

"But we haven't got time, Mamma," the girl retorted hotly. "We have no time left at all. To have survived all these—these horrors and then to die would be a bitter pill to swallow, would it not?"

"Amelia is right," the General said slowly. He held out his hand to her and she knelt at his side, instantly submissive and ready to apologize but he waved her to

131

silence. Turning to Alex, he went on with conviction, "And so are you, my young friend. Between you, you have resolved my doubts. I owe it to this noble garrison to do everything in my power to save them. Send the *jemadar* back to his regiment tonight. Tell him that I will give my word that a pardon shall be granted to every sepoy who returns to the Company's service within the next twenty-four hours, and that I will use my best endeavors to see that they also receive a fitting reward— more I cannot promise."

"It might be advisable to extend the time limit for their return, sir," Alex suggested. "The *jemadar* will have to make his offer cautiously . . . perhaps to a few individuals at a time. And he will have to bring us their answer, so that we can make arrangements to guard against the possibility of treachery."

"True. Then make what arrangements you see fit, Colonel Sheridan."

Alex bowed. "I will, sir—in consultation with Captain Moore, of course. And as to my other suggestion . . . may I have your permission to make the attempt to reach Allahabad?"

"As to that—" The General hesitated, white brows coming together in an anxious pucker. "I must defer my decision. I am sorry, Sheridan—I appreciate your zeal and self-sacrifice but you are needed here. We cannot spare officers of your experience from our defense." Both Alex and Amelia started to speak but he shook his head and said, with something of his old decisiveness, "No, you cannot change my mind, either of you. We are not yet reduced to desperation—if we should be, then I'll avail myself of your courageous offer, perhaps. Although I think that a native messenger would stand a better chance of getting through than any European. . . ." Again he hesitated, his frown deepening. "I intend to make one last appeal to Sir Henry Lawrence. The man who got through to Lucknow and returned with Sir Henry's reply—Ungud —is here and he is willing to make a second journey. I have also received the offer of a volunteer—a man named Shepherd, a senior clerk in the Commissariat Office—who has said he will endeavor to make his way to the city here and bring back information as to the Nana's intentions. He has a house in the General Gunj and knows the city well—and he will go in disguise, of course. I shall instruct him to contact the Nunneh Nawab—Mohammed Ali Khan—who is faithful to us and whom I trust. Let us see how he fares, shall we, Sheridan, before taking more desperate measures?"

"Yes, sir, of course." There was obviously nothing to be gained by further discussion and Alex prepared to take his leave. "Thank you for seeing me, sir. I trust your wound will soon heal and that you will not be caused too much discomfort from it."

"I am in no pain," the General assured him. "Tomorrow I shall prepare a letter for Sir Henry and give Shepherd his instructions. In the meantime . . ." He settled back on his mattress with a sigh. "We should get what rest we can. I don't think we shall suffer any attacks *this* night but, in any case, most of us have learnt how to sleep through cannon fire, if we've learnt nothing else." He closed his eyes and was asleep before Alex left the room. Amelia Wheeler went with him to the door.

"My father is worn out," she said. "And in quite a lot of pain, although he won't admit it. But he will do everything in his power, Colonel Sheridan, and I promise I won't allow him to forget your offer."

Alex thanked her and returned to his post.

At dusk, the guns ceased fire and a party of native officers, bearing a flag of truce, approached the entrenchment to request permission to remove their dead. This was granted and, after agreeing to a cease-fire, the native officers saluted and returned to their own lines. Burial parties from both besiegers and besieged went about their melancholy task uninterrupted, and the well outside the entrenchment opened to receive its two hundred and forty-seventh recorded victim.

133

That night the guns were silent, and the absence of snipers and a short but heavy shower of rain enabled those within the entrenchment to drink their fill for the first time in almost three weeks. Many stripped to the skin during the downpour, letting the rain water cool their tortured bodies and wash some of the filth and dust from their skins and, when it was over, the men at the parapet—with the exception of the sentries, who were changed every hour—slept peacefully and well, undisturbed by the sudden alarms by which their sleep was usually broken.

But, as always, when the new day dawned, it was heralded by the familiar thunder of the guns and, as the sun rose, the temperature rose with it and the brief lull was over. Once more musketry fire raked those who attempted to draw water from the well; shells screeched overhead and round-shot thudded against the tottering buildings and bounced their deadly way across the compound. Three children were hit by snipers and it was necessary to clear the unfinished barrack blocks of a horde of skulking intruders. The ghastly stench of putrefaction from dead horses and bullocks rotting on the plain added the fresh torment of a plague of flies, and Francis Whiting reported anxiously that the rain of the previous night had undermined the mud wall in places and flooded the old hospital drain.

With two of Ashe's three guns disabled and reserves of ammunition for the remaining seven all but exhausted, the position was critical.

"We couldn't hold off another attack like yesterday's," John Moore told Alex wretchedly. "The devils could walk in here, for all we could do to prevent them." He moved his injured arm gingerly, ashen-faced and clearly in pain. He was closer to despair than Alex had ever seen him, even his faith and courage strained to the limit and beyond. "I've been the rounds, Alex," he went on, brushing wearily at the flies which buzzed about them in a persistent cloud. "And, counting ourselves, we could raise about fifty reasonably fit men for a sortie, and they're all willing to join us. It's our last chance and I truly believe that it would succeed, if only the General would give his consent to it . . . but he refuses. In God's name, what are we to do?"

"I think," Alex said, "you should have that arm of yours dressed. You—"

"Dressed?" Moore retorted irritably. "It should come off, my dear fellow, but the surgeons have no instruments with which to take it off . . . or had you forgotten that?"

"No, I hadn't forgotten," Alex answered quietly. He offered his hand. "Come on—you're going sick for twenty-four hours. You need sleep—unless you have it, you won't be able to lead a sortie, John, you'll collapse. The General will not refuse his consent when the time comes—he told me as much, when I spoke to him last night. When he accepts that our situation is hopeless, he'll agree to whatever desperate measures any of us may propose."

"Are you certain of that?"

"Yes, I am. So for God's sake be sensible—let me take you to the surgeons. At least they might be able to relieve your pain."

It was a measure of the gallant Moore's despair that he offered no further objections and Alex left him in Emmy's care in the main guard building.

135

CHAPTER SIX

Writing his final appeal for help to Sir Henry Lawrence, on the evening of 24th June, General Wheeler gave a brief and bitter account of his garrison's brave resistance and the peril in which they now stood. Tears blurred the closely written lines as he read them through and then penned his last, accusing question: *"Surely we are not to be left to die like rats in a cage without any attempt being made to bring us succor?"*

He could say no more. The decision must be left to Lawrence, but his heartbroken protest had to be committed to paper, so that, if the message reached Lucknow, posterity might know that his small, heroic garrison had fought and died in the best traditions of their service, defeated only because they had been abandoned to their fate by those on whom they had depended for aid.

Dr. Boyes, waiting silently at his elbow, took the small spill of paper from him. Having inserted it in Ungud's right ear with a pair of rusting tweezers, he took the messenger to the Brigade Major, Captain Williamson, to be smuggled out of the entrenchment as soon as darkness fell.

To his second messenger—the Commissariat clerk Shepherd—the old General issued defiant instructions, staking his all on a gambler's throw. He gave the names of several of Cawnpore's influential citizens and ordered, "Go first to the Nunneh Nawab, Mr. Shepherd. He is faithful to us and I trust him. Tell him to endeavor to cause a rupture among the rebels. Tell him also to spread the rumor abroad that we have ample provisions for another month at least, that we are in good heart and, above all, that we expect speedy help from Allahabad and Calcutta. If the Nawab—or any others who are well disposed to us—can cause the rebels to break off their attacks on our position or go away from the station, you are authorized to promise them pensions for life and lavish rewards. The reward could be as high as a lac of rupees."

The clerk's eyes widened. He started to speak and then broke off and the General, guessing his thoughts, added pointedly, "You, too, will merit high reward if you come back to me with correct information as to the Nana's intentions, Mr. Shepherd—or with definite word as to the arrival of reinforcements from Allahabad or Lucknow. But if you should be taken by the Nana, be very careful that you do not let him know the true state of our defenses, or that we are discouraged, you understand?"

Shepherd assured him that he understood perfectly. "Have I your leave to go tonight, sir?"

"Whenever you are ready with your disguise, Mr. Shepherd. May God have you in His keeping!"

When the dark-faced clerk left to make preparations for his departure, General Wheeler limped over to his mattress and sank down onto it wearily. The other occupants of the room—his wife and daughters and the wounded postmaster, Roache, to whom he had given his son's *charpoy*—were sleeping and he yearned to follow their example, to find oblivion, to forget, even for a few hours, the problems which beset him. The problems he could not solve, since they had no solution; the guilt he could not shake off, the responsibility for the garrison's terrible losses, and his grief for those who had given

137

their lives in this three-week-long siege to which he had committed them. The loss of his son . . . oh, merciful God, how that loss haunted him! He would gladly have laid down his own life, if Godfrey's could have been spared; he would willingly have submitted to any suffering if, by so doing, he could have saved his son.

But Godfrey was dead, his poor young body one of hundreds rotting in the well outside the entrenchment, his life's blood still staining the wall of this room, where his mother and sisters daily averted their eyes from it and where he . . . The old General tried vainly to fight down his rising nausea and the weakness it brought with it. He would *have* to relinquish his command, he told himself; he was too ill, too stricken with grief, too worn out to continue to make decisions and to shoulder responsibility for the lives and deaths of other men.

He sat up, controlling his retching at last. Tonight he had taken two decisions—vital ones, perhaps, if Lawrence relented and sent him the two hundred European soldiers for whom he had pleaded, and if the clerk, Shepherd, managed to persuade the Nawab to take the action he had outlined. If they did not, then he would have failed and would be in honor bound to hand over command, either to Moore or to Sheridan. Moore, of course, would lead the fit men of the garrison on a do-or-die sortie against the enemy guns if command were entrusted to him. It might succeed by its sheer daring but how many of the half-starved specters who manned the mud walls days and night would be fit to undertake such a sortie? And if they failed, what would happen to the women? No! He shuddered, feeling a cold sweat break out over his face and body. He could not give Moore his way although, in his heart, he understood and was deeply in sympathy with the motives which had caused Moore to propose a sortie—he wanted to die like a soldier. But so did they all, the wounded and the sick, and if they were left defenseless, the consequences were too hideous to contemplate.

Besides, there were the women, the women and children —he looked across at the sleeping faces of his wife and daughters and knew that, whatever the pressures put upon him, he could not permit any action which might leave them to the Nana's mercies. Since Ungud's story of the slaughter of the Fategarh fugitives had been confirmed by other informants, he had known that he could never accede to Moore's request.

Sheridan, then? He was a brave man and a fine soldier, who had acquitted himself well throughout the siege but . . . Sheridan could not assume command *and* make the attempt to contact Neill in Allahabad. He had offered to go and the decision to accept his offer was the third vital decision which, as garrison commander, he would have to make. The General moved restlessly on his uncomfortable pallet. He had planned, however, to wait until the result of Shepherd's mission was known—Shepherd's and, of course, that of the *jemadar*, who had also been sent to cause disaffection among the Nana's sepoy troops. One or other of them should report back to him within the next twenty-four hours; if they failed in their endeavors, then he would have to send Sheridan on the well-nigh impossible attempt to reach Allahabad. All the previous messengers he had despatched to contact Neill's relief column had failed to get past the Nana's patrols and, from Ungud and his other informers, he had heard what their fate had been. For purely humanitarian reasons, he was reluctant to accept Sheridan's offer or, indeed, to ask any of his British officers to go, but . . . He sighed unhappily.

As his daughter Amelia had argued so vehemently, they were all facing almost certain death—what was the death of another brave man on his conscience, when already there were so many? He . . .

"General Wheeler!" the Major of Brigade, Williamson, was shaking his arm and he sat up, rubbing at his red-rimmed eyes.

"Ah!" he exclaimed gruffly. "Have you sent Ungud and Shepherd on their way, Captain Williamson?"

The Commissariat Officer nodded, his mouth tight. "Yes, sir, they've both gone. But the *jemadar* is back, sir —Ram Gupta. The Pandies sent him back."

"The *Pandies* sent him? What the devil do you mean?"

Williamson shrugged despondently. "They must have learnt what he was doing, sir. The unfortunate fellow is barely alive and he can't tell us anything—they cut his tongue out and blinded him, as well as hacking off both his hands. They delivered him to us under—under a flag of truce, sir." He swallowed hard, obviously sickened by what he had seen. "I did not want to disturb you, sir, but I thought you would wish to know."

"Yes," the General acknowledged. "I did, I . . . thank you."

When Williamson had gone, he lay back, closing his eyes again, but sleep continued to elude him, for now there was yet another brave man on his conscience—a sepoy, this time, and as a sepoy general he could not but be proud that it was so. The 56th had been a good regiment and . . . He heard a faint rustling sound in the far corner of the room. His daughter Amelia tiptoed across and, dropping to her knees beside him, gently smoothed the spare white hair from his forehead.

"I thought you were sleeping, child," he said reproachfully.

The girl smiled down at him. "But *you* are not, dear Papa. Is your leg troubling you?"

"No," he denied. "It gives me no pain. Did you hear what Captain Williamson told me?"

She bowed her head. "Yes, I heard. The poor *jemadar!* They are turned into fiends, the sepoys—and we always believed them so docile and trustworthy! Papa, you—" There was a catch in her voice, a sudden note of fear. "If . . . if the worst should happen, if we are defeated, you . . . you will not let us fall into their hands, will you?"

His brave Amelia, the General thought, sick with pity;

140

she had flinched from nothing throughout the past three weeks but now, and with reason, she was afraid. God help her, God help all the women! His gnarled old hand tightened about her slim one. He could not answer her but, fumbling beneath his pillow, he found his Adams' pistol and slipped it into the pocket of her dress. "Your mother," he began. "Your mother and Charlotte . . . it has six shots and—"

"I understand, Papa," Amelia said quietly. There was a little silence and then she asked, still quietly, "Will you now give permission to Colonel Sheridan to attempt to get through to Allahabad?"

"Tomorrow, Amelia," he promised. "If there is no word of relief by tomorrow evening, I'll let him go."

She nodded, satisfied. "Dear Papa, lie down, will you not, and let me soothe you to sleep?" She bent over him and he felt the hard outline of the pistol pressing against his side as her fingers moved, with skilled gentleness, about his forehead and then down, to knead the aching muscles of his neck and shoulders.

General Wheeler slept at last but, even in sleep, there was no peace for him because the faces were there, the faces of those who had died, haunting even his dreams. The bluff, jovial face of Sir George Parker, the Civil Magistrate, blackened and contorted in the agonies of the sunstroke and apoplexy that had killed him; of Stephen Williams, Colonel of the 56th, and of his pretty, fair-haired wife; of Robert Prout and of Alec Jack, his Brigadier and friend, who had gone the same way. All the men had been, like himself, veterans of the Sikh wars, grown gray in the Company's service and looking forward to honorable retirement . . . but he had brought them death. He had refused to listen to their advice; they had begged him to make his stand in the strongly built Magazine but, instead, he had insisted on their joining him in the mud-walled entrenchment, which Azimullah Khan, the Nana's Moslem aide, had so contemptuously called his "Fort of Despair." His was the guilt; the decision had been his although, perhaps, it was shared with those who had promised him reinforcements and failed to send them. Given two hundred more British bayonets, he could have held even the Fort of Despair—he could hold it now, if the reinforcements came. God in heaven, would they ever come? Were he and the gallant men and women of his garrison to be left—as he had told Lawrence they were—without aid, to die like rats in a cage at the treacherous hands of the Nana?

The face of his son Godfrey blotted out the other faces and finally the old General slept the sleep of exhaustion. It was daylight when he was awakened by a voice calling his name and he sat up, blinking uncertainly at the men who were crowding about him. Moore was there, he saw, and Vibart and Whiting. . . . And his wife and daughters had left the room. His first thought was that they had come to bring him news that the relief column had been sighted but a glance at their expressions told him that it was not so.

"Well?" he demanded hoarsely. "What is it, gentlemen?"

Moore answered him. "A Eurasian woman, a Mrs. Henry Jacobi, sir, has brought this letter from the Nana. She says that he is offering us terms, sir."

The General put out a shaking hand for the letter. He read it slowly, unable at first to take it in; then, at a second reading, its meaning became clear. Addressed, not to him but to "The Subjects of Her Most Gracious Majesty, Queen Victoria," the message ran: *"All those who are in no way connected with the acts of Lord Dalhousie* and are willing to lay down their arms, shall receive a safe passage to Allahabad."*

---

*Lord Dalhousie, Governor-General from 1848-56. He implemented the policy of "annexation by right of lapse" by means of which the East India Company had acquired vast tracts of land from native princes and landowners who had no direct heirs. The Nana's claim to Baji Rao's pension was refused under this policy.

It was unsigned but General Wheeler had no difficulty in recognizing the handwriting and the autocratic style as Azimullah's. He thrust the single sheet of paper into Moore's hand and said, suddenly angry, "This is not even correctly addressed! It is arrogant and insulting and, as such, merits no reply. In any case we cannot deal with underlings—this is Azimullah's work. The Nana must sign it himself before I will consider it. By whom was it delivered, did you say, Captain Moore? A Eurasian woman?"

"A Mrs. Henry Jacobi, sir. One of the Nana's captives, I believe, whose children are being held at the Savada House with a number of other Christian prisoners. Most of them were hiding in the city when they were taken." He looked at Edward Vibart and the cavalry officer took up the story.

"I admitted Mrs. Jacobi to the entrenchment, sir. The Pandies stopped firing on us a couple of hours ago and then we saw this woman approaching, waving a handkerchief and calling out to us, in English, not to shoot. She was very distressed and . . ." Vibart hesitated. "She told me, sir, that if we rejected these terms, the Nana would execute her children."

Cold rage hardened the General's heart. "*All* our lives are at stake," he retorted brusquely. "And these are terms for a vanquished enemy. We have not been defeated, therefore we shall *not* lay down our arms." He gestured to the letter. "The Nana must sign that before I will treat with him. Furthermore he must give us his most solemn oath that he will abide by whatever conditions are finally agreed between us for the evacuation of this garrison to Allahabad—otherwise we shall stay and fight him. Don't you agree, gentlemen?" He glanced from one to the other of them and then to the postmaster, who rose from his *charpoy* and limped over to join them.

No one spoke until Moore said, with evident reluctance, "We have provisions for only three more days, sir. And if the rains break, what is left of our defensive wall will be washed away. We cannot hold this place any longer."

The General's anger slowly evaporated. There were also the women and children to be considered. . . . He bit his lower lip, remembering the pistol he had given his daughter Amelia and the use to which he had told her to put it. If there was any chance of saving them, he had to take it—but they could not surrender unconditionally. They must retain their arms, not only because British honor demanded that they should but because they would have to defend themselves on the way to Allahabad. He turned to Moore.

"Send Mrs. Jacobi back to the Nana with the letter, if you please, Captain Moore. Provided that he signs it, we will receive his representatives to negotiate conditions of our evacuation. Then call a conference of senior officers to decide what conditions we can accept and have them put in writing. The Nana will have to sign them also."

John Moore came to attention. "Very well, sir. Shall we agree to a cease-fire, in the meantime?"

"Yes, certainly." The old General's voice was very tired. "You will have to conduct the negotiations on my behalf, Moore. I cannot walk and if they see me thus . . ." He did not complete his sentence but Moore nodded in understanding. "We must have a free exit and march out under arms. And we shall require carriages, to convey the women and children."

"I'll do my best, sir," Moore promised. He nodded to the other two and they withdrew.

That evening, Mrs. Jacobi returned with the letter correctly addressed and with the Nana's signature appended to it. In the gathering darkness, two hundred yards behind the frightened, barefooted woman, Azimullah Khan and Jwala Pershad, commander of the Nana's cavalry, waited with an escort of *sowars*. Mowbray Thomson went out, with Ensign Henderson, to direct them to one of the unfinished barrack blocks; Azimullah greeted him in Eng-

144

lish and the *sowars* demanded insolently that he speak his own language.

In the rubble-strewn barrack and in Hindustani, negotiations for the surrender of the Cawnpore garrison were begun, between the Nana's two representatives and Captains Moore and Whiting, on behalf of General Wheeler, and Roache, the postmaster, on behalf of the civilians.

II

Alex, at the General's behest, took no part in the negotiations. His brief interview, soon after these had started, left him with no illusions as to Wheeler's feelings.

"I do not trust the Nana, Colonel Sheridan," the old man told him, with bitter frankness. "But I must not let slip any opportunity to save the lives of our women and children. If it were not for them, I should not treat with the enemy or contemplate surrender. As it is, I intend to obtain the most solemn guarantees, in writing, from the Nana to ensure that we shall be permitted to march out unmolested and that suitable conveyance shall be provided to take us all by river to Allahabad. However—" he paused, eyeing Alex searchingly. "I may still require you to try to contact Colonel Neill, should the negotiations break down or the Nana refuse to agree to the conditions I have directed Captain Moore to impose. I take it you are still willing to make the attempt?"

Alex felt his mouth go dry but he answered quietly, "Yes, sir." The General had voiced his own feelings, his own fears and mistrust concerning the Nana and his henchmen but, with every hour that passed, his chances of escaping from the entrenchment were becoming more hazardous. A ring of infantry encompassed them and his observations with a telescope had revealed strong patrols of cavalry to the rear of the watching sepoys. It would be impossible now to adopt the disguise he had originally planned; his only chance would be to pass himself off as a sepoy, mingle with those who were seeking to guard against any attempt at escape on the part of the garrison and then, if he could, steal a *sowar's* horse and resort to bluff. He explained this and saw the General's white brows come together in an anxious pucker.

"You would don their uniform?" he asked.

"Yes, sir. Their uniforms are pretty irregular. I've taken *Jemadar* Ram Gupta's. It's bloodstained but that would probably aid my deception. In any case"—Alex wryly indicated his empty sleeve—"I should have to try to pass myself off as a casualty, in order to hide this."

"And you will require to shave," the General reminded him. "I have a razor and water here—please make use of them while we're waiting for news of the negotiations." He sighed. "The razor was my late son's. I—my daughter will fetch it for you and give you what aid she can. Amelia!"

Amelia appeared from the shadows, the razor in her hand. It was a luxury to remove the unsightly stubble from his cheeks but, even with Amelia's skillful assistance, the task took some time and his face, Alex realized with some dismay, after inspecting it in General Wheeler's cracked mirror, would have to be darkened to an even tan if he were to have any hope of avoiding detection.

"You should shave your head, Colonel Sheridan," Amelia advised, eying him critically. "Leaving just a single long tuft of hair in the center, as the Hindu sepoys do. And I will bring you a lamp—lampblack would darken your face sufficiently to pass muster, I think."

The lampblack was successfully applied but, with his face now as dark as his body, Alex could not bring himself to follow the rest of the girl's advice. He was a British officer and a Christian, he reminded himself, and would carry his disguise no further; his hair was already cropped short, like that of most of the other defenders, and could be hidden under Ram Gupta's tightly wound *pugree*. He left the weary old General dozing restlessly and went in search of Emmy, finding her in the Main Guard caring, as usual, for the wounded. *Chattis,* brimming over with

146

dust-clouded well water, stood about the room and Emmy greeted him happily, face, hands and close-cropped hair freed at last of the accumulated dust and dirt of the three-week siege, her small, famished body clad in a clean dress.

"Oh, Alex!" Her voice shook. "Even if the negotiations break down—as pray God they won't—we can be grateful for the cease-fire. It has enabled us to quench our thirst, to wash our persons and our clothes—to feel clean again! And for these poor men"—she gestured to the rows of wounded men—"it has meant the difference between torment and a measure of comfort. For some it has meant the difference between life and death. The Crimea was never as bad as this, Alex. You . . ." She broke off, regarding him with furrowed brows. "You've stained your face!"

"Yes," he admitted, reaching for her hand and drawing her to him.

"Does that mean that you—that the General is sending you to find Colonel Neill after all? Overland, not by river with us? I thought, I hoped . . . Oh, darling, must you go?"

Alex shook his head. "Only if the Nana refuses his agreement to our conditions, Emmy."

The brief happiness faded from Emmy's dark eyes. "Then there really is a chance that he may refuse?"

"There was always that chance, my love. The General is insisting on the most stringent guarantees before he will order our evacuation—and he is right. The Nana has betrayed us once. Conditions are to be set down in writing —the Nana will have to take an oath that he will adhere to them."

"Do you think he will?" Her voice was a small whisper of sound, heartbreaking in its plea for reassurance, and Alex responded to it with a conviction he did not feel.

"Yes, darling, I think so."

"Thank God!" Emmy choked on a sob. "Oh, thank God!"

147

When she left him to return to the makeshift hospital, she was smiling, her hopes revived. And there seemed every reason for hope when, at noon, John Moore informed the General that Azimullah and Jwala Pershad had agreed to all the conditions for which he had asked. The agreement, drawn up in writing, had been taken back to the Nana for ratification.

"We are to hand over all money, guns and magazine stores, sir," Moore said. "But we march out under arms, with sixty rounds of ammunition apiece. The Nana is to provide carriage for our wounded and for the women and children to the Suttee Chowra Ghat, where covered boats will be waiting. They are to be provisioned and we may inspect them as soon as they are prepared—probably this evening. And, as you stipulated, sir, the Nana will guarantee, under his seal and signature and giving his most solemn oath, that our garrison will be permitted to proceed to Allahabad unmolested."

The General listened with eyes closed, lying back on his mattress. He said, without opening his eyes, "So be it, Captain Moore. If the Nana signs that agreement, I will do likewise."

The agreement, duly signed and sealed, was brought to the entrenchment by Azimullah, early that afternoon, with the information that four hundred coolies were already at work preparing and provisioning the boats. As earnest of the Nana's good intentions, a supply of provisions for the garrison's immediate use was on its way to the entrenchment.

The news that their long ordeal was almost at an end was received joyfully by the entire garrison. Even the wounded smiled through their pain; the children, like small, emaciated ghosts, gathered round the cooking fires and choked down mouthfuls of *chapatti* and bowlfuls of lentil stew, brimming panikins of water clutched in their bony little hands. The women washed and searched for

148

changes of raiment, exclaiming eagerly over a tattered shawl or a torn petticoat; the men shaved and poured water over their sweating bodies; soldiers donned again the scarlet jackets they had earlier discarded and cleaned their rifles: a few even raked over the ashes of the burned-out hospital, hoping to find their lost medals.

Only the weary old General lay weeping on his mattress, refusing all Amelia's pleas to try to eat or at least to allow her to shave him. Alex went to him once but left again, without having made himself heard; he returned to the compound, to find John Moore and Francis Whiting engaged in an altercation with Jwala Pershad.

"He's insisting that we evacuate the entrenchment tonight, Alex," Moore said, almost speechless with anger. "I've told him that it is quite impossible. We can't move four hundred people, including wounded and sick, in a few hours—besides, we have not yet inspected the boats."

"Is this the Nana's demand, Jwala Pershad?" Alex questioned curtly. "Or your own?"

"Not mine, Sahib," the cavalry commander answered with well simulated innocence. "But my men are anxious. They say now that the British have washed and dressed and have had time to rest, they will not go away. They have held out for so long—now they will be able to hold on longer."

"We have agreed to go, we have given our word and the General Sahib has set his hand to the agreement," Alex reminded him.

"True, Sahib, we know this. But my men are witless dogs, they do not believe written words. They——"

"Then convince them—you are their commander. Do you take orders from your *sowars*?"

"If you will hand over your guns to them and the treasure," Jwala Pershad said sullenly, "then they will believe that you intend to leave Cawnpore. I myself, with two of my officers, will remain as hostages within the entrenchment, if you will comply with our wishes, Sahib.

Otherwise . . ." He spread his hands in an elaborate shrug, dark eyes on Alex's face. "I cannot promise that our guns will not speak again and if they do, they will annihilate you."

Francis Whiting laid a hand on his arm, jerking the man round to face him. "If you push us to the last extremity," he threatened, his tone cold, "we have powder enough in our magazine to blow both your force and ours into the Ganges . . . and by heaven, we shall use it!"

"Tell him," John Moore intervened quickly, "that we will be ready to leave at dawn and not before. If he obtains the Nana's agreement—and his *sowars'*—to this, I will request the General to let him remove the treasure this evening, on the terms he suggests. But not until *after* we have inspected the boats."

Whiting translated, in a flat, controlled voice. The Indian officer departed, supposedly to consult the Nana, but returned, with suspicious alacrity, to announce that his master was willing to postpone the evacuation until the following morning.

"The boats are ready for inspection," he added blandly. "Horses and an escort await the sahibs who will undertake the inspection."

Athill Turner, Henry Delafosse and Ensign Wainwright of the 32nd were deputed to go with the escort. They came back, just before sunset, to report that twenty-four boats had been provided, each 30 feet long by 12 feet across the thwarts, with the stern part roofed over with thatch. Not all had been provisioned and, as yet, a number lacked their straw awnings, but coolies were working on these tasks and the three officers expressed the opinion that all should be in readiness by the following morning. The boats were at present lying at the Customs Ghat but were to be moved to the agreed mooring place as soon as work on them was completed.

Accordingly, all that had been saved of the Government treasure—a lac and a half of rupees—and the battered, almost completely disabled guns were handed over and Jwala Pershad and two of his officers yielded themselves up as hostages.

So far the terms of the agreement were being meticulously honored but Alex was uneasy and, with the coming of darkness, he left Emmy to her preparations for their departure and went with Francis Whiting, into the compound. Outside the guard had been increased, ostensibly for their protection; the sepoys' cooking fires flickered like so many fireflies a scant sixty yards from the walls of the entrenchment and, from where he stood, the jingle of bits and the creak of leather could plainly be heard as a cavalry patrol passed along Cantonment Road, heading south towards the road to Allahabad. The unfinished barrack blocks, which the garrison had guarded so tenaciously, were packed with the Nana's troops, including Number Four, which Mowbray Thomson had been compelled to vacate during the afternoon.

"*Will* they keep faith with us, Alex?" Whiting asked, breaking the silence that had fallen between them. "Will they really allow us to go to Allahabad unmolested?"

"I wish to God I knew!" Alex answered morosely. "My wife asked me the same question this morning and I did not know how to reply to her. They say one should trust a snake before a Mahratta, don't they? So far the Nana seems to be keeping his word . . . perhaps all he wants is for us to evacuate this place and leave him in undisputed possession of Cawnpore. He'll claim it as a victory."

"No doubt. My God, I wish we could have stayed and fought it out with him—made a sortie and taken his guns, as poor old John wanted to!" Whiting's voice shook in angry frustration. "It's too late for regrets, of course, but if we'd occupied the Magazine, instead of this place, we shouldn't be treating with the Pandies now or having to trust the word of a Mahratta. Or if Neill had managed to get to us, even yesterday—What held up those damned reinforcements from Calcutta, I wonder?"

"The state of the country, lack of transport, failure to appreciate the gravity of the situation—unpreparedness. That most of all, Francis. Sir Henry Lawrence was the only one who *did* prepare."

"And he refused us help! He's fifty miles away, with European troops, but he sent us nothing, not a single man. He—"

"How could he?" Alex sighed, recalling the last conversation he had had with his old chief in Lucknow. "He had to put his own people first. Whatever help he had sent us would have weakened his own position—irreparably, perhaps—and it might not have reached us. He only has one European regiment. If he'd sent us half of them, how could he have got them across the river, without guns and with the Pandies holding both banks and every boat within miles? Suppose he had sent the two hundred Europeans the General asked for and lost them before they even got to us, as he very well might have done? He would have risked losing Lucknow, as we have lost Cawnpore, for lack of British soldiers to defend it. Damn it, Francis, with Delhi—as far as we know—still in the Pandies' hands and Lucknow lost as well, surely you must see what the result would be? The whole country would rise against us, not only the sepoys! Lawrence has *got* to hold Lucknow, whatever happens to us. The reinforcements from Calcutta and Neill's column will have to relieve *him*, now that we're out of the reckoning. Pray God they do—and soon!"

He had spoken vehemently and Francis Whiting stared at him in some surprise. "I suppose you are right," he conceded. "All the same—'rats in a cage,' the General called us, did he not? Well, that's what we are . . . and we're committed. There's no going back now—we've no choice but to trust the Nana. I take it the General has resigned himself to surrender? He's not sending you to look for Neill?"

Alex shook his head. "No, he's not sending me but I

confess I'm tempted to go. If it weren't for my wife—"
He glanced over the parapet. There were so many sepoys
out there in the darkness now that it would have been
simple enough to lose himself amongst them, wearing
Ram Gupta's uniform. Only that morning, he had sent
out his bearer, Mohammed Bux, in the guise of an escaped prisoner, bidding him hide in the city until he
could make his way to his own village near Lucknow. The
man had mingled with Azimullah's escort, apparently
without exciting suspicion; it could be done but . . .
there was Emmy.

"Every day I've thanked God that I haven't a wife or
children here," Whiting said, guessing his thoughts. "What
you married men have had to endure doesn't bear thinking about. We could have held this infernal place, or
broken out and fought our way to Lucknow, if we hadn't
had those unfortunates to consider. It was having to watch
them suffer and die that was our undoing, Alex—and the
children were the worst, God rest their innocent souls!
Do you know how many of us are left? I had to count
heads this morning, when we were estimating the conveyances we should require to evacuate our people to the
river and the number of boats."

"How many?" Alex asked, his throat stiff.

"Four hundred and thirty-seven, my friend, of whom
seventy are sick and over a hundred wounded. I fear . . ."
A young officer approached them and he broke off. "Yes,
what is it?"

"Captain Moore requests your attendance in the General's room, sir—yours and Colonel Sheridan's, if you
please." The boy hesitated and then added diffidently, "It's
to decide the order of march for tomorrow, sir, and the
allocation of boats."

They followed him in silence across the dusty, foul-
smelling compound and, from the parapet behind them,
came the sentry's familiar shout of "All's well!"

To Alex the words sounded cruelly ironic in these circumstances, but he controlled himself and, his face a

153

blank mask, entered the *pucca*-roofed barrack to hear General Wheeler saying, with grim determination, "All who can march must do so, Captain Moore. We leave with the honors of war and that no one shall deny us!"

CHAPTER SEVEN

By dawn on Saturday, 27th June, as a procession of elephants, bullock carts and palanquins came towards them across the sandy plain, the survivors of the Cawnpore garrison were ready to evacuate their entrenchment. They had made such preparations as time and their enfeebled state would permit, and their hopes were high as they waited patiently for the conveyances to reach them.

The Nana Sahib had kept his word, they told each other, he had sent eighty palanquins and *doolies;* the boats were waiting to take them to Allahabad and soon, very soon, their long ordeal would be over. Some of the women wept for joy, clutching their children to them; some knelt to pray and to give thanks for their deliverance. A few, observing that the Nana had sent his own elephant, with a gold-encrusted *howdah,* for General Wheeler's conveyance to the river, called down blessings on their enemy's head. He was honoring the agreement he had signed—surely he could not intend to betray them?

The Nana Sahib had, however, made other preparations for their reception at the riverside. All night, while an army of coolies had toiled to roof the waiting boats with fresh thatch, another and larger army of sepoys and

155

golundazes had been busy at the Suttee Chowra Ghat under the direction of the Nana's elder brother, Bala Bhat, the commander of his bodyguard, Tantia Topi, and Azimullah Khan, his young Moslem aide.

They had worked without fear of discovery, for the Ghat—an open, dusty landing place at the river's edge, a hundred and fifty feet long and about a hundred feet in width—lay two miles east of the entrenchment, well screened by groves of neem and pipal trees. The road, skirting the New Cantonment and the Artillery Bazaar, approached it across a wooden bridge which spanned a wide ravine, with high ground on either side as it descended to the Ghat—barren, rocky ground, dotted with prickly pear and offering no cover for fugitives until the tree-line was reached.

A small, white, stone-built temple—Hurdeen's—stood on a mound overlooking the moored boats, and here divans and cushions had been arranged, to enable the Nana Sahib and his commanders to watch the embarkation in some degree of comfort. As yet it was empty, but beyond it, in the ruins of a house once occupied by a merchant named Christie, a gun had been placed, so as to command the whole line of boats, which had been hauled into shallow water, their keels almost touching the sandy river bottom.

A second gun—prudently withdrawn during the British officers' inspection of the landing place the previous evening—was once more in position a quarter of a mile downriver, in a temple known as Bhugwan Dass, after its builder. A third, a nine-pounder, was hauled on to the Koila Ghat, eight hundred yards below the Temple of Bhugwan Das and, distributed between them and hiding amongst buildings and trees, Tantia Topi had positioned a strong force of infantry, armed with muskets. Four hundred yards across the river, on the Lucknow shore, a battery of bullock-drawn, six-pounder guns unlimbered and waited, the gunners joined in their vigil by a regiment of irregular cavalry and by the 17th Native Infantry,

156

newly arrived from Azimghur, where they had mutinied early in June.

A letter, dated that evening and signed by the Nana*, accepted the offer of their services and the looted treasure they had brought with them, and informed their commander, *Subadar* Bhoondho Sing, that: "At this time there are absolutely no English troops remaining here; they sought protection from the Sirkar (ruler) and said, 'Allow us to get into boats, and go away.' Therefore the Sirkar has made arrangements for their going and by ten o'clock tomorrow these people will have got into boats, and started on the river.

"The river on this side is shallow, and on the other side deep. The boats will keep to the other side, and go along for three or four *koss*. Arrangements for the destruction of these English may not be made here; but as they will keep near the bank on the other side of the river, it is necessary that you should be prepared, and make a place to kill and destroy them on that side of the river and, having obtained a victory, come here. . . ."

Azimullah smiled, as he read this letter and then sent it across the river by one of the 17th's sepoys. Well satisfied with their preparations, he and Bala Bhat went to report to the Nana, leaving Teeka Singh and Tantia Topi to supervise the masking of the guns. The boatmen had their instructions; nothing could go wrong. The sun rose and they waited, with growing impatience, for the appearance of the hated *feringhis*.

Outside the entrenchment, in addition to the heavy sepoy guard, a mob from the city had gathered, eager for plunder, but it took time to load the wounded and sick into the *doolies* and palanquins which had been sent for them and the British officers sternly refused to accede to the sepoys' demands that they make haste. In accordance

*Among correspondence found by Brigadier James Neill, on taking command command of the reoccupied city of Cawnpore.

157

with the General's last order, John Moore prepared to lead an advance guard of thirty men under arms to the *ghat*. They were the fittest he had and he lined them up, to form a barrier between the crowd and the fatigue parties, which—since the *doolie* bearers offered them no assistance—were compelled to carry the wounded from the makeshift hospital in the quarter-guard building and then, as gently as they could, lift them into whatever conveyance was available.

Alex, who had overall responsibility for the loading of the wounded and sick, was deeply moved when he recognized the gallant John McKillop—one time "Captain of the Well"—whom he had believed dead, being carried out on a blood-soaked mattress. Brave and uncomplaining as ever, the magistrate managed to summon a smile but Alex, afraid that the jolting of the uncaring *doolie* bearers might prove more than even his stoical spirit could endure, had him placed in one of the bullock carts which had been earmarked for the women and children. Emmy, to his relief, agreed to go with him and Alex helped her into the cart, shocked by her evident fatigue.

"I'll wait for you, Alex," she told him, anxious eyes on his face. "I won't go on board until you come."

"No, my love." He shook his head, his tone one that brooked no argument. "There'll be no shade on the landing *ghat*—at least the boats are roofed. You're done up, you've been on the go all night—rest while you can, in one of the boats. I'll find you. But I may be delayed, I have to see all the wounded safely on their way. If we should miss each other—"

"We'll meet again in Allahabad," she finished for him bravely. But her eyes were brimming with tears when he kissed her and he watched, his own eyes moist, as the bullock cart moved ponderously off down the white, dusty road.

Dear God keep her safe, he prayed silently. Let no harm come to her—she has been so splendid, so courage-

158

ous, and she has worn herself out, caring for others, giving no thought to herself. She . . .

"Don't worry, Colonel Sheridan, Lucy and I will go with your wife." Alex turned, recognizing the voice but not the lined, white face of Mrs. Chalmers. The gaunt young woman beside her—her daughter Lucy, he could only suppose—looked at him blankly, her eyes grown imbecile, her slack mouth curving into a strange, secret smile. There was an empty bundle cradled in her arms and, when she spoke, it was in response to a voice or voices only she could hear.

"No," she said. "No . . . don't take him away. I'll look after him, I'll keep him safe. Please . . . let me hold him."

Alex, shouting to the bullock cart driver to halt, was conscious of a knife twisting in his heart as he helped Lucy and her mother into it, but Emmy's face lit up when they joined her and he could not but be glad that he had been able to accept Mrs Chalmers' offer. He returned to the line of waiting *doolies* and Mowbray Thomson, sweating under the weight of a tall civilian with a bandaged head, whom he had carried out single-handed, called to him urgently.

"Yes? Anything I can do, Tommy?"

Thomson deposited his burden. As the *doolie* moved away, he said, lowering his voice, "The General's coming out. They're having to carry him, he can't walk and he can't possibly ride two miles on the Nana's elephant. He'll have to go in a *doolie*. He says his wife and daughters are to use the elephant—he wants the advance guard to march off now and lead the column."

Alex bit back an exclamation of dismay. Without Moore's thirty resolute riflemen, it would be difficult, if not impossible to hold back the mob of bazaar riff-raff who were clamoring to enter the entrenchment. Heaven knew they would find little of value now among its battered, tottering buildings but their presence would impede the evacuation of the wounded.

"How many more to bring out?" he asked.

Thomson shrugged. "Oh, not that many. We'll manage ... let the poor old man have his guard of honor. He's earned that, at least, and it may be the last he'll ever have."

"Very well, if you say so." Alex crossed to where Moore was standing and passed on the General's request.

"Right, Alex, we're ready. Watch those swine from the city, though, won't you, when we've gone?" Moore looked deathly pale but he called his men to attention and, as General Wheeler emerged, leaning heavily on the shoulders of Dr. Harris and the young cavalry surgeon, Boyes, they brought their worn-out rifles to the present and stood there rigidly until their commander has been helped into his palanquin. The Nana's *mahout*, who had sat stony faced and seemingly deaf to all demands that he bring his animal to its knees to enable its passengers to mount, now did so—impressed by the guard of honor—and Lady Wheeler and her two daughters were assisted onto the *howdah*.

"Advance party!" John Moore's voice was firm and strong. "Slope ... arms! Left ... turn. By the right, quick march!"

His small party bore little resemblance to Queen's soldiers in their torn remnants of uniform and their ragged nankeen; many of them were barefooted, with bandaged limbs, but they marched with their heads held high down the long, dusty road, and the sepoys watched them with grudging respect.

The General had been right, Alex thought; it *was* a question of honor, although—he frowned angrily as he saw a mob of townspeople surging towards the entrenchment. Glimpsing a native officer, he shouted to him to post a guard to halt the threatened invasion. To his credit, the man did his best, but the mob was not to be gainsaid and the sepoy guard, after a few halfhearted attempts to stop them, stood aside and let them in. Other sepoys, with yells of derision, followed them and for several minutes pandemonium reigned, as a crowd of several hundred erupted into the entrenchment, halting the flow of wounded. Finally, with the aid of some men of the 56th and the native officer, Alex restored order and the flow was resumed.

Mowbray Thomson came out at last, with Edward Vibart, and announced that the hospital had been cleared. The sepoys of the 56th, recognizing him, clustered round him with touching pleasure and, not to be outdone, a dozen of Vibart's *sowars* trotted up, saluted and volunteered to escort him and his wife to the boats. Their pleasure and the respect they showed appeared to be genuine and Alex, free now to leave the entrenchment, did so thankfully, his earlier fears and doubts lulled, if not quite dispelled.

Anxious to catch up with Emmy and reassure her of his continued safety, he set off at the best pace he could manage after the slow-moving procession of carts and *doolies*, accompanied by Henry Delafosse and a private of the 84th, a husky young Irishman named Murphy, who had been helping to carry wounded.

"It all seems to be going according to agreement," Delafosse said, changing his Enfield to his left hand in order to wipe the sweat from his dust-grimed face. "The only trouble we had in the entrenchment—apart, of course, from the arrival of those rapacious swine from the city sewers—was when a sepoy of the First tried to relieve George Kempland of his rifle. George told him he could have its contents if he liked but not the rifle and the fellow skulked off."

"I'm sorry those blasted *budmashes* were let in," Alex apologized. "I did manage to put a guard on the entrance—sepoys—but they are very much out of hand and their own officers can't control them."

"Their discipline is appalling," Delafosse agreed. He grinned at Murphy. "Glad to be getting out of here, Paddy?"

"Oi am that, sorr," the boy assured him. "Niver so glad to get out of anywhere in me whole loife! All the

161

same, though, 'twas a grand night we had the last time we wuz here, was it not, sorr?" They were passing the Garrison Church, still some way behind the last *doolie,* and Murphy gestured to the compound where their raiding party had spiked the rebel 24-pounder almost a fortnight before. "We fairly caught the bastards *that* night, sleeping at their guns and..." He broke off and said, a puzzled note in his voice, "What's that now, for ony sake? Over there, sorr, do you see, at the back of the compound?"

They halted, following the direction in which the Irishman was pointing and a vulture rose, on flapping wings, to make an ungainly flight to the compound wall.

"It's just a vulture," Henry Delafosse began. "There's plenty of work for them here, the filthy—"

"Indians remove their bodies," Alex reminded him, suddenly and instinctively alarmed. "Cut across into the compound, Murphy, like a good lad, and see what it is."

Murphy obediently clambered over the low wall and vanished behind the burnt-out ruin of the church. He returned a few minutes later, retching violently.

"Well?" Delafosse demanded impatiently. "What was it?"

Murphy made an effort to control himself. "Colonel Ewart, sorr," he managed, "and his lady. They..." He could not go on.

"I'd better go," Alex said. "Colonel Ewart was badly wounded. I saw him into a *doolie* myself—the last one. His wife went with him on foot. They may need help and—"

"There's nothing you can do to help them, sorr," Murphy whispered fiercely. "And if I was you, I wouldn't look. They're both dead—hacked to pieces, sorr, and the poor old lady... Mother of God! 'Twas fiends out of hell killed her, sorr, and that's the truth."

Fiends out of hell or sepoys? Alex asked himself bitterly, as he and Delafosse, after a shocked inspection of the two bodies, resumed their interrupted journey. The white-haired Colonel of the 1st Native Infantry had been unarmed, disabled by a wound in the stomach and in so much pain that it had taken a long time to move him from the entrenchment and into the *doolie*. Some sepoys of his regiment had volunteered to carry him, Alex recalled, promising that they would take better care of him than the coolies and Ewart, moved by their solicitude, had thanked them with tears in his eyes.

He mentioned this to Delafosse, who shrugged helplessly. "He wasn't popular with his men, you know. Bit of a martinet, by all accounts, poor old devil."

"Then you think it was an isolated incident? They were paying off old scores?"

"God, I don't know, Alex. I suppose so. *They* were carrying him and none of the coolies were armed. We checked to make sure."

"Nevertheless, I think we'd better catch up with the rest of the column. There are a number of women who set off to walk and may have dropped behind," Alex said grimly. "If they intend treachery, we'd better find out before anyone boards those boats." There were armed men marching at intervals beside the column but he was worried. He had told Emmy to board as soon as she reached the *ghat*... He broke into a shambling run and the other two followed him. Winded and sweating profusely, they drew level with a group of women, plodding wearily along, their feet shuffling in the dust; but Ashe and two young ensigns were with them and the artillery officer assured them cheerfully that all was well.

"They promised they'd send one of the bullock carts back for us and they've kept their word. Look"—he pointed—"it's coming now." He brought his party to a halt and the women thankfully sat down at the road verge to await the cart's arrival. Alex gave them his water bottle and then, drawing Ashe aside, told him of Colonel Ewart's murder.

"An isolated inevident—Henry's right. The poor old

163

fellow wasn't popular with his men, particularly the Moslems." Ashe shrugged, mopping his heated face with the sleeve of his shirt. "As far as I can see, they're all keeping to the letter of the agreement—even exceeding it. I asked for water a little while ago and the *bhistis* were sent back at once. Truly, Colonel, I don't believe they intend to betray us. I mean, they could have slaughtered the lot of us in the entrenchment last night, if they had any such intention—once we'd surrendered our guns, we couldn't have done much to prevent them, could we? Besides, why go to all the trouble of procuring twenty-four boats, roofing and victualling them, if they don't mean to let us go? Rather an elaborate and costly farce, surely, sir?"

It was a logical argument, Alex was forced to concede. "We should have taken quite a few of them with us, Georgie," he pointed out. "If they *had* attacked us last night."

"And so we shall at the *ghat*," Ashe asserted confidently. "We're all armed, we'll give a good account of ourselves and they damned well know it. They won't try anything."

"Scattered, divided amongst forty boats—with the women and children unprotetcted?"

"Even so." Ashe patted the stock of his Enfield. "Anyway, there's nowhere to go but forward now, is there? We've *got to* trust them. But if you've any serious doubts, sir, why not mention them to the General? He's just ahead—in that palanquin over there, do you see? And Lady Wheeler and the two girls are with him, on the Nana's elephant."

Alex sighed. The boy was right about one thing though, he thought unhappily—there was nowhere to go but forward. On to the Suttee Chowra Ghat, where the boats were waiting. . . . He glanced behind him. Francis Whiting and their small rearguard were now in sight; Vibart, with his wife and two children, was seated in a bullock cart, surrounded by about a dozen of his *sowars*, and

Mowbray Thomson was marching with the sepoy guard which was bringing up the rear. He was talking to his men and, as Alex watched, he saw two of them lift him on to their shoulders and start to carry him, laughing like children, as they pretended to stagger under his weight. For heaven's sake, he chided himself, they could not behave like that if they were contemplating betrayal! The bond between a good officer and his men had always been a strong one in the old days, and here, surely, was proof that it still existed? Poor Ewart's murder had been an isolated incident, a crime perpetrated by a few men who bore him a personal grudge; the First Native Infantry had a high proportion of Oudh men in its ranks—Moslems, who had served the deposed King, Wajid Ali. They had joined the Company's army as the alternative to penury and had never been noted for their loyalty to their new masters.

The bullock cart creaked to a standstill and, as Ashe and his two ensigns went to help the women to climb into it, Henry Delafosse asked, frowning, "Are you going to speak to the General, Alex?"

Alex shook his head. "It would be to no avail now, Henry. As Georgie Ashe says—we've nowhere to go but forward."

"They'll need guns, if they attack us on the *ghat* ... and there were none there when we made our inspection yesterday evening." Delafosse forced a smile. "We made a very thorough inspection, I give you my word. Well ... shall we press on? There will be wounded to load into the boats."

They walked on briskly, passing the lumbering, gaudily painted elephant, from whose *howdah* Amelia Wheeler waved in friendly greeting. Crossing the bridge over the ravine, Alex paused to look down to the landing stage, three hundred yards below him. He could see nothing, at that distance, to excite suspicion. The boats were in shallow water but, in the absence of the rains, the river level was exceptionally low and it had obviously been necessary to bring them as close as possible to the bank, in order to embark the wounded. Each boat had a crew of nine or ten; the men were in their places, offering no more help with the loading of their craft than the sullen palanquin coolies had offered earlier. But they were there, he saw, as he started to descend at a jog trot to the *ghat*, ready to take up their oars when the loading should be completed.

There were no gangplanks, which was clearly making the embarkation of the sick and wounded difficult, but most of the women and children appeared to be wading out and a number of men—Moore's advance guard, presumably—were standing waist deep in the muddy water, giving what assistance they could. Others clambered into the boats and, as the wounded were carried across—or, still lying on their mattresses, were passed from man to man—they were hoisted aboard, the inevitable rough handling wringing cries of anguish from even the most stoical.

The first four boats were loaded—overloaded, Alex decided, studying them anxiously—their keels resting perilously close to the sandy bottom, which meant that they would have to be manhandled into deeper water. At the previous night's conference, it had been decided that no boat should move off until all were embarked and that no particular order should be observed in loading, save that each must carry a complement of armed men for protection during the voyage downriver. Edward Vibart was to command the leading boat and give the signal to cast off, when all were to make for the Oudh shore with all possible speed. Emmy was presumably in one of the first four boats, since she and her cargo of wounded had been among the first to leave the entrenchment, but the boats were so crowded that it was impossible to pick out individual faces and, more anxious than ever now to find her, Alex broke into a run.

"I'm going to look for my wife," he told Delafosse. "I'll be near the loaded boats if I'm needed."

166

"I'll come with you," the younger man said. "Because it looks as though all those first four boats are going to have to be pushed out into the stream." He gestured to the now half-empty *ghat* and to the throng of townsfolk gathered at vantage points on the high ground to witness their departure. "Not many of the Nana's troops in evidence, are there? That's all to the good. But they've posted a hell of a strong guard on the bridge, d'you see?"

Alex glanced back over his shoulder. The Nana's elephant and the palanquin bearing the General had just completed their descent from the road, with Ashe's bullock cart just behind and, forming up to their rear, on the bridge, as Delafosse had said, and for some distance below it, were about a hundred sepoys, with more marching down from the road to join them. Those on the bridge were holding back a mob of curious sightseers—the same mob, probably, which had invaded the entrenchment in search of plunder—and he was not sorry to see the sepoys dealing firmly with them at last.

Edward Vibart came running along the *ghat*, his escort of *sowars* at his heels, their horses reined back so as to keep pace with him as he made for the leading boat. Two of them carried his two little daughters on their saddlebows and his wife was mounted behind a bearded *rissaldar*, who lifted her down, with striking gentleness, when they drew level with the boat. Taking a child by each hand, she started to wade out to it and Alex glimpsed Emmy at last, beneath the thatched awning, as he went into the water to help Mrs. Vibart climb on to the canting deck. The boat was so full that there was barely room for the new arrivals but two officers yielded their places to her and she and the children scrambled on board, followed by Vibart himself.

"Better find a boat, Alex," the cavalry Major called to him. "Some of those behind us aren't full. Don't worry about your wife—we'll look after her and we can sort ourselves out when we reach the Lucknow bank."

"We'll push you off," Alex offered. "You're well and

truly aground at the moment." He moved closer to the boat and heard Emmy's voice, vibrant with relief, calling his name. He put out his hand to her but, before she could grasp it, the *rissalder* who had dealt so gently with the wife of his onetime commander, shouted something he could not catch and, as if this had been the signal for which they had been waiting, the boatmen dropped their oars and dived into the water. They had barely reached the *ghat* when the first shot rang out and turning in swift alarm, Alex saw that every boat in the long line had been deserted by its crew. He saw also, with a sinking heart, that there were sepoys behind every rock and bush on the slope above them. More appeared among the ruins of a deserted village on the edge of the ravine, and the rearguard posted at the bridge were running down the steep slope, their muskets no longer leveled at the mob from the bazaar but at those they had purported to protect ... and the mob came howling at their heels.

Above the frightened cries of the women and a ragged volley from the men in the boats—aimed, for the most part, at their fleeing crews—a bugle shrilled, loud and clear, from the small white temple overlooking the landing stage, in which the Nana and his staff were seated. This, too, Alex's dazed mind registered, must have been a signal for the hidden guns to be run out, since it was followed, seconds after, by a burst of cannonfire. A savage hail of canister and flaming carcasses descended on the helpless line of moored boats. Several of the straw-thatched awnings were already on fire and that covering Vibart's boat was set alight by one of the carcasses; tinder-dry, it blazed up, filling the boat with a cloud of thick, suffocating smoke.

Frantic with anxiety for Emmy, Alex floundered through the water and, finding Delafosse and the two officers who had given up their places to Mrs. Vibart and her children, he yelled to them to help him push the boat off. They did so, heedless of their own safety and, with their combined efforts, managed to get the ungainly craft out into midstream, while some of those aboard it tore at the blazing thatch with their bare hands. But volley after volley of musketry was taking its toll of them and, to his horror, Alex saw Emmy fling herself into the water in a desperate bid either to escape the flames or reunite herself with him—he could not be certain which until, managing at last to reach her, he felt her arms close convulsively about his neck.

"Alex ... oh, Alex, my dearest love ..." Her small, thin face, drained of the last vistage of color, blurred in the reflected glare from the water. "Alex, I—" The shouts and screams and the incessant musketry fire swallowed up her words. Her lips moved soundlessly but the love she bore him was in the dark, pain-filled eyes she raised to his; her heartbroken regret was there, plain for him to read, even in that moment of terrible pandemonium and blind, unreasoning slaughter. He did not realize that this was to be their parting, this the end for them until, dragging his gaze from hers, he saw that her life's blood was draining away into the muddy, churned-up water of the Ganges. There was a hideous, gaping wound in her breast, just below the heart, through which an artery was pumping a pulsating stream of scarlet. Like a man demented, he crushed her to him with his single arm but she did not speak again, although the blood went on flowing, resisting the frantic efforts he made to staunch it and he knew, suddenly, that she was dead when her arms relaxed their hold and he felt her go limp against him.

Then the hidden guns ranged on some target further afield and some of the *sowars* of Vibart's regiment spurred their horses into the shallows, cutting and hacking with their sabers at any threshing bodies within their reach. One of them lunged at Emmy's lifeless body and Alex turned, forced to release her, recognizing the bearded *rissaldar* behind whom Vibart's wife had ridden down to the *ghat*. A savage fury filled him, lending him maniac

169

strength as the *rissaldar* came at him, saber flashing above his turbaned head. He stepped aside, avoiding the up-raised blade and, as it descended, he wrenched that weapon from the *rissaldar's* grasp with such force that the fellow was unseated. He fell into the water and Alex, without compunction, took his head from his shoulders with the razor-sharp blade. Two others rode at him; he used the riderless horse as a shield and, abandoning the saber, took the *rissaldar's* pistol from the saddle holster and emptied it into the face of the first of them. The second backed away, jerking brutally at his horse's head; the animal reared and he, too, slithered into the water, to be trampled senseless by its iron-shod hooves.

Someone, he had no idea who, yelled his name and Alex saw that there was a boat, miraculously floating free on the sluggish current only twenty yards from him. He struck out for it instinctively and several hands came out to drag him aboard. He lay for a moment, gasping, on the smoldering deck timbers, hearing bullets whining overhead like angry hornets and then, from beside him, an Enfield spoke and Henry Delafosse said, with cold satisfaction, "Got you, you swine!"

"Henry—" His voice was a harsh croak, unrecognizable even to his own ears. Delafosse did not hear him and, raising his head, Alex saw that he was reloading his rifle, lying prone on the deck a foot or so from him. Edward Vibart was in the stern, also busy returning the enemy's fire, and two men of the 84th, one of whom was the boy Murphy, were working the stern oar in an effort to propel their clumsy craft towards the mud flats of the Lucknow shore. They were making some progress but the boat was so low in the water that it frequently grounded on sandbanks and the men lining the deck had to drop their rifles and fend it off with poles wrenched from the burnt-out awning. Two other boats were astern of them, experiencing similar difficulties, but the steady and accurate fire they contrived, between them, to maintain kept the rebel marksmen on the Cawnpore bank at a respectful distance.

In midstream, at last, with the river widening, the musket fire from the shore, although it continued, became less deadly. Alex checked his Adams and, with the aid of a wounded man lying close by, who offered his assistance, dried out and reloaded it. A pistol was useless at this range, of course, but he felt happier when he knew that it was again in working order and tucked into the waistband of his tattered overalls. If he had been able to use it when Emmy . . . He felt his throat tighten, as he remembered and, in sick despair, stumbled to the stern of the boat to take a turn at the sweep, in the hope of distracting his thoughts. The sun blazed down, reflected back by the water and he was soon drenched with sweat and almost blinded by the glare. When, after twenty minutes or so, a big Bengal Artillery gunner volunteered to relieve him, Alex accepted the offer thankfully and slumped down beside Vibart, who said bitterly, "Out of twenty-four boats, it looks as if only three got away! I daren't let myself think about what is happening back there, to the ones who did not get away. They were killing the children, Alex—little, innocent children. And my *sowars* were at the forefront of the massacre, when only this morning . . ." Tears were streaming down his cheeks. "Only this morning, they—"

"I saw what they did, Eddie," Alex told him. "I killed your *rissaldar* for you."

"The poor old General," Vibart went on. "They stopped his palanquin sixty yards from the nearest boat. He never even reached it—they hacked him to pieces when he was trying to drag himself to the water's edge."

"And Lady Wheeler and the two girls?"

"I don't know, I didn't see them but someone said they got to a boat. Not that it will have helped them, poor souls." Vibart hesitated. "Your wife—was she . . ."

"She died in my arms," Alex told him harshly.

"I'm sorry, I . . . what is there to say?" Vibart gestured

171

wryly to his own wife, who sat with the two wide-eyed, terrified little girls clasped in her arms, staring into space in the terrible silence of deep shock. "Perhaps she's better off than Melanie, if the truth were known. Perhaps all of them back there are better off now than we are, God knows. Our agony may just be prolonged. But I confess I want to live, Alex—I want to live for only one reason."

"I imagine your reason is the same as mine. I want to see the Nana driven from Cawnpore." Alex's voice shook. "I want to see him hunted as a fugitive, from whom even his own people will turn in loathing and disgust. And if I live, I'll help to hunt him down—that I swear, by all I hold sacred."

Vibart laid a hand on his knee. "Yes," he said thickly. "Those are my sentiments also. The Nana of Bithur is the vilest of assassins and by this day's work, he has put himself beyond the pale. *Some* of us must live, Alex, if only to tell the story of his betrayal and to ensure that justice is meted out to him. We've no choice but to fight on."

But it was a bitter, cruel battle they would have to fight, Alex knew. Within a few minutes of his conversation with Edward Vibart, the boat again grounded on a sandbank and, as seven or eight of them went over the side to endeavor to push it off, a heavy fire was opened on them from a six-pounder which, drawn by bullocks, had been following them on the Cawnpore bank. Up to his waist in water, his shoulder against the boat's side, Alex heaved and tugged. The round-shot shattered their steering oar and cries from astern told them that one of the other boats had been hit. A dozen swimmers, including Mowbray Thomson and Francis Whiting, maneuvered the sinking boat alongside; the dead were thrown overboard to make space for a fresh influx of passengers and, when at last they had freed their craft from the sandbank, it was so heavily overladen that it seemed unlikely that it could for long remain afloat.

The shore gun started to rake them with grape, wounding several and killing, among others, the heroic John McKillop; but their fighting ranks had been doubled and, with the addition of such practiced marksmen as Whiting and Thomson, they held the gun team at bay. Concentrating their fire on the bullocks, they succeeded in disabling two of them and, as they rowed frantically with spars and even pieces of wood torn from the boat's sides, they saw that the six-pounder, although keeping up the chase, had been noticeably slowed down.

A fresh shock awaited them when they neared the mudflats on the Lucknow bank, however. Two guns opened on them from behind a mango grove and cavalry galloped up to the water's edge to fire volley after volley from their carbines into the listing boat. The exhausted boat's crew returned their fire and Alex, assisting Vibart in the stern to manipulate a makeshift sweep, came near to despair when their efforts succeeded only in setting them once more aground on a sandbar. Vibart, taking his turn to go over the side to haul it off, was hit in the left arm by a musket ball. They dragged him back on board; someone contrived a rough bandage from his shirttail and, white with pain, he lay for over an hour in a semiconscious state. His wife, still clasping her two small children in nerveless arms, seemed unaware that he had been wounded and, out of pity, no one told her; but Charles Quinn, still disabled by the wound he had received four days earlier, pulled himself up beside her and took one of the children in his arms.

Some time after midday, the third boat, which had been following them, was seen to be swamped and sinking; a few of the men aboard managed to swim over to them and, as they were hauled on to the deck, one of them gasped out the distressing news that there were no other survivors. It was impossible to ascertain whether or not his information was correct; the current was wayward and sluggish, their own boat so low in the water that it was also in danger of foundering and any attempt to turn it against the current would, almost certainly, have resulted in its sinking. They could only press on, ridding themselves of the weight of their dead at intervals, so as to make more room for the living. One of the survivors from the third boat was St. George Ashe and when, at long last, they drew out of range of the guns, he told them, in a harsh, bitter voice, that John Moore had been among those killed at the Suttee Chowra Ghat.

"Poor fellow, he was trying to get our boat free of the sand—he and five or six of the fellows who formed the advance guard were in the water—and a sepoy of the First took deliberate aim at him and shot him through the heart." Ashe's voice broke. "He was the best and bravest man I've ever known or ever shall know. And now he's dead, shot by one of those foul swine of Pandies, on the orders of the foulest of them all, who broke his sacred oath and betrayed us! They killed the poor old General too—a *sowar* of the Second Cavalry hacked his head off and held it up for the rest of the filthy traitors to see. And they cheered him, they actually cheered him." He could not go on; burying his blistered, blackened face in his hands, he wept . . . but there was no comfort any of them could offer him.

CHAPTER EIGHT

All day the ghastly, unequal chase went on; cavalry cantered after them along both banks; infantry kept up a ceaseless fire of musketry, and the guns on the Lucknow bank limbered up and joined the pursuit, sending grape and canister after them whenever they were within range. Quinn was shot in the arm; Mowbray Thomson knocked unconscious when a musket-ball ploughed through his scalp and both the Paymaster of the 3rd Cavalry, Captain Seppings, and his wife were wounded—she very painfully through the thigh and Alex, now plying his sweep with young Murphy, tried vainly to shut his ears to her screams. A surgeon named Macauley, who had joined them from the sunk boat, managed at last to quieten her and then he, too, took a bullet through the arm.

They had no food; the provisions stowed the previous night had evidently been removed after the inspection, and all that passed their lips until nightfall were sips of muddy, bitter-tasting river water. With the coming of darkness, they gained a desperately needed respite. There was no moon; the guns ceased fire and the volume of musketry because less intense and so inaccurate as to do them little harm. But the boat again ran aground when they had traveled an estimated five or six miles downriver, and they were now so exhausted that the effort to refloat it seemed beyond them. Both Alex and Vibart stumbled into the water to pit their shoulders and their single arms against the recalcitrant vessel; shifting it at last, they were only just in time to avoid a burning boat which the sepoys on the Cawnpore bank set adrift, in the hope that it might fall foul of them. Flaming arrows, each one tipped with charcoal, presented the next hazard and they were compelled to jettison what was left of their straw-thatched awning when this was set alight.

Dawn found them still afloat, but they realized that they had traveled only four instead of the six miles they had believed, and the boat seemed, to their anxious eyes, to have settled dangerously low in the water. The pursuit had, however—if only temporarily—been abandoned and, greatly cheered by this, the rowers bent to their skeleton oars with a fresh will, while others set about the melancholy but now routine task of putting the dead overboard.

It was Alex who sighted the natives bathing at the river's edge, two hours later. They were obviously harmless villagers and he suggested that they attempt to make contact with them, to which, after a brief discussion, the other officers agreed. A native drummer was put ashore, with a handful of rupees to purchase food and, if possible, to bargain for the services of a few boatmen. After a nerveracking wait, the man returned emptyhanded. The villagers had promised food, he said, and had taken the money but . . . He hesitated, eying them miserably.

"Well?" Mowbray Thomson prompted, his voice strained.

"They say, Sahib, that there are soldiers at Nuzuffghur, two miles below us, to whom orders have been sent to seize us," the drummer told him. "And also that Babu Ram Buksh, the *zamindar* of Dowriakhera, on the Oudh side, has engaged with the Nana Sahib that no *feringhis* shall be permitted to escape from his territory. He, too, has armed men waiting and the villagers are afraid to

176

help us. They will give us *chapattis* and some rice but that is all."

The food did not appear. They waited, with fading hopes, and finally decided to go on.

"Some of us must live, Alex," Edward Vibart said. "Whatever it costs. Our betrayal *has* to be avenged." He leaned, with eyes closed, on the oar they shared and then, bracing himself, started to haul on it once more with grim, tight-lipped determination. "I have a brother in Fategarh, you know—the boy went there to visit his fiancée. I hope he's safe, at least." Overhearing him, Francis Whiting offered a scrap of torn paper for his inspection.

"I've set down a very brief account of our misfortunes, Eddie," he explained. "If both you and Alex would oblige me by signing it, I'll put it in a bottle and cast it into the river. Who knows—by the grace of God, someone may find it, your brother, perhaps, or someone from Neill's column. It seemed a good idea, in case none of us survives, to put the facts on record."

Vibart sighed, appended his name with the pencil Whiting produced and passed it to Alex in silence.

Nuzuffghur was a small fishing village on the Cawnpore bank; a pleasant, peaceful-seeming collection of stilted huts and mud houses built among the trees and marked by a white stone temple to the Hindu god Hanuman, the steps of which descended gracefully to the river's edge. The current carried the boat down to it and, despite their efforts to steer clear of obstruction, a long sandbar in midstream proved their undoing. A fusillade of shots rang out and sepoys appeared from behind the screening trees and on the steps of the temple. They directed a vicious fire on the boat's occupants, as they struggled to haul and push its keel free of the glutinous mud. Beside him, waist deep in water, Alex saw Edward Vibart stagger and almost fall, blood from a wound in his unbandaged arm staining the surface of the water in slowly spreading circles. From the deck above, Francis Whiting

177

reached out to aid him; between them, they got him into the boat and, leaving him there, Whiting himself slid into the water to take his place.

"One good heave should do it," he said breathlessly. "She's nearly off now and Tommy's got a pole out on the other side. Those villagers were right, weren't they, Alex? There's the best part of a regiment on the bank there and a gun to the—" His voice was abruptly silenced by a musket-ball, which struck him in the back of the head. He was dead when Alex, abandoning his hold on the boat's stern, made a frantic grab at his shirt. The boat cleared the bar and, as he scrambled back on to its deck, he saw Francis Whiting's body, caught in a freak current, go whirling shorewards as if, even in death, he were determined to face and bring retribution to his enemies.

On deck, Vibart lay moaning softly and poor Quinn, now also wounded, had been forced to let the child he had been holding escape from his embrace. She stumbled unsteadily to her father's side, a frail little ghost of a child in a torn dress, sobbing her terror. A knife twisted in Alex's heart as he caught and restored her to her mother, unable to find any answer to her pathetic question, "Oh, sir, why are the sepoys still firing at us? Did they not promise to leave off?"

Back once more at his sweep with the Irish lad, Murphy, he looked for the gun Francis Whiting had warned him about and saw it being unlimbered on top of a high bank, twenty yards beyond the temple steps.

"'Tis going to rain, sorr," Murphy told him. "Let us hope them sods don't keep their powder dry!"

Alex glanced skywards and noticed, with surprise, that the bright sunlight of the morning and early afternoon had faded. The sky was gray and overcast, pregnant with rain, and he found himself praying fervently that the threatened cloudburst would come in time to save them. Miraculously, it did; the six-pounder discharged only one round and then the heavens opened and the rain came down in blinding torrents, driving both gunners and infantrymen to seek shelter, their quarry, for the time being, forgotten. So heavy was the downpour that even the rowers had to leave their oars and bail; there was no shelter in the open boat but the chilly sheets of rain refreshed their stiff and aching bodies, and the wounded welcomed the fall in temperature and the temporary numbness induced by the cool water in which they lay.

Their respite lasted until late afternoon. The rain passed over and at sunset the chase was resumed, this time by a boat considerably larger than their own, with a lateen sail spread to catch the evening breeze and a dozen boatmen at the oars. It was manned by fifty or sixty well armed sepoys, whose fire disabled Athill Turner, killed a Light Cavalry officer named Harrison, and inflicted minor wounds on several others. The enemy craft was gaining rapidly on that of the British fugitives when, looking back to measure the distance between them, Alex saw to his joy that it had run aground on a sandbank close into the shore. The light was going and, seeing no sign of any other pursuit, he steered for the shallows, his call for volunteers answered by twenty weary but vengeful men.

The sepoys had not expected their quarry to turn on them and half of them, impatient to float their craft before darkness hemmed them in, were in the water, their backs to shore, making so much noise that they heard nothing until the British Enfields spoke. It was a swift attack and a bloody one, with no quarter given, and only about six or seven escaped. Alex, with Mowbray Thomson, Delafosse and Ashe, climbed into the captured boat, hoping to find food but, although well stocked with arms and ammunition—which they appropriated—there was nothing eatable on board.

The boat itself was in better condition than their own but it was stuck fast on the sandbank and, their efforts to get it off being unsuccessful, they contented themselves with its oars and the sail, which they carried back through the shallow water to display to the anxious Vibart. The

179

oars were of great assistance when they were once more afloat and heading downriver but they were all so worn out by their exertions that the rowers slept at their oars and Alex, sharing the sweep with Sergeant Grady of the 84th, lapsed more than once into a semiconscious state. Waking, with a start, in darkness, he realized to his dismay that the boat had again grounded. Within minutes of this discovery, rain lashed down with almost hurricane force and, with the flood, the boat freed itself. Two oars were lost when the increased force of the current snatched them from the weary hands of the men to whom they had been consigned and the sail, which they had rigged with so much effort, became uncontrollable in the sudden gusts of wind sweeping across the river and they were compelled to lower it.

At Thomson's suggestion and with infinite difficulty, they draped it on poles in place of the thatched awning and across the open deck, in the hope of affording some sort of shelter for the wounded. Several of them were in a bad way and, leaving Grady to steer, Alex, with Ashe and Delafosse, did what they could to ease their suffering. It was little enough and a man named Blenman, who had been shot through the groin, repeatedly begged them to give him the merciful release of a bullet. They had no dressings; scraps of cloth torn from their clothing and soaked in rain water were the only palliatives they could offer and Blenman's agonized pleas became harder to resist as the night wore on. To their relief, he sank into a stupor and died about an hour later.

Athill Turner, wounded in both legs, lay with a rifle propped against the thwart in front of him; Edward Vibart, both arms disabled, lay on his back endeavoring to keep a lookout, so as to permit the fitter men to rest, and neither uttered a complaint, but the moans and cries of the dying and the frightened sobbing of the children were an added torment and Alex was thankful when Murphy offered to relieve him at the sweep. He fell asleep instantly, too spent to be conscious of grief, too exhausted to remember what had gone before or even to care what fate might lie in store for him.

The horrors of the past two days faded and he was with Emmy, walking in the beautifully kept rose garden of the Commissioner's house at Adjodhabad.

"Alex." He heard Emmy's voice, as clearly as if she were beside him. "Alex, I'm going to have a child. Oh, darling, I'm so happy! He'll be a son, I know, and we'll call him William, after William Beatson. You're pleased, darling, aren't you—as pleased and happy as I am? Oh, Alex, I love you!"

He stirred restlessly, feeling the sun on his face, instinctively aware that the boat was aground again. The sound of firing and the whine of bullets passing overhead shocked him into full wakefulness and he dragged his stiff and rain-wet body to the stern. Wren and Daniel, of the Light Cavalry, were both wounded, he saw, and poor young Macauley, himself white with pain, was attempting to staunch the bleeding from Daniel's shattered forearm.

"We must have drifted out of the navigable channel during the night," Vibart told him despairingly. "Look, we're in a siding—and stuck fast, I fear, in full view of that village. The villagers must have seen us coming and sent for help—there are sepoys and some Oudh irregulars and a whole mob of matchlock men—Babu Ram Buksh's, no doubt—on both banks. And they killed Georgie Ashe —the swine put a bullet through his head just now, when he and Wren went over the side to try to get us off. We're finished, Alex . . . we can't go on. We shall have to surrender in the hope that at least they'll spare the women and children."

"They did not spare the women and children at the Suttee Chowra Ghat," Alex reminded him. "And there are still about—what?" He counted heads "About a dozen of us unwounded."

Vibart sighed. "Well, if you want to make an attempt

to drive them off, you have my blessings and my prayers. But—"

"A last sortie," Mowbray Thomson put in. He squatted down beside Alex, measuring the distance to the bank with narrowed eyes. "The do-or-die sally poor old John was always talking about before we felt the entrenchment, eh? What about it, Alex? Shall we die like fighting men, taking some of these blasted Pandies with us?"

"For God's sake, why not? What have we got to lose?" Alex felt his heart lift at the prospect. "We'll give 'em something to remember us by—we'll have at 'em with the bayonet." He thought of Corporal Henegan and his cracked lips twisted into a smile. "The swine never could stand up to cold steel!" He looked round at the gaunt gray faces of the Queen's soldiers, exhausted, unshaven, famished specters of men, in their tattered uniforms and their bandages, most of them barefooted. Sergeant Grady and the big gunner, Sullivan, were already fixing bayonets to their rifles and, from somewhere in the bottom of the boat, Henry Delafosse had retrieved his sword. He offered it, eyes bright with the light of battle.

"You can use this, can't you, Alex? I'm sticking to my rifle." He grinned. "Right, boys—who's with us?"

They slipped over the side, fourteen of them—Thomson, Delafosse, Grady, two Bengal Artillery gunners and the rest men of the 32nd and the 84th—and those of the wounded who could still hold a rifle prepared to give them covering fire.

"We'll be back for you, God willing, Eddie," Alex promised. "Hang on as long as you can."

They reached the shore without suffering any casualties and their first charge drove back a crowd of sepoys, who—as those in the boat had been—were taken by surprise and fled in terror before the maddened, desperate assault of what they had evidently imagined to be a party of helpless fugitives, whose surrender was imminent. A mob of natives, armed with clubs and matchlocks, attempted to surround them but they cut their way through

182

without the loss of a man and, breathless but triumphant, fired a volley into a troop of horsemen, which emptied several saddles and caused the rest to join the sepoys in ignominious flight.

They reloaded and pressed on, driving all opposition before them. Then Alex halted them, anxious to return to the boat with its cargo of wounded, but the mob they had scattered earlier had reformed and he saw, with dismay, that their retreat was cut off.

"Come on!" Delafosse urged. "One more charge does it!"

Stumbling with weariness, they turned and cut their way for the second time to the river bank but the boat had vanished.

"It will have refloated, without our weight, and drifted downstream," Alex said, hoping against hope that this was true. He led them on, striking inland to avoid following a curve in the river; the cavalry keeping pace with them but just out of range, the matchlock men harassing them from the rear and the infantry retreating before them, pausing occasionally to fire spasmodic and ill-aimed volleys in their direction. About a mile downstream from their original landing place, they sighted the river again but, apart from a few small fishing boats drawn high up on the mudflats, it was deserted. A line of sepoys, now firing from cover, barred their advance, and on the opposite bank, they could see others positioning themselves to contest any attempt they might make to cross the river.

"This is it, Alex old man," Mowbray Thomson said regretfully. "The boat must have fallen into their hands. How about making a stand over there?" He pointed to a small, stone-built temple among the trees to their left and Alex nodded his assent, too winded to speak. They fired a volley into the menacing line of sepoys and gained the shelter of the temple with a concerted rush, losing Sergeant Grady, who went down under a hail of bullets. Some of the other men were wounded but thirteen of them reached the temple, and for almost an hour, they defied all efforts to evict them, picking off any attacker who showed himself in the narrow aperture of the temple doorway.

The end came when, unable to protect the sides and rear of their small stronghold, they heard logs and bushwood being heaped against its walls. The airless darkness of its interior started to fill with smoke and the crackle of flames told them that the wooden roof had caught alight. The men were starting to cough and retch, and as a beam crashed down from the blazing roof, Delafosse said hoarsely, "The swine have licked us, Alex. We can't stay here—they're making it too hot for us."

"There's the river," Alex reminded him. "A few strong swimmers might have a chance."

"If you think it's worth a try, I'm game. But how many of us are strong swimmers? You, Tommy . . . fine. How many more?"

Several voices answered him. "I'm not," Alex stated flatly. He took the Adams from his belt. "Those who can swim, make a dash for the river. The rest of us will give you covering fire and hold them off as long as we can. Get into midstream and don't try to land until you're clear—pray God you make it." He added, remembering Vibart, "Some of us *must*, if the Nana's to get what he deserves. Bless you, my boys—it's been a privilege to serve with all of you."

"And you, Alex my friend," Mowbray Thomson told him warmly. He stripped off his shirt, his eyes streaming; Delafosse, Sullivan and Murphy followed his example. With two privates of the 84th and a gray-haired gunner, they picked up their rifles and moved towards the door of the temple.

"Now!" Alex yelled, his voice a harsh croak. They charged out through the blazing brushwood, half-blinded by smoke and the sepoys who were stoking the fire fell back before their leveled bayonets. Seven men reached the water and hurled themselves into it. Two had swum only

184

a few yards when they were hit but five were in midstream, striking out for their lives, when Alex looked for them, Thomson's fair head just in front of Murphy's dark one. Then he was fighting for his own life, he and the five men with him, their backs to the river, the high-pitched whine of the Enfields mingled with the crackle of the Pandies' muskets.

A *sowar* of the irregular cavalry in a yellow *achkan* rode at him, saber raised. Alex pressed the trigger of the Adams and brought him down; he fired again and wounded the horse of a native officer but the man slid from the saddle and came at him, with two mounted men at his heels. He shot the *jemader* and the first of the *sowars* but the other lunged at him, knocking him off balance and he was conscious of an agonizing pain, which started on the left side of his head and spread until it seemed to envelop his whole body.

From somewhere, a long way away, he heard a scream, which went on and on, waking ghastly echoes in his head. Dimly he realized that he was lying on his back, with a great weight on top of him, pinning him down, and he heard the thud of hooves, galloping past, and it seemed, over him. After that a black void opened and he sank into it, thankful for the oblivion it brought him.

The sun was setting when, slowly and painfully, consciousness returned. In the subdued light, as he peered about him, he could see only vague shapes—what appeared to be a tree in the distance and beyond it the shell of a gutted building. The temple, of course—the one in which they had sheltered and the Pandies had set on fire. There were vultures on the tree and strutting, satiated, in front of the ruined temple. . . . Alex struggled to sit up, memory returning, as he cautiously raised his head. A heavy weight held his legs as if in a vise, and after another struggle, he managed to wrench himself free and to identify the weight—and the stench beginning to emanate from it—as the dead body of a horse. Its rider,

185

a *sowar* in a yellow *achkan*, lay a few feet from it, also dead.

There were other bodies scattered between the temple and the river bank and the vultures were at work on some of them; more of the foul birds rose on flapping wings, disturbed by his sudden movement as he started to limp towards the temple, looking warily about him in search of hidden enemies. But the living were his enemies, not the dead and there was no one left alive here, save for himself . . . there were no Hindu bodies, either, he saw. Only the Moslem *sowars* and the British dead had been left to the vultures; the villagers, being devout Hindus, had carried off those of their own kind for cremation and the proper funeral rites. Filled with a cold anger at this evidence of their callousness, Alex searched for and found the men who had been with him, and summoning all his strength, dragged them, one after the other, to the river and cast them in.

On his last journey, which took him right up to the temple steps, he saw a horse tethered to a tree behind it. The animal was wounded in the neck, but apart from this, it appeared to be in fair shape, and when his self-imposed task was completed, he returned to examine it more carefully. It was a black countrybred, with a good deal of Arab in it, and standing a little under sixteen hands, it reminded him of his own purebred charger, Sultan, which he had been compelled to leave in Lucknow. Until this moment, he had been so intent on removing the bodies of his men from the predators which infested the temple *ghat*, that he had given no thought to the problem of how best to make a bid for escape, but the discovery of the horse set his dazed mind working.

He felt curiously lightheaded and almost carefree, unable to move at more than walking pace, and there were, he realized, odd gaps in his memory, which he could not fill in, try as he might. There was an odd tingling sensation in his head, which also puzzled him, and putting up his hand to investigate the cause, he was astonished when

186

his searching fingers encountered a deep cut that had laid his skull bare from temple to ear and continued across his left cheek to the corner of his mouth. He felt no pain and the bleeding, which had probably been profuse, judging by the extent and depth of the wound, had long since ceased. Shock and concussion, he decided, must be the cause of his strange state, combined with lack of food. But he was in danger—that, at least, he knew—and it would behoove him to get as far away from this place of the dead as he could. The horse would carry him; it was a *sowar's* horse, wih a carbine in the saddle boot, only . . . He looked down at the stump of his right arm. He could neither use nor load a carbine; he would have to arm himself with a saber and . . . yes, find his Adams pistol.

Slowly, like a sleepwalker, Alex returned to the river bank. His search for the pistol was successful; he stumbled on it, lying in the sand, close to the body of the *jemadar* in the yellow *achkan*. He squatted down, still without haste, and with infinite effort, cleaned and reloaded the pistol. He took the *jemadar's* saber and was about to return, with his newly acquired weapons, to fetch the horse when another memory, dredged up from the depths of his mind, made him pause. He had been asked, by General Wheeler, to make an attempt to get through to Allahabad; to make contact with Neill and his relief column. . . . Yes, that was it, of course it was! And he had planned to do so in the guise of a sepoy, because the road to Allahabad was patrolled by the Nana's troops, his cavalry, and no European had any chance of getting past them.

He bent, and with some distaste, stripped the *jemadar's* body of its uniform. The *achkan* was stained with blood but so was his own ragged shirt; the exchange would be to his advantage and he made it, pleased to find that *achkan* and the voluminous white pantaloons were a comfortable fit, the fellow's soft, hand-tooled leather boots equally so. He wound the green *pugree* about his head,

187

thrust the Adams into his swordbelt, and as an afterthought, opened the *jemadar's* food pouch. It contained *chapattis,* some dried meat and a bag of *dhal.* He wolfed the meat and the *chapattis,* collected another pouch and a bag of grain, and mounting the horse, set off across country just as darkness fell, in search of a safe refuge in which to spend the night.

II

Six miles downriver, natives on the Oudh shore had persuaded the four exhausted swimmers—Thomson, Delafosse, Murphy and Sullivan—to come ashore. They had been fearful at first, having been so often deceived, but the natives had thrown down their matchlocks in earnest of their good faith and assured them repeatedly that their Rajah was a friend of the British.

They could not go on; poor Sullivan was wounded in the back and at his last gasp and the fifth man who had escaped with them had been taken by their pursuers an hour or so earlier. They stumbled up the bank and their rescuers fetched blankets in which, after allowing them to rest for a time, they carried them to their village, where the headman received them with a kindness they had ceased to expect from any native. He gave them a meal, provided them with *charpoys* and let them sleep. Next morning, soon after 5 A.M., the Rajah, Drigbiji Singh, sent a party of his retainers, with ponies and an elephant, to transport them to his fort at Moorar Mhow. After partaking of a meal of buffalo milk, *chapattis* and native sweetmeats, they set off, arriving at nightfall at their destination.

Once again they slept and the following morning a native doctor dressed their wounds and a tailor furnished them with fresh clothing and native-made shoes. Three times during their month-long stay at Moorar Mhow, messengers came from the Nana demanding the surrender of their persons, but Drigbiji Singh sent them back emptyhanded. On 29th July, when they had recovered and he considered the roads safe, the Rajah sent them under escort across the river, and meeting a patrol of the 84th Foot after traveling some nine or ten miles, they marched to Cawnpore on the 31st.

III

The luckless wounded in Edward Vibart's boat were captured by the followers of Babu Ram Baksh, *zamindar* of Dowriakhera, within a short while of the landing of the fourteen fit men at Sheorajpore. True to his promise, the *zamindar* sent them back to the Nana in bullock carts. They reached Cawnpore on 30th June, passing by the scene of the massacre at the Suttee Chowra Ghat on their way, their hopeless, pain-dimmed eyes gazing on the charred shells of the boats which still floated in the muddy water. Bloated bodies lay at the water's edge—the bodies of their friends and comrades, unrecognizable now—abandoned to the vultures and the prowling jackals, and to the human predators, who had stripped them of everything of value before turning their backs on the carnage.

The Nana had called a halt to the slaughter after an hour or so and had ordered that the women and children who had escaped the bullets and *tulwars* of his soldiers were to be spared. A hundred and twenty-five dazed and mud-spattered souls were dragged ashore, many of them wounded, and mocked by grinning sepoys and jeered at by the bazaar *budmashes,* they were taken in open carts to the Savada Koti, a brick building close to the Nana's camp, in which Mrs. Jacobi and a number of other female captives were being held. One or two of the younger women and some Eurasian girls were seized by the *sowars* of the Light Cavalry—contrary to the Nana's orders—and carried off to the city.

No aid was given to the sick and wounded for three days; they lay moaning on the bare floor of their prison with nothing but water and a few handfuls of coarse grain

189

to keep them alive. With a single exception, the men who had not been butchered out of hand as they stumbled back to the *ghat* were taken out and executed, soon after their arrival at the camp. The exception was Lieutenant John Saunders, of the Queen's 84th who, with half a dozen men of the advance guard, had put up so stubborn a resistance that he was only taken when all the rest of his party had been killed or disabled. With an escort of *sowars* guarding him closely, he was brought before the Nana for sentence to be passed on him, and defiant to the last, he drew a six-shot Adams pistol which had been concealed on his person. With this, he killed two of his guards and wounded a third, and breaking free, attempted to bring down the Nana himself with his last remaining shot. Unhappily for him, he fired well wide of his target, and being again overcome, was subjected to the most fiendish punishment.

On the Nana's personal instructions, the unfortunate young officer was nailed to planks laid on the ground and had his ears, nose, toes and fingers hacked off. Thus, bleeding and in agony, he was left in the full glare and heat of the sun and it was not until further painful mutilations had been inflicted on him the following day that, at long last, death released him from his torment. Men of the Light Cavalry cut his body to pieces with their sabers and his remains were left there, unburied, as a warning to any others who might attempt to dispute the Nana's will or threaten his life.

The evening after the massacre, the Nana held a review of his troops on the plain close by the Savada Koti. To the beat of drums and the firing of salutes—plainly audible to the unhappy women captives—he was formally proclaimed Peishwa of the Mahrattas. The sacred mark was affixed to his forehead; he appointed his brother, Bala Bhat, Governor-General of Cawnpore and Jwala Pershad was made Commander-in-Chief, and after speeches praising his army for their courage in gaining victory over the British, he promised them a lac of rupees as reward and retired to his tent. The imprisoned women, hearing this, wept. . . .

On the third day of their incarceration, a native doctor was sent to minister to the wounded; they were given clean clothes and their diet was improved, but cholera had now broken out among them and five of these saved from the Suttee Chowra Ghat died. The survivors from Edward Vibart's boat, all wounded and almost starving, were dragged roughly from the jolting bullock carts outside the prison and the women ordered to go inside. The men, with seventeen others captured on the Oudh shore by the irregular cavalry, were told by Teeka Singh that they had been condemned to death. The onetime *rissaldar* turned a deaf ear to the pleas of some of his *sowars* to spare the life of their paymaster, Captain Seppings; the wounded captain was permitted to read a brief prayer and then, with the young wife of the Light Cavalry surgeon, Dr. Boyes, clinging so frantically to her husband that her hands could not be prised loose, the execution was brutally carried out by sepoys of the 1st Native Infantry.

The rest of the women were driven at musket point into the misery of the Savada Koti, their tears evoking only derision from their captors. Next day the Nana broke up his camp and took up residence in the Old Cawnpore Hotel in the Civil Lines, close to the Assembly Rooms. The women and children, now numbering 122, were taken to a yellow-painted brick building thirty yards from the hotel. It was flat-roofed and comprised two main rooms, each about twenty feet by ten feet, with four dark closets at the corners, less than ten feet square. The doors and windows—with the exception of the entrance—were secured by wooden bars, and in the walled courtyard which surrounded it, a heavy guard of sepoys was posted.

The house, built originally by a British officer for his native mistress, was known as the Bibigarh—the House of Women—and had previously been used by a native clerk employed in the medical department.

With the addition of some forty more women and children—a second party of fugitives from Fategarh, who had endeavored to make their escape by river—and other captives, brought in from the city and surrounding districts, there were over two hundred Europeans in the small, yellow-painted House of the Women, and it had become unpleasantly overcrowded. In the airless heat of July, without *punkas* or adequate sanitation and with only straw for bedding, the hapless women suffered the worst torment most of them had yet had to endure. All had been bereaved, many had seen their loved ones butchered in front of them; they did not know for what purpose the Nana was holding them prisoner, and as each day dawned, they feared that an order might come for their execution. Rescue seemed to them now as impossibility; they no longer dared even to hope that the relief column, for which they had waited so long, might be on its way to them from Allahabad or Calcutta.

True, they were fed; the native doctor did all in his power for them, and they had the services of a *bhisti* and a sweeper; but the woman from the Nana's household, Hosainee Khanum—*ayah* to his courtesan, Adala —who had been put in charge of them, told them nothing. She hinted that any who might wish to join the Nana's harem would be well treated but, beyond this, she offered them little hope of release. They lived with fear; death or the fear of death was always with them, and the sepoy guards, squatting under the *moulsaree* tree in the compound or smoking their *hookahs* beside the well, smiled at them mockingly when they begged to be told whether they were to live or die.

Many, tried beyond endurance, lay on the matting-covered floor and prayed for death; one of them, although no whisper of her fate reached them, had already found release in the only way left to her. Amelia Wheeler, the General's young daughter, had been taken from the Suttee Chowra Ghat by a *sowar* of the 2nd Native Cavalry, Ali Khan, and hidden in a house in the bazaar. It was his intention to convert her to the Mohammedan faith and take her as one of his wives but she proved obstinate in her refusal to forsake her own religion. Returning one night, fortified by *bhang* and accompanied by two of his comrades, Ali Khan attempted to break down her resistance.

Amelia, proud daughter of a sepoy general, took out the pistol her father had given her, days before, in the entrenchment. She had not been able to put it to the purpose for which her father had intended it—her mother and sister had been butchered in their boat—but now she snatched the weapon from the bosom of her dress. It contained six shots, her father had said; she used up four of them on her tormentors and the fifth, as her father had told her she must, she reserved for herself, her hand quite steady as she depressed the trigger.

IV

Alex left the ruined bungalow of an indigo planter, in which he had spent the night of 29th June, mounted the *sowar's* horse, and with a pale, watery sun to guide him, set his face in the direction of Allahabad.

He rode for eleven days, at times drenched by heavy rain, at others mercilessly burned by a blazing sun. He took an indirect route, through villages within sight of the river and by rutted bullock tracks, which meandered aimlessly through cultivated fields, sometimes traveling in a circle, in order to avoid concentrations of troops and occasionally, in the hope of meeting the British relief column, along parts of the Trunk Road.

Had he been in his normal senses, he would have been more cautious but the odd, carefree indifference to danger he had felt on recovering consciousness at the temple *ghat* persisted; he rode without fear of molestation and no one attempted to molest him. In India, among the unlettered peasants, a strange, wary respect is paid to madness, and to the villagers, who gave him food—and even to some of the native troops he encountered—it

193

was evident that the tall *jemadar*, with the hideously scarred face and light, staring eyes, was far gone in madness. Frequently, indeed, he was; talking to himself and to the gallant beast that carried him, memory returning in jumbled flashes and then vanishing again, so that even his own identity occasionally eluded him and he had no idea for what purpose he was traveling. He knew only that he was under orders to make contact with a column commanded by Colonel Neill—a column of the Madras Fusiliers, believed to be marching from Allahabad—and that it was important that he find them. But when, on the evening of the eleventh day of his long journey, he met a patrol of irregular cavalry spread out across an open plain and was fired on, he did not suppose them to be British and his first impulse was to endeavor to escape.

They swiftly surrounded him, however, and when the officer in charge of the patrol rode up, pistol in hand, he realized thankfully that his journey was over. The stern order, in English and then repeated in Hindustani, woke a latent echo in Alex's bemused brain and he answered, an authoritative note in his voice, in English, "All right, my young friend—put your pistol away—I'm a British officer. Are you from Colonel Neill's column?"

"From the advance column—Major Renaud's, sir. Colonel Neill is in Allahabad but General Havelock's force is following us." The young cavalry commander, after a momentary hesitation, holstered his pistol and motioned to his *sowars* to rein back. He introduced himself as Lieutenant Palliser and asked, "May I know your name, sir, and where you're from?"

Alex's hesitation was also momentary. "My name is Sheridan, brevet Lieutenant Colonel, late Third Light Cavalry . . . and I'm from Cawnpore. That is to say, I—"

"*Cawnpore*, sir?" Palliser stared at him in stunned surprise. "We heard that the garrison had fallen—that General Wheeler had surrendered and that you'd all been wiped out. The reports came from native informants,

194

of course, and some of them were conflicting, but we heard there's been a massacre and ..." He recovered himself. "I'd better take you to Major Renaud at once. He's anxious for reliable news and so, I feel sure, is the General. We're expecting him to rendezvous with us here in the next day or two."

"General Havelock, did you say?" Alex questioned.

"Yes, sir. Government got him back post haste from Persia, I believe, to take command of the force which is to—I mean *was* to relieve Cawnpore. We'll retake it, of course, and then I suppose push on to Lucknow."

"Is Lucknow also under siege?"

Lieutenant Palliser turned his horse towards the river. He nodded. "Yes, since the thirtieth, we understand. The garrison made a sally to Chinhat and suffered a serious reverse. Sir Henry Lawrence commanded in person but he was deserted by his native cavalry and artillery and his force only just managed to fall back on the Residency. We heard a rumor that Sir Henry himself had been mortally wounded and then another, which claimed he was dead—but neither has been confirmed. It's to be hoped that it's not true."

Indeed it was, Alex thought, another gap in his memory sadly filled. Palliser talked on as they rode back to the Fusiliers' camp but Alex scarcely heard him. The mists were closing about him again; his vision dimmed, then cleared, and dimmed again.

"We have four hundred Europeans—Blue Caps and Eighty-Fourth, sir—three hundred Sikhs and two guns, in addition to my detachment of cavalry, of whom there are a hundred. The rest of the Fusiliers have joined the General, apart from a detachment under Lieutenant Spurgin, about a hundred strong, who are coming up river by steamer in support. The main force consists of the Sixty-Fourth and the Seventy-Eighth Highlanders, and four hundred of the Eighty-Fourth, with Captain Maude's horse battery and a very small detachment of volunteer cavalry, under Captain Barrow. The arm we're shortest of is cavalry and, of course, transport has been a problem. We—"

"What delayed Colonel Neill for so long in Allahabad?" Alex asked thickly.

"Delayed him, sir?" The boy sounded at once surprised and faintly indignant. "Why, mutiny—in both Benares and Allahabad. Colonel Neill had to restore order before he could move on. He'd only just done so in Benares when news came from Allahabad that the Sixth Native Infantry had risen and murdered most of their officers—the Colonel and his Blue Caps marched seventy miles in three days, and only just arrived in time. They'd looted the Treasury of three lacs of rupees and were running riot, with the Europeans shut up in the Fort. But the Colonel put it down, sir. He hanged hundreds of the swine and blew the rest from guns—to make an example of them. It was necessary, believe me, sir, and it worked. The Sikhs remained loyal and most of my chaps as well. But it took time, of course, because the whole area was in revolt and—"

Alex, groaned, feeling his control slipping from him, as once again memory stirred and a vision of young Ensign Stirling's face flashed into his mind. Stirling, with his field telescope, crouching twenty feet above Number Four Block, in what Mowbray Thomson had called his "crow's nest," scanning the Allahabad road for some sign of the relief column, for some sign that would give them hope. But Neill and his relief column, if young Palliser were to be believed, had been hanging mutineers and blowing them from guns . . . He choked and the breath was strangled in his throat, the pain and confusion of his thoughts suddenly more than he could bear.

"Are you all right, sir?" his companion inquired anxiously. "You look as if . . . We're just at the camp now, sir, and Major Renaud's tent is only fifty yards from us."

Alex did not answer him. He slid from the saddle and was unconscious when two *sowars* carried him into Major Renaud's tent. The Fusilier major listened in silence to his cavalry commander's report and sent for a surgeon.

"He's apparently from Cawnpore, from General Wheeler's garrison, Doctor," he said, when the surgeon had completed his examination. "A Lieutenant Colonel—brevet rank—named Sheridan, according to Palliser, and as you may imagine, I'm extremely anxious to hear his story. The General will be, too, I'm sure. How is the poor fellow?"

"He ought to be dead," the surgeon returned bluntly. "In all my experience—which is now considerable—I've never seen a man who was in such a state and still able to sit a horse, as he's been doing for—how long? Ten days, more perhaps. I'm amazed that he could even give a rational account of himself to Palliser . . . but I fear he won't be able to tell you anything more for several days. Possibly even a week."

"A week? Oh, damn! You're sure of that, I suppose?"

The doctor shrugged. "One cannot be sure of anything in a case like this, Major. The poor fellow has a saber cut seven inches long across the head and face—the brain's been exposed and there could be multiple skull fractures, I don't know yet. He has a recently healed bullet wound in the right shoulder and he is very near to starvation, with all the complications that go with it— I tell you, it's a wonder he's alive! And I can tell you something else, too."

"What's that?" Renaud asked.

"That the reports concerning Wheeler's garrison are probably true—they've been wiped out—if Colonel Sheridan's physical state is anything to go by. But I'll have him moved to the hospital tent and I'll do my best to patch him up by the time the General gets here."

"Thanks, Docor," Sydenham Renaud acknowledged. "Do the best you can. Because we'll have a battle to fight within the next couple of days—though not before the General joins us, if I can help it. The Nana is reported to have over three thousand troops occupying Fatepur." He sighed. "And I've also had a report from a spy that he's holding two hundred women and children in Cawnpore—survivors of the garrison, one presumes, and one must also presume that he's holding them as hostages." He gestured to the unconscious Alex. "That poor devil may be able to tell us if it's true. If it is . . . "

The doctor's face drained of color. "I understand," he said quietly. "As I said, I'll do my very best. At present his greatest need is sleep. He has a strong constitution. He may live but I'm making no promises."

General Havelock's force marched into Renaud's camp at Batinda, four miles from Fatepur, the following evening, led by the pipes of the 78th Highlanders. They had marched through torrential rain and pitiless sun and were suffering badly from fatigue and exposure. The long, slow-moving baggage train which followed in their wake did not arrive until long after the troops, and their dapper little General—aware that his total force numbered only twelve hundred men, with eight guns—had hoped to permit them a day's rest before leading them into battle. The Nana's troops, however, elated by what they deemed their victory over General Wheeler at Cawnpore and imagining that only Renaud's handful of men opposed them, were eager to do battle.

Bringing two guns and a strong force of infantry forward, with cavalry on either flank, they opened a cannonade on Havelock's front. He held them with a hundred Enfield riflemen of the Queen's 64th until the rest of the men had finished their breakfast and then launched a counter atack. With Maude's guns in the center, covered by skirmishers, and the rest of his infantry, all armed with Enfields and deployed into line of quarter distance columns, he advanced, disconcerting the rebels with the range and accuracy of the Enfields. Maude's guns, skillfully handled, disabled those of the enemy and then, pushed through a swamp to point-blank range on their right flank, opened so deadly a fire on them that they broke into precipitate flight, abandoning twelve guns and the town of Fatepur to the swiftly advancing British. It

198

was a battle fought with Enfield rifles and cannon and won, by Havelock's tired and footsore soldiers, without the loss of a single man. Pursuit was, unhappily, impossible since only Barrow's eighteen volunteer cavalrymen were available. To the distress of young Lieutenant James, his irregulars had refused to charge and the General ordered them disarmed and sent back to Neill at Allahabad. But the tide had turned for the British at last; the enemy had been ignominiously routed by an army half its size, with heavy losses in guns and men—and, only fifty miles ahead, lay Cawnpore.

Havelock was delighted; his tired troops had acquitted themselves magnificently in their first major engagement. Brasyer's Sikhs, of whom there had been some doubt, had fought like tigers beside their British comrades; the Enfield rifle had proved its vast superiority over the rebel's Brown Bess muskets, and for Francis Maude's splendid artillerymen—many of them gray-haired pensioners—no praise could be too high. On 13th July the little General permitted his force a day's rest, gave the town of Fatepur over to sack and himself spent most of the day in earnest prayer. The following day he pushed on, fighting two successful engagements and taking the village of Aong for the loss of only 25 killed, of whom, sadly, the gallant Renaud was one.

The next obstacle was the Panda Nudi river, 70 yards wide and swollen to an unfordable torrent by the rains. A cavalry reconnaissance revealed the enemy to be rallying and endeavoring to blow up the bridge, six miles ahead. Aware that, if they succeeded in their attempt, his progress to Cawnpore would be indefinitely retarded, the General called on his troops for a fresh effort. Exhausted by a five-hour march and a severe action, fought under a nearly vertical sun, the men were lying down, awaiting their long delayed breakfast, but they sprang up at the word of command and grimly pushed on.

The road ahead ran through groves of mango trees and, as the head of the column emerged from these and came in sight of the bridge, the rebels opened cannon-fire on them, with 24-pounder guns. But their position was badly chosen. The bridge was at the apex of a bend in the river, which curved toward the advancing column, and behind the bend they were massed in a dense body, with their guns mounted on the approach to the bridge. Havelock ordered his infantry to lie down in their ranks and Maude's guns, moving swiftly, unlimbered on the right, close to the stream, to envelop the enemy battery with a deadly concentric fire.

The mine exploded prematurely and, to the intense relief of the little General, ineffectively; he yelled at his infantry to go forward and, covered by riflemen on the bank, the right wing of the Fusiliers carried the bridge with their bayonets. With the river behind them, the exhausted soldiers flung themselves on the ground to rest, too spent now even to eat the food they had earlier been compelled to cram into their haversacks untasted. But Cawnpore was now only a few miles ahead and the whisper passed, from man to man, that more than two hundred British women and children were alive and held captive by the Nana. . . .

Alex had wakened to the thunder of the guns, late that afternoon, his body refreshed but his memory wiped clean. He could tell General Havelock nothing; a dark curtain shrouded the events of the past month, and try as he would, he could not pierce it. Filled with a strange restlessness, he disregarded the surgeon's advice and insisted on returning to duty and Captain Lousada Barrow welcomed him to the thin ranks of his volunteer cavalry —eighteen men, planters, civil officials and unemployed officers. With his heavily bandaged head, his emaciated, deeply sunburnt body and his borrowed horse, he was not, he realized wryly, a recruit anyone else was likely to welcome—but Barrow was glad of any man who could ride.

He slept on the bare ground with the rest of the men, his horse tethered beside him, and again dreamed happily of Emmy and the golden days when they had first taken up residence in Adjodhabad.

V

In Cawnpore, as the thunder of the British guns came inexorably nearer, the Nana Sahib trembled, and railed at the men he had once so extravagantly praised for their courage and devotion. His generals and advisers had lost their arrogance now; Azimullah was visibly terrified; Tantia Topi had had his elephant blasted from under him by Maude's guns at Fatepur; Teeka Singh had twice led his cavalry in humiliating retreat and Jwala Pershad's tactics had failed to match or even counter those of the British General, whose contemptible little force was carrying everything before it. The Moulvi of Fyzabad alone remained confident of the final outcome and it was he who advised the abandonment of Cawnpore, to enable the Nana's army to regroup north of the city, where reinforcements from Oudh would join them.

"We should leave no witnesses behind, Nana Sahib," he added, his voice cold. "No one who might tell the *feringhi* of what occurred at the Suttee Chowra Ghat, to fill the hearts of their soldiers with vengeful hatred. Order the captives killed, for your own safety."

The Nana looked at the faces about him and they met his gaze stonily. "They could be used as hostages," he objected.

"We dare not free them," his brother, Bala Bhat, stated with conviction. He rose. "Shall I give the order?"

The Nana's puffy face paled but, after a brief hesitation, he inclined his head. "So be it, my brother. Bid the guards shoot them." As an afterthought, he went on, "Order also that the *babus* and everyone who can speak and write English have their right hands and noses cut off."

"I will attend to it," the Governor-General of Cawnpore promised. Wincing with the pain of the bullet wound he had received at the Panda Nudi bridge, he summoned his escort and left the hotel, two servants running beside his carriage, holding a scarlet umbrella above his head.

Late that afternoon, the 15th July, the serving maid, Hosainee Khanum, whispered to one of the captives in the Bibigarh the warning that the Nana had ordered their execution. The poor captives had been in their prison now for eighteen days and the sound of Havelock's guns had revived the hope that, at last, rescue was at hand. Weeping, some of them called to the *jemadar* of their guard, Yusef Khan, to ask him if the Nana had indeed ordered that they must die, but he denied it. The girl, he admitted, had brought such an order, but he and his men had refused to obey.

"You have nothing to fear at our hands," he assured them. "But so as not to incur the Nana's wrath, we will fire a few musket-balls into the walls." The sepoys duly did so and the frightened women thanked them tearfully. But Hosainee had vanished and, still apprehensive, some of the women tore strips from their dresses and petticoats, with which they attempted to secure the door. Then, clasping their children to them, they waited, praying that the British relief force would reach them before Hosainee's return.

At five o'clock, the girl returned and there were five men with her; two were Hindu peasants of low caste, two Moslem butchers in stained white robes, and the fifth wore the red uniform of the Nana's bodyguard, and the girl addressed him as Sarvur Khan. He ordered the *jemadar* to march his guard outside the compound and, when this had been done, two other men—one a *sowar* in the service of the Moulvi of Fyzabad—took their places at the door and, at a nod from Savur Khan, put their shoulders to it and burst the pathetic wisps of cloth which had held it shut against them.

"You know the Nana Sahib's command," Savur Khan reminded them harshly. *Tulwars* unsheathed, the men followed him into the shadowed room. . . .

It was dark when they emerged and the heartrending

cries and shrieks which had issued from the shuttered windows of the Bibigarh had faded into a deathly silence. The building remained closed that night and none approached it.

Next day, a party of low caste *jullads*—men normally employed in the extermination of dogs—were sent to remove the bodies of the slain and cast them into the well at the far side of the compound. A few women and one or two children, who had survived the previous evening's slaughter, were ruthlessly butchered or flung, still living, among the dead now piled high in the well.

The Nana did not enquire as to their fate. The treasure he had amassed during his forty-day reign as Peishwa was hastily loaded on to elephants and into bullock carts and, under heavy escort, he fled to Bithur before the British troops reentered the city. Five thousand rebels followed him.

VI

It had been a bitter battle, fought with tenacious courage all through the heat of the day against an army of eight thousand Pandies, who had fiercely contested each village and each mile of the way. Spurred on by the thought of the women and children—those poor sufferers, who had endured so much and whose lives must, at any sacrifice, be saved—the Highlanders of the 78th, led by their pipers, hurled themselves at the enemy's entrenched positions, the sun glinting on the bright steel of their ferociously jabbing bayonets. The riflemen of the 64th flattened themselves to the ground, then rose and advanced firing; the 84th, with memories of comrades who had defended the Cawnpore entrenchment, took guns at bayonet point and neither they, nor the Sikhs who fought beside them, gave quarter to any gunner who had the temerity to stand by his gun. In their famous blue caps and "dirty" shirts, the young Fusiliers fought grimly;

they had Renaud, their commander, to avenge, and they had had their baptism of fire.

And always the order was "Forward!" Shells burst and round-shot thinned the advancing ranks; a 24-pounder held them, until it was blown up by Maude's guns at point-blank range from the flank; then a howitzer from the enemy center ranged on the charging 78th, forcing them to take cover behind the causeway carrying the road.

Havelock himself rallied them, his sword held high above his head as a storm of shell burst round him. "Another charge like that wins the day, Seventy-Eighth!" he exhorted them and the red-coated line reformed, at his bidding, and stormed the howitzer's emplacement, their pipes keening above the nose of battle.

The rebels started to fall back, covered by their cavalry, and in vain Lousada Barrow begged Havelock to allow his volunteer horse to charge them. Permission was finally given and the nineteen volunteers spurred forward joyously, Alex with them. Two hundred and fifty yards from the massed rebel cavalry, their commander shouted to them to charge.

"Give points, boys—damn cuts and guards!"

Reminded of the charge of the Heavy Brigade at Balaclava, Alex felt his heart lift; so had the Dragoons charged the might of the Russian cavalry division, their sabers in the "straight arm engage" and held with rock-like steadiness, so that the speed and momentum of their advance had carried them through. His reins lying loose on his horse's sweat-streaked neck and his saber in his single hand, he galloped straight at the ranks of white-robed rebel horsemen, riding knee to knee with a yelling civilian clerk on one side, with a bearded Scottish planter of sixty-five on the other, and they crashed into the enemy line, sending it reeling. Only when the *sowars* were in retreat and four of their horses had fallen beneath them did Barrow yell to them to reform and retire. The General himself cantered to meet them.

"Gentlemen volunteers," he told them. "I am proud to command you!"

At last it was over; the Nana's army had made their last stand, falling back to where a giant, 24-pounder howitzer blocked the road into Cawnpore and they glimpsed the Nana himself some distance to the rear, watching the battle from his elephant. With casualties mounting and only eight hundred men in line, his own horse shot under him, Havelock showed his mettle. Mounted on a borrowed hack, he sent his son to replace the commander of the 64th, who, under a ghastly rain of shells from the howitzer, were in danger of breaking ranks, and himself trotted over to the line of desperate, exhausted men. Facing them, he gave his orders with a smile.

"The longer you look at it, men, the less you will like it. Rise up! The Brigade will advance, left battalion leading."

They had obeyed him, running forward, flinging themselves to the ground when the howitzer and its supporting gun spoke, then charging on again, leaving their dead and wounded behind them, to fire a shattering volley and then leap, with plunging bayonets, into the mob of cringing gunners.

Maude's battery completed the victory, lashing the fleeing rebels with vicious salvoes of grape.

It was dusk when they set off to march the last two miles into Cawnpore and they cheered their little General as he stood at the roadside to watch them pass.

"Don't cheer me," he said, when he could make himself heard. "You did it all yourselves!"

The report from spies sent forward to reconnoiter the approaches to the city finally halted them. The women and children were dead; they had been massacred by the Nana's orders—there was no longer the need for undue haste.

On the morning of 17th July, an advance guard of the 64th entered Cawnpore and marched through its ravaged, empty streets to the Bibigarh to investigate the truth of the spies' report.

EPILOGUE

Alex Sheridan stood, sickened and white to the lips, outside the small, flat-roofed building in which the captives had been housed.

Memories came flooding back; the shock and horror of what he had seen parted the mists that had mercifully clouded his brain and deadened his emotions for the past seventeen days. Now he remembered them, remembered the faces and he saw Emmy's face again, floating away from him in the muddy water of the Suttee Chowra Ghat and knew that, for as long as he lived, he would never again forget, would never be able to forget.

Nothing he had seen could match what lay behind him in the room he had just left; he had passed within sight of the entrenchment and felt no emotion, had ridden through streets of roofless gutted houses and looked on the wanton destruction of the city of Cawnpore unmoved. . . . Now he could only weep, and find no relief in tears.

The place was a charnel house, inches deep in blood, with here and there a woman's bonnet, shoes, the frilled muslin frock of a child, books, a torn Bible and, still hanging from the door, the flimsy rags with which a vain attempt had been made by those who had perished there to bar it to their murderers. The walls were scarred with saber slashes and the marks of bullets, with sword cuts low down, where some poor crouching woman or a tiny child had tried to ward off the blows aimed at them by their brutal assassins.

He could not bring himself to cross the fifty feet between the door of the house and the well; others had done so and none more than once. A tough, hardened sergeant of the 64th had said, fighting down nausea, "I've faced death in every form but never anything like this. If they shot me for it, I could not look down that well again."

Alex started to move away and then halted, seeing a blood-flecked prayerbook in the grass at his feet. He bent and picked it up and read in the flyleaf: *"Psalm 18:41."* His hand shaking, he knelt, the book on his knee, and slowly turned its pages, to find the verse indicated. It read: *"They cried, but there was none to save; even unto the Lord, but He answered them not. . . ."* Blindly he let the book fall back into the foot-deep grass. Had it all been in vain, he asked himself bitterly, the defence of the entrenchment, the battle they had waged in Vibart's boat, the long, hopeless flight, with their pursuers always close at their heels? He was alive but these poor innocents were dead, hideously, barbarously butchered by men without pity. They . . .

A short distance from him, three of the 78th in their scarlet jackets and tartan, squatted down, dividing something between them. It was a tress of fair hair, Alex saw, and each man was counting the number that had fallen to his share.

"A rebel shall die for each one of these," a red-bearded corporal vowed passionately. "I swear it, on ma mither's grave!"

Alex approached them, his hand outheld and, when they hesitated, eying him uncertainly, he said harshly, "I was one of this garrison—these were my friends."

"You . . . aye, sir." The corporal laid a lock of hair on his palm. Attached to it was a torn scrap of paper, on which was scrawled in pencil: *"Melanie Vibart, aged four years."*

"Likely you'll have known the puir wee lassie, sir?" the corporal suggested diffidently.

"Yes, I did." His throat stiff, Alex placed hair and label in his breast pocket and turned away, not wishing to let the Highlanders see that he wept.

"Some of us must live," Edward Vibart had said. "Our betrayal *must* be avenged. We've no choice but to fight on."

He would avenge this most terrible of betrayals, he vowed; he would fight on and, God willing, hunt down and bring to justice the man who had been the architect of it all.

Within an hour, he was with the advance party marching towards Bithur, but the Nana Sahib had fled and his palace was deserted. . . .

GLOSSARY OF INDIAN TERMS

Achkan: knee-length tunic
Ayah: nurse or maid servant
Babu: clerk, loosely applied to those able to write
Bazaar: market
Bearer: personal, usually head, servant
Bhang: hashish
Bhisti: water carrier
Brahmin: high-caste Hindu
Cantonments: European quarters, residences, civil or
    military, usually military
Chapatti: unleavened cake of wheat flour
Charpoy: string bed
Daffadar: sergeant, cavalry
Dhal: flour
Din: faith, Moslem war cry "For the Faith!"
Doolie: stretcher or covered litter
Eurasian: half-caste, usually children of British fathers and
    Indian mothers
Fakir/Sadhu: itinerant holy man, Hindu
Feringhi: foreigner, term of disrespect
Ghat: landing place, river bank, quay
Godown: storeroom, warehouse
Golandaz: gunner, native

Gram: coarse grain, usually fed to horses
Hanuman: Hindu monkey god
Havildar: sergeant, infantry
Jemadar: native officer, all arms
Khitmatgar: table servant
Lal-kote: British soldier
Lines: long rows of huts for accommodation of native troops
Moulvi: teacher of religion, Moslem
Nana: lit. grandfather, popular title bestowed on Mahratta chief
Oudh: kingdom of, recently annexed by Hon. East India Company
Paltan: regiment
Pandy: name for mutineers, taken from the first to revolt, Sepoy Mangal Pandy, 34th Native Infantry
Peishwa: ruler or king of the Mahratta race
Poorbeah: from the East, an inhabitant of Oudh
Pugree: turban
Raj: rule
Rissala: cavalry
Rissaldar/Rissaldar-Major: native officer, cavalry: RSM
Ryot: peasant small holder
Sepoy: infantry soldier
Sowar: cavalry trooper
Subadar/Subadar-Major: native officer, infantry: RSM
Sweeper: low-caste servant
Tulwar: sword or sabre
Vakil: agent
Zamindar: landowner

HISTORICAL NOTES ON EVENTS
COVERED IN THE SEPOY MUTINY

The outbreak of mutiny in the three native regiments stationed in Meerut on Sunday, 10th May, 1857 and the subsequent seizure of Delhi by the mutineers, aided by native troops of the garrison, was the first act in a tragedy which was to cost the lives of countless men, women and children in the Bengal Presidency.

There can be little doubt that the Meerut uprising was premature. Those who, for months past, had been plotting sedition had, in fact, chosen the end of May as the date on which the Army of Bengal was to break out in open rebellion against the East India Company's rule and they, as well as officials of the Company, were taken by surprise. Meerut was the one station in all India which had a strong British garrison but, due to the inept handling of the situation by the Divisional Commander, Major General William Hewitt, not only did the revolt succeed but Delhi, with an entirely native garrison, was permitted to fall into the hands of the mutineers without a single British soldier being sent from Meerut to prevent it. As a result, British prestige suffered an almost mortal blow and Delhi, ancient capital of the Moguls, became the focal point of the revolt, its recapture essential if the whole of India were not to be lost.

In 1857, Britain was still recovering from the toll taken of her fighting strength by the Crimean War; she was about to embark on a war with China and had recently been fighting in Burma and Persia. India had been drained of white troops; there were only 40,000—exclusive of some 5,000 British officers of native regiments—whilst the sepoys of the three Presidency Armies (Bengal, Madras and Bombay) numbered 311,000, with the Army of Bengal accounting for 150,000 of these. The territory for which this Army was responsible included all northern India, from Calcutta to the Afghan frontier and the Punjab.

The Punjab had only lately been subdued, following the two Sikh Wars of 1845-6 and 1848-9, and there was a constant threat of border raids by the Afghan tribes, so that most of the Queen's* regiments were stationed at these danger points and on the Burmese frontier, with 10,000 British and Indian troops in the Punjab alone.

The 53rd Queen's Regiment of Foot was at Calcutta; the 10th at Dinapur—400 miles up the River Ganges; the 32nd was at Lucknow and a newly raised regiment, the Company's 3rd Bengal European Fusiliers, at Agra. The Meerut garrison, 38 miles from Delhi, consisted of the Queen's 60th Rifles—1,000 strong—and 600 troopers of the 6th Dragoon Guards, with two batteries of artillery.

Both the Governor-General, Lord Canning, and the Commander-in-Chief, General Anson, took action as swiftly and decisively as they could when news reached them of the disasters in Meerut and Delhi. From Government House in Calcutta, Canning summoned all available reinforcements. He recalled British regiments from Persia and Burma, sent for troops from Madras, Bombay and Ceylon and dispatched a fast steamer to Singapore, to intercept the convoy then on its way from England to

*Queen's—from England, British soldiers, serving in India.

China. Virtually all troops had to come by sea and, aware that delay was inevitable, Canning requested the Chief Commissioner of the Punjab, John Lawrence, to send every British soldier he could spare to swell the ranks of the Delhi Relief Force.

This Force was being assembled in Ambala by General Anson but the Commander-in-Chief was greatly hampered by lack of transport. The East India Company, in the interests of economy, had dispensed with the military Transport Establishment at the conclusion of the Sikh Wars, leaving the Army to depend on hired civilian contractors, who were expected to provide coolies, carts, ammunition tumbrils and *doolies* for the sick and wounded, as well as a vast number of beasts of burden, all of which had to be commandeered from their normal civilian employment and ownership. It was impossible to obtain these at the speed which the emergency demanded and the collection of provisions presented similar problems. The countryside was unsettled and the native cavalry, which usually assisted with the collection, were unreliable and, in some cases, openly mutinous. To add to Anson's difficulties, he could no longer depend on the Delhi arsenal to supply the guns and munitions he required, since Delhi was in the hands of the mutineers. The weapons of war had, in consequence, to be brought from Phillaur and Ferozepore—many miles to the north —and once again lack of transport caused frustrating delays.

The unfortunate Anson, bombarded by urgent telegraphic instructions from Lord Canning and similar urgings from John Lawrence to advance immediately on Delhi, did the best he could with the means at his disposal. Within six days of the fall of Delhi, he had sent the first echelon of his hurriedly gathered Relief Force to Karnaul and had ordered the Meerut garrison to join his force at Baghpat, a few miles from Delhi. By 27th May, Anson himself, worn out by his efforts, had succumbed to an attack of cholera and his place as Commander-in-

Chief was taken by General Barnard, who had served with distinction in the Crimea.

A force of 2,400 infantry, 600 cavalry and 22 light field guns was at Karnaul, lacking adequate medical supplies, heavy guns, reserves of ammunition, provisions and tentage, but Sir Henry Barnard nevertheless gave the order to begin the 70-mile march to Delhi. On 30th May, the Meerut force, under the command of Brigadier-General Archdale Wilson, fought and won the first battle of retribution against a vastly superior number of mutineers, with heavy guns, which disputed their passage at the Hindan River Bridge. Fighting with superb gallantry, two squadrons of the 6th Dragoon Guards, a wing of the 60th Rifles, one horse and one field battery and a few loyal native cavalry routed and put to flight six thousand rebels and captured five of their guns. After fighting a second successful engagement next morning, Wilson made his rendezvous with General Barnard, as instructed, at Baghpat.

Still barely 4,000 strong, the combined relief force continued its advance and at the village of Badli-ka-Serai, six miles from Delhi, found 30,000 rebels in a strongly entrenched position, with 30 guns, waiting to oppose them. At dawn on 8th June, the British attacked with such courage and vengeful ferocity that, with the loss of only 200 killed and wounded, they drove the enemy from their entrenchments at the point of the bayonet, inflicting over a thousand casualties and capturing 13 guns. The mutineers retreated in disorder to Delhi and Barnard led his victorious troops back to the Ridge where, with the Union Jack once more flying from the Flagstaff Tower, plans for an assault on the city were eagerly discussed, as the various strongpoints which overlooked it were occupied. Next day the famous Guides, commanded by Major Daly, joined the force, having marched down from the Punjab—a distance of 500 miles, which they had covered in 27 days—adding three troops of cavalry and six companies of infantry to its number.

Although fully aware of the tremendous psychological effect the capture of Delhi would have on the rest of India—and particularly on those native regiments that had not yet joined the mutiny—General Barnard was not blind to the fact that a formidable obstacle faced him. The city walls extended for seven miles and were of massive construction, 24 feet high and protected for two miles by the River Jumna and, for the rest of their length, by a ditch, 25 feet wide and 20 feet deep. Over a hundred guns were mounted in bastions at strategic points, each holding 9 to 12 guns of heavy caliber, served by well-trained gunners, with 24-pounders covering the gates by which an assault force would have to enter. Behind the walls were a large, fanatical population and an estimated 40,000 sepoys and police, whose numbers were augmented almost daily by fresh waves of mutineers from other stations, now flocking to join in the revolt.

Barnard's force was too small to do more than maintain a precarious hold on the two-mile-long Ridge, where their positions were under constant attack. He could not invest the city or prevent reinforcements from entering it and his few light field guns could make no impression on the towering walls of the Red Fort. He was short of munitions and supplies of every kind and had no reserves, whilst the defenders had a limitless supply of arms, taken from the arsenal on the Ridge when Brigadier Graves had been compelled to abandon it, on 11th May. Nevertheless, elated by their initial successes at the Hindan and at Badli-ka-Serai, his troops were eager to attack and Barnard, against his better judgement, permitted an attempt to carry the city by assault to be made on 13th June.

"The place is so strong," he wrote to Lord Canning, *"and my means so inadequate, that assault or regular approach are equally difficult—I may say impossible— and I have nothing left but to place all on the hazard of a die and attempt a* coup-de-main, *which I purpose to do. If successful, all will be well. But reverse will be fatal, for*

216

I have no reserve on which to retire. . . . I see nothing for it but a determined rush and this, please God, you will hear of as successful."

The attack was badly planned and coordinated, however, and had to be abandoned. General Barnard decided reluctantly to await the arrival of a siege train and badly needed reinforcements. Both, due to the herculean efforts of John Lawrence, were on their way from the Punjab but, as the original relief force had been, they were hampered by lack of transport. The effect of the British failure to recapture Delhi was, predictably, a spate of mutinous outbreaks throughout northern India.

In Oudh, the situation grew hourly more critical. Sir Henry Lawrence, Chief Commissioner of the recently annexed province, had made good use of the weeks of inaction which had followed the Meerut mutiny. He had fortified and provisioned the Residency at Lucknow, in anticipation of a siege and, as the first signs of trouble began to manifest themselves among the native troops, he ordered all women and children to take refuge within the fortified area. On 30th May, having asked for and obtained plenary military powers, he took resolute action when four of his native regiments rose and drove them from their lines at the head of the Queen's 32nd. Next morning, after a sharp engagement on the racecourse, he pursued them for ten miles and took 60 prisoners. His courageous leadership not only averted a massacre but also induced several hundred sepoys to remain loyal, including virtually all the Sikhs of the garrison. With 600 women and children and a total of a thousand Europeans capable of bearing arms—among them 153 civilians—Lawrence prepared to defend his Residency, aided by some 700 loyal native troops and pensioners, only a few of whom subsequently deserted to the rebels.

In Cawnpore, 53 miles to the northeast, the garrison commander, the 75-year-old Major General Sir Hugh Wheeler, had also made preparations for a place of shelter and refuge in which to protect his noncombatant

Europeans, of whom 375 were women and children and 74 invalids of the 32nd, left behind when the regiment moved to Lucknow. His command consisted of four native regiments—the 2nd Native Cavalry, and the 1st, 53rd and 56th Native Infantry—with 60 British artillerymen, 60 men of the 84th Queen's and 15 Madras European Fusiliers. To these, when the native regiments finally rose, were added 30 of their officers and a handful of young railway engineers and civilian volunteers.

Wheeler's choice of a site for a defensive stand was made contrary to the advice of the majority of his officers, who believed that the Magazine—a strongly-built, walled-in enclosure at the river's edge six miles north of the military station—would better have served the purpose. It contained ample stores of guns and ammunition and could, his staff officers argued, be defended almost indefinitely. The old General overruled them and, instead, elected to occupy two newly built European barracks, one a hospital, round which he ordered an earthwork parapet, with gun emplacements, to be constructed. His chosen site was on open ground near the road from Allahabad and the south, along which he expected his promised reinforcements to come, at the end of their 700-mile march from Calcutta. In addition, it was very close to the cantonments occupied by the British civil and military residents and therefore easier to reach, should a sudden crisis arise, than the Magazine.

There, however, its advantage over the latter ended. The barrack buildings were of thin brickwork, one had a roof thatched with straw, and the parapet, for all the frantic labor put into its construction, was little more than a mud wall, far from bulletproof and incapable of withstanding a determined assault. Wheeler had eight 9-pounder guns mounted at intervals along the parapet and laid in stocks of ammunition and provisions for twenty-five days. There was a good well within the enclosure and, in the belief that the sepoys, if they mutinied, would make at once for Delhi, the old General was satisfied that he could hold off any attacks made by riff-raff from the city until relief reached him—or until the news that Delhi had been recaptured put an end to the threat of mutiny.

Against the repeated advice of Sir Henry Lawrence, he continued to put complete trust in the Maharajah of Bithur—better known by his Mahratta name of the Nana Sahib—with whom he and his wife were on terms of close personal friendship. When it became evident that neither the fall of Delhi nor the hoped-for reinforcements were likely to prevent the mutiny of his four native regiments, Wheeler called on his friend the Maharajah for assistance. Receiving this, in the shape of 300 men of the Nana's own bodyguard, he entrusted the defence of the Treasury and the Magazine—with its priceless store of arms—solely to them. So convinced of their trustworthiness was he that, when the first hundred men of the 84th Queen's Regiment reached him from Calcutta on the 3rd June, he sent half of them on to Lucknow, together with some reserves of the 32nd, to aid in Lawrence's defense, believing their assurance that other reinforcements were close on their heels.

The Madras European Fusiliers had landed in Calcutta on 24th May and he received word that they were proceeding upcountry with all possible speed, by rail, road and river steamer. Their commander, Colonel James Neill, an experienced Crimean veteran, entered Benares on 3rd June and would, General Wheeler was certain, lose no time in pressing on to Cawnpore and Lucknow.

On 4th June, he wrote to inform Sir Henry Lawrence that all noncombatant civilians had been ordered into the entrenchments, adding: *"Trust in any of the native troops is now out of the question. . . . It is said that the 1st Native Infantry is sworn to join (the mutiny) and they speak of its going off this night or the next morning . . . doing all the mischief in their power first, this to include an attack on our positions. . . ."* The rest of his letter was a bitter expression of resentment at the news that Lt. General Sir Patrick Grant, Commander-in-Chief of the

Madras Army, had been chosen to succeed General Anson in preference to himself. He was fifteen years senior to Grant, so that his resentment was understandable when he wrote: "*I can but serve under him but it is a poor return for above fifty-two years of zealous service to be thus superseded. My name with the Native Army has alone preserved tranquility thus up to the present time and the difficulties that I have had to contend with can only be known to myself. . . . I have performed subaltern duty in going the rounds at midnight because I felt that I gave confidence. . . . I write with a crushed spirit, for I had no right to expect this treatment. . . ."* The letter ended with the alarming admission that "*We can offer protection to nothing with our entrenchments. . . .*"

Despite his final statement, the old General made no attempt to blow up the Magazine and when, as predicted, the four native regiments rose early in the morning of 5th June, the Nana's bodyguard permitted them to possess themselves of the £100,000 contents of the Treasury and of the arms stored in the Magazine. The mutineers—almost certainly because of the high esteem in which their commander was held—offered no violence to their officers, and 80 men of the 56th N.I. entered the entrenchment to pledge their loyalty to the old "Sepoy General."

The rest, after a brief orgy of arson and looting, prepared to march on Delhi, 268 miles to the northwest, dragging their treasure and their looted guns behind them. They had traveled as far as Kalianpore, six miles outside Cawnpore, when the Nana Sahib revealed himself in his true colors. Invited by the native officers to become their leader, the Maharajah gave them a qualified assent and, in callous betrayal of the trust General Wheeler had reposed in him, he rode after the mutineers to persuade them to return to Cawnpore. . . .

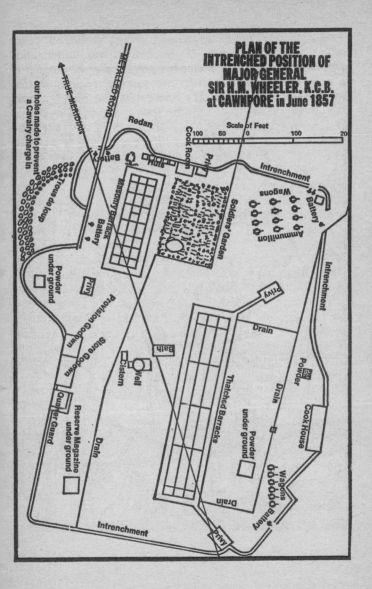

PLAN OF THE
INTRENCHED POSITION OF
MAJOR-GENERAL
SIR H.M. WHEELER. K.C.B.
at CAWNPORE in June 1857

Scale of Feet

100   50   0   100   200

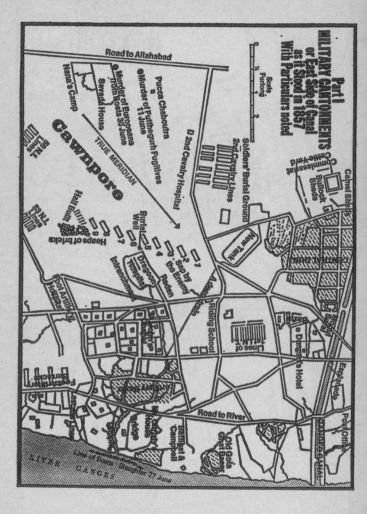

Part I
MILITARY CANTONMENTS
or East Side of Canal
as it Stood in 1857
With Particulars noted

Scale
½ Furlong

Road to Allahabad

Nana's Camp

Pucca Chabootra
● Murder of Futtehgurh Fugitives
● Murder of Europeans
    from Boats 30 June
Sayadi House

TRUE MERIDIAN

Cawnpore

58 N.I. Lines

56 N.I. Lines

1 N.I. Lines

□ 2nd Cavalry Hospital

Soldiers' Burial Ground

2nd Cavalry Lines

Commissariat
Cattle-yard

Bullock
Sheds

Camel Sheds

Hall Burn

Heaps of bricks

Burial
Well

Dragoon
Hospital

Intrenchment

9
8
7
6
5
4
3 Sap by
  the Enemy
2 Redan
1

New Tank

Adjan tank

Riding School

Lines of N.I.

Director's Hotel

Esplanade

Post Office

Post Artillery
Hospital

Assembly
Rooms

Foot Artillery
Barracks

Judges House

Massacre
Ghat
House

Road to River

Battiger &
Campbell

Old Gola
Ghat Bazar

GANGES CANAL

LIVER   GANGES

Line of Boats Slaughter 27 June

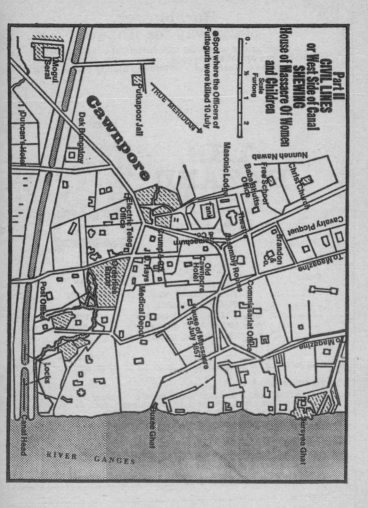

Part II
CIVIL LINES
or West Side of Canal
SHEWING
House of Massacre Of Women
and Children

Scale
0. ¼ ½ 1 2
Furlong

● Spot where the Officers of
Futtegurh were killed 10 July

TRUE MERIDIAN

Cawnpore

Putkapoor Jail

Mogul
Serai

Dak Bungalow

[Dulcan's] Hotel

Nunneh Nawab

Free School

Baba[ghutts]
Office

Masonic Lodge

Christ Church

Cavalry Picquet

Electric Telegraph
Office

Bank

Theatre

Grandon
& Co.

To Magazine

Crump & Co

J. D. Hays Medical Depot

[Orderian]
Bazar

Assembly Rooms

Old
Cawnpore
Hotel

Commissariat Office

Post Office

House of Massacre
15 July 1857

To Magazine

Locks

Suttee Ghat

Surajee Ghat

Canal Head

RIVER   GANGES